Carole Matthews is an internationally bestselling author and her unique sense of humour has won her legions of fans and critical acclaim throughout the world. *A Compromising Position* and *A Minor Indiscretion* were both Top 5 *Sunday Times* bestsellers. Film rights in *A Minor Indiscretion* and *For Better, For Worse* have been sold to Hollywood. Carole has presented on television and is a regular radio guest. When she is not writing novels and television scripts she manages to find time to trek in the Himalayas, rollerblade in Central Park, take tea in China and snooze in her garden shed in Milton Keynes.

To read exclusive short stories by Carole Matthews and receive her monthly email newsletter visit www.carolematthews.co.uk or contact her direct at cmatthewsmail@aol.com

'Carole Matthews writes of the travails of romance, relationships and motherhood with hilarity, tenderness and despair . . . a story loaded with laughter, tears and hope. This is one to share with your girlfriends' Adriana Trigiani

'Matthews is one of the few writers who can rival Marian Keyes' gift for telling heart-warming tales with buckets of charm and laughs' *Daily Record*

'Touching. Feelgood. Funny' *Heat*

'A feel-good tale . . . fun and thoroughly escapist' *Marie Claire*

'Hilarious . . . saucy, but nice' *Daily Express*

'Will have you giggling from the start . . . hilarious' *OK!* magazine

Also by Carole Matthews

A Whiff of Scandal
More to Life than This
For Better, For Worse
A Minor Indiscretion
A Compromising Position
The Sweetest Taboo
With or Without You
You Drive Me Crazy

Let's Meet On Platform 8

Carole Matthews

HEADLINE

First published in 1997
by HEADLINE BOOK PUBLISHING

First published in paperback in 1998
by HEADLINE BOOK PUBLISHING

17

ISBN 0 7472 5794 9

Typeset by Avon Dataset Ltd, Bidford-on-Avon, Warks

Printed and bound in Great Britain by
Clays Ltd, St Ives plc

HEADLINE BOOK PUBLISHING
A division of Hodder Headline PLC
338 Euston Road
London NW1 3BH

To Mum
for all we've been through together

And for Steve

With grateful thanks to Clare, Darley and Elizabeth for believing in me and to Pauline, a true and trusted friend.

Chapter One

It was the hole in her tights that made Teri start crying. She looked at them in desperation as sheer as they were. The tights were black with added Lycra 'For Working Legs' and she'd paid £7.99 for them. Seven whole pounds and ninety-nine pence for one pair of tights – and now look at them! Perhaps they would have lasted longer if she'd bought the ones for *non*-working legs.

Her knee was scraped and bright scarlet blood was oozing through the grey grit-encrusted skin. She hadn't had a scabby knee since she was ten, when she'd fallen off the swings in the local playground in the unenlightened days before the Council used knee-friendly landing areas like squishy black rubber or shredded tree bark. It seemed even more cruel when she had managed to negotiate the icy pavements of Euston Road – which, at this moment, were probably suitable for Torvill and Dean to practise on – without an undignified incident.

To help matters along, her briefcase – seeking to exact some minuscule revenge, as only briefcases can – had decided to shed its contents, and her papers blew fussily along the platform in the frantic funnelled breeze from departing trains. *Including hers*.

'Oh hell, I'm really sorry. Here, let me help you.' His

voice was like being stroked with velvet. Okay, so it was a very romantic-novel type of thing to think in the circumstances. But it was true. The voice was soft and soothing and held the faint trace of a quiet, reassuring Scottish burr whose corners had been knocked off by too many years spent in the Home Counties. He looked sort of romantic hero-ish, too. Probably tall, though it was hard to tell as he was crouched over her briefcase carefully gathering its contents to his chest, while the last breathless stragglers hoping vainly to catch the 18.07 for all stations to Milton Keynes pushed heedlessly past them.

'I was rushing to catch the train,' he explained. 'I just didn't see you. I'm sorry.'

'Shit,' Teri said, fishing in her pocket for a tissue. There was one lurking in the corner but she could tell by its disconcertingly crispy feel that it was far too disgusting to pull out in public. 'I'd gathered that,' she said, summoning as much sarcasm as she could manage after having been savaged by such a cute-looking kitten.

'I feel terrible.' He put her papers inside her briefcase and clipped it shut. 'But probably not quite as terrible as you,' he added hastily.

'You'll miss your train.' She sniffed and wiped her eyes with the back of her hand. Although he had stooped to her level, she looked up at him. There was definite eye-contact. Lots of it. His eyes were greeny-gold and bordered with dark-brown rims – as if someone had carefully and lovingly outlined them with brown felt-pen to make the whites look Persil-white. They were soft and warm and she could tell he laughed often. At the moment, they positively oozed concern. Either he was genuinely mortified or he was the leading light in his local amateur dramatics group.

'It's already gone.' He produced a clean white handker-chief from inside his coat with the air of an accomplished magician. Somehow it looked more suave on him than it did on Paul Daniels. 'It was an all-stopper anyway. Here.'

Teri took it reluctantly. She had no idea that men under fifty carried handkerchiefs. It was the equivalent to wear-ing a string vest on chilly mornings or socks with garters or, even worse, those metal armbands that held shirt-sleeves up that were otherwise too long. This hanky looked far too clean to wipe dirty things with. Hesitantly, she dried her eyes.

'Now fold it over and do your knee,' he instructed.

She looked at him to check that he was serious.

'Go on,' he urged.

It was a long time since she had been treated like a four-year-old – probably not since she was four, in fact. And it was even more mind-boggling that, for the moment, she didn't resent it.

Teri dabbed gingerly at the blood and grit, totally ruining the immaculate white linen. She winced. 'Ouch.'

He frowned. 'I think you need to get that properly cleaned up.' He offered her his arm. 'Here, let me help you to your feet.'

He slipped his arm under hers and lifted her easily to her feet. Teri's knees buckled. 'Oh God, I think I've sprained my ankle!' The tears sprang afresh to her eyes. 'That's just about a perfect *sodding* end to a perfect *sodding* day,' she said with feeling.

'Let me have a look.' She hopped round on her good leg, holding on to his back while he examined her ankle. 'No bones broken, but I think your diagnosis is right. Looks like you've twisted it.'

'Are you an expert then?'

He stood up and rubbed his hands together. 'No, but I've watched *Match of the Day* often enough to know when someone's really hurt and when they'll be running around the pitch the next minute as if nothing's happened,' he replied earnestly.

The fount of all useless knowledge straightened up and raked his fingers through his hair. It's amazing the details you notice when you're in pain, Teri thought. His hair was dark and wavy, slightly flecked with grey. Late-ish thirties, she guessed. It was receding slightly at the sides, giving a hint of the baldness that would rob him of his youthful looks later in life. But then nobody was perfect. She should know. She'd dated more men than she'd had low-calorie, low-fat dinners and still hadn't found Mr Right. She'd been through all of the other Mr Men though, in a short history of painful relationships – Mr Lazy, Mr Greedy, Mr Bump, Mr Completely Selfish, Mr Looking-for-Mother-Substitute and Mr Downright Pervert – but, as yet, no Mr Right.

'If I hold you under the arms, could you manage to hop to the public loos? They're not far – just at the end of the station.'

It was possibly the most original chat-up line she'd heard recently – if indeed that was what he was trying to do. And it was certainly better than the one all the double-glazing and space-age vacuum-cleaner salesmen used when she answered the door to them – the very original 'Is your mother at home?'

Perhaps other thirty-year-old women went all skittish and malleable when they were 'mistaken' for teenagers and instantly signed up for lorry-loads of UPVC windows they had no need of, and extortionately priced vacuum cleaners that would ruin your carpets within two years. In her book it earned them nothing more than a withering glare and a faceful of door sandwich.

'Can you manage this?' He passed her handbag to her and gripped her briefcase in the same hand as he held his own.

Teri nodded and hung on to him. 'It would help if you could just relax your grip a bit,' he said breathlessly, as he shifted her weight to his shoulder. 'I've nothing against blue, but I'd rather my face wasn't that colour just at the moment, thanks. Otherwise, we might not make it to the ladies' loos.'

'Sorry, sorry,' Teri said. God must have a really warped sense of humour to put her in this predicament with the most decent-looking man she had bumped into in ages – quite literally. 'You really don't need to do this, you know.' It was hard to hop and talk at the same time.

'Call it a salve to my guilty conscience. And anyway, there isn't another train for twenty minutes.'

'I'm glad to be able to fill in the time for you.'

'Oh sorry, I have the knack of saying the wrong thing.' He looked like a scolded schoolboy.

'Then let's just concentrate our efforts on getting me to the loo in one piece.' Hopping up the steep concrete slope from Platform Eight back on to the main concourse at Euston was an experience Teri wasn't keen to try again in a hurry. But, as usual, in the rush-hour no one gave her a second glance. All commuters worked on the same premise. If they simply looked the other way there was no chance that they could be called on to provide assistance which would delay their flight from the City to the relative sanity of the suburbs – for the few brief hours of respite before they turned round and did it all again.

She hopped to the turnstile at the entrance to the

ladies' loo and rummaged in her handbag for her purse. 'I've got a twenty-pence piece,' he said, and thrust it in the slot before she could protest. He gently pushed her towards the turnstile barrier. 'I'll wait here. Take your time.'

The loos were not very clean – not enough to warrant a twenty-pence entrance fee, anyway. Teri looked at her face in the smeared mirror. Or more accurately, her smeared face in the smeared mirror. Wiping the panda-circles of mascara from under her eyes, she noted regretfully the decreasing amount of white on the borrowed linen handkerchief that she still clutched like a security blanket. She dragged her fingers through her hair and fluffed it up hopefully. It fell flat to her head instantly. She would bet a pound to a penny that Julia Carling didn't have bad hair days. Especially when she had Mr Fanciable of the millennium dancing attendance on her – even if it was in slightly less than romantic circumstances.

'A nice young man asked me to give you these, dear.' A white-haired old lady who looked incredibly like Barbara Cartland – without the pink – thrust a packet of tights into her hands.

'Thank you.' Teri raised her eyebrows appreciatively. Thoughtful with a capital T. 'Wait.' Teri touched her arm. 'How did you know they were for me?'

'He told me to look for the dishevelled woman with a scabby knee,' she replied sweetly. 'It had to be you, dear.'

'Thanks.' Teri smiled a tired smile. 'Yeah – thanks a bunch,' she muttered under her breath to the old lady's retreating back.

One attempt at trying to lift her foot into the wash basin whilst balancing on her good leg told her that it was far too acrobatic a manoeuvre to consider in a tight skirt, considering the indignity she had already suffered. And the paper towels were too rough to bathe her knee with, so Sir Galahad's handkerchief was pressed into service again, then she dried her knee under the hot-air blower that was thankfully broken and was blowing cold. As an afterthought she gave the sodden stained handkerchief a cursory blast.

Teri nipped into one of the cubicles to change into the new tights and meditated on what kind of man would even think to go and buy her a replacement pair. Okay, they weren't anything flash, no Lycra, no Tactel for velvet softness, no satin sheen for enhanced elegance, no elastane for a perfect fit. But they were the right size – although with one size you couldn't go too far wrong – and the right colour – again with black you were pretty safe. At least he had noticed.

And so what if his description of her had been a little less than flattering; it was accurate. He could have said 'attractive, but *temporarily* dishevelled woman', it's true. But then Teri was a firm believer that actions speak louder than words. While she was there, and contemplating deeply, she made use of the facilities. If they were going to charge you twenty pee for a pee, the least you could do was make sure you got value for money.

He was still waiting outside. Which was just as well because he had her briefcase. But she wouldn't have been surprised if he'd disappeared. He could have just dumped it and cleared off. He could have just dumped *her* and cleared off, too. He'd done enough already really – despite the fact it was his fault she had been knocked down in the first place.

He was lounging against the glass wall of the sunbed

salon tucked incongruously into the corner opposite the toilets. How many people clamoured to top up their tans in the salubrious setting of Euston Station was another one of life's little mysteries that deserved further consideration at a later date.

She hopped towards him. 'Thanks for the tights.' She showed him her knee, which through thickish black nylon looked perfectly presentable.

'I hope they were okay. I didn't know if you wore tights or . . .' he blushed '. . . or well, the others, you know.'

It was years since she had seen a man blush. They didn't any more, did they? God, it was endearing. Carrying a handkerchief and blushing – this one was a prize. 'Well, you wouldn't, would you?' she teased.

'I got them in Knickerbox,' he said by way of explana-tion, gesturing towards the glass kiosk filled with pastel shades of frillies in every shape and size imaginable, marooned in the middle of the concourse. 'They have nice things in there.'

'Really?' Teri arched her eyebrows. His skin flushed to a deeper shade of beetroot. She wondered briefly if he was a pervert.

He cleared his throat. 'We'd better move it or we're going to miss this train, too. How's the ankle?'

'I'll live.'

'Come on then, take my arm again.' It had in fact improved to two limps and a hop and they struggled back to the platform for the next train. He paused to look at the display board.

'Which stop?' he asked.

'Leighton Buzzard. And you?'

'Milton Keynes. This one will do us. It leaves in five minutes on Platform Eight.'

They set off again. 'Look, you're helping me marvellously. . .' Teri paused for breath, '. . . with my Long John Silver impersonation.' Limp, limp, hop. 'And I don't even know your name.'

'Jamie,' he puffed. 'Jamie Duncan. I'd shake your hand but you don't seem to have one free.'

'I'm Teri Carter, that's T-E-R-I,' she said breathlessly, trying to co-ordinate breaths and hops to synchronised intervals. 'Pleased to meet you. I think.'

The train was sitting waiting patiently and already most of the seats were taken in the first few compartments. 'There are two together in here.' He opened the door.

'Look, I'll be fine. You've done enough.'

'I insist. My guilt complex still hasn't gone.'

They both sat down gratefully, opposite each other, and Jamie dropped the briefcases on the floor with an exaggerated sigh of relief. 'Thank goodness for that! I'm not sure which is heavier – you or your briefcase.' Several newspapers in the surrounding seats lowered to look briefly at the object of his derision.

'Well, next time you decide to knock a woman over, choose a smaller one!'

'Sorry.' He winced. 'Put your foot up here. It stops the swelling if you elevate it.' He indicated the seat beside him.

'More information gleaned from *Match of the Day*?'

'*Casualty*.'

'I didn't have you down for a *Casualty* watcher.'

'I'm not. My secretary tells me all about it – usually in its full Technicolor glory. She's obsessed with watching operations.'

'*Animal Hospital* is her favourite.' He gave Teri a sideways smile. 'If you'd been a pregnant rhinoceros I'd have known exactly what to do.'

'That's very encouraging, but it probably would have involved more than a pair of black tights and a strong shoulder.'

Jamie shrugged. 'Infinitely more.' Again, he patted the seat next to him. 'Foot.'

Obligingly, after adjusting her skirt to provide a modicum of modesty she raised her foot. He touched her ankle, stroking the swollen area gently. His fingers were cool against the hot skin that throbbed through her tights. Why was her mouth suddenly dry? It was probably delayed shock. She should have bought a drink from the End of the Line Buffet.

'I don't like the look of that.' He tutted and shook his head ponderously. 'I don't like the look of that at all.' His eyes travelled up to her knee. 'Does it hurt anywhere else?'

'Only when I laugh,' Teri said tartly and wriggled her skirt down.

The guard blew his whistle and there was a succession of slamming doors. Their carriage door was wrenched open and a sweating businessman with a florid face and a wet, bald pate squeezed himself on to the seat next to Jamie, smiling genially at him as he lowered his bulk, sandwiching her foot with his bottom. Casually, Jamie lifted her foot and put it on his lap as if it was something he did every day.

The businessman dabbed his face with a handkerchief that was considerably more grubby than Jamie's had previously been – although it was probably a good match for it now.

Teri didn't know which would be more embarrassing, to move her foot away or leave it there throbbing as acutely as her temples. The train jerked out of the station and she decided to leave it there for the time being until she could devise a way to extricate it without drawing too much attention to herself.

'So what do you do when you're not discussing *Casualty* or *Animal Hospital* with your secretary?' she asked, more in an attempt to deflect his eyes from her legs and the fact that one of them was resting ever so comfortably in his lap than out of sheer unadulterated interest.

'I'm a Database Manager for an insurance firm – the Mutual and Providential.'

'That's interesting.'

Jamie smiled. 'That's polite.' He had perfect white teeth, like the ones in a toothpaste advert. The sort of teeth that meant you needn't care less whether there was added fluoride or chloride or bromide – the sort of teeth that made you want to get your own teeth very, very close to them and have first-hand experience of that fresh-breath ring of confidence.

'It's actually the most boring job in the entire universe,' he went on. 'That's why I spend my days discussing the latest load of twaddle on television with my secretary.'

He wasn't touching her foot any more, which somehow made it worse. She couldn't relax, because it might flop and nestle somewhere more intimate than it was now. Hell, she was going to get cramp at this rate.

'What do you do?' he asked.

'I work in television.'

'Oh hell! Sorry.'

'That's all right.' Teri laughed as he flushed again. 'Most of it *is* a load of old twaddle. I work for City Television. And I can't claim any credit for the actual programmes. Like you, I'm at the boring end.'

'I didn't think there was a boring end in television. I

11

thought it was all glamour and luvvies and *dahlings* and free booze.'

'If you can make coffee and count you could do my job.' It hurt more than her ankle did to admit that, and she wondered why she'd told him. Why was she sitting here in a rush-hour commuter train with a stranger, her foot resting just centimetres away from his groin, letting him know about the frustrations of her job? She was one step away from telling him her whole life story!

In ten years of commuting, Teri had never had a conversation with anyone else. She saw the same faces every day, year in, year out, rain, hail and snow – and never a word was spoken. There might be the odd person with whom she was on nodding terms, and once, about three years ago, a woman who ran the Brides' Book at John Lewis in Oxford Street had accidentally prodded her with her knitting needle just outside Berkhamsted and they had chatted amicably for the rest of the journey. She had told Teri that she was knitting a matinée jacket for her new grandson and Teri had wondered if babies still wore white matinée jackets knitted by their grandmas. After that they had been on good nodding terms, which included a smile, but that was about it. She hadn't seen the woman recently and had assumed she'd retired – or died.

'You're probably underselling yourself.' His voice broke into her thoughts.

She shook her head. 'No, but I don't intend to be at the boring end for ever.'

They whistled through a tunnel, the wind buffeting against the windows making conversation impossible. The train was cold as they always are in winter – it's only in summer that hot air belches out relentlessly from beneath the seats – and Teri stared out of the window into the street-light-flecked darkness. The aroma of cooking biscuits from the McVities' factory hadn't twitched her nostrils tonight as it usually did. It normally started her taste buds tingling and her stomach rumbling so that the first thing she did when she got through the door was head for the jar where the Jaffa Cakes were kept and immediately eat three to sate her appetite until it was time for her calorie-counted meal. But not tonight. Tonight her stomach was churning but she certainly couldn't put it down to the enticing smell of biscuits. Perhaps it was Jamie. She hoped to God he wasn't a mind-reader.

He looked at her and winked. It was a reassuring kind of wink. A little shiver had travelled down her spine for a moment, but fortunately, this wasn't a wink that said, 'yes, I *am* a mind-reader'. It was just a wink. His face didn't move at all, just his eyelid squeezed languorously over his eye.

They were definitely feline, his eyes. They reminded her of one of her mother's cats – a long-haired white one with ginger ears called Sooty, which spoke volumes about her mother's state of mind. If anyone had winked at Teri on a train before, she would have hit them squarely on the head with the *Daily Telegraph*. Tonight, the *Telegraph* lay unopened in her traitorous briefcase and she just smiled back.

As the train slowed into Leighton Buzzard, she reluctantly removed her foot.

'Better?' Jamie asked.

'Much.' The puffed skin was swelling over the top of her shoe most attractively. 'Thanks for your concern.'

'It's the least I could do.' He stood up and picked up both briefcases.

'I can manage, thanks.'

'I want to see you safely home.'

'But you live in Milton Keynes! You'll have to wait for the next train.'

'You won't be able to drive.' It was a reasonable assumption. 'Is your car at the station? Or is someone meeting you?'

'No, neither. I walk.' She realised as she said it that walking home would be impossible. 'It's about fifteen minutes,' she added lamely.

'Then we need to get you into a taxi.' Jamie ushered her off the train, hand firmly under her elbow. Teri winced as she hit the platform awkwardly. He helped her towards the footbridge which led from Platform Four to the exit. The bridge looked as if it was made of Meccano and was painted bright red, which added considerably to the effect. They made slow progress. One limp, one hop. Was that an improvement or had it got worse?

'I'm not a mugger or a rapist,' he said thoughtfully as they inched their way along. 'There's no need to worry.'

'Thanks for that character reference,' Teri puffed. 'It hadn't crossed my mind until then.'

'Unless, of course,' he hesitated. 'If there's someone waiting for you and it would be difficult . . .'

'No, there's no one waiting,' Teri answered truthfully. 'Well, at least I don't think so. I'm sharing my house with a very close friend at the moment; I can never tell whether she's going to be there or not.'

'A *very* close friend?' A dark look crossed his face.

Teri laughed. 'Not *that* sort of close friend!'

'I'm sorry – for a moment I thought you meant—'

'I know what you thought! You don't need to spell it out. I might work in television but I'm not that trendy. Clare and I were at school together,' Teri explained. 'Her husband's just run off with some teenage bimbo and she's staying with me.' They took the steps one at a time, Teri clinging on to both Jamie and the handrail for support. 'Though how he found anyone more bimbo-ish than Clare it's hard to imagine. She's a trolley-dolly – sorry, *flight attendant* – at Luton, hence the irregular time-keeping.'

His arm was strong around her and his skin still held the faint scent of a citrus aftershave that said expensive. She was glad she'd agreed to let him take her home. Not that he actually gave her a lot of choice, but she could have invented some excuse for getting rid of him if he'd shown imminent signs of turning into a nerd. She'd had a lot of practice in the past.

It took ages to struggle over the bridge to the cheerful red station that looked as if it had been modelled on a pair of Christopher Biggins's glasses. To add to the bitter cold it had started to drizzle, but thankfully there was a solitary taxi still left at the rank when they emerged from the station. It was a Mercedes – one that had seen considerably better days, and its interior had been brightened by the touching adornment of nylon leopardskin seat covers. Instead of the ubiquitous fluffy dice hanging from the mirror, the driver had installed a yellow-and-black-striped fluffy bee with the legend BUZZ OFF stitched on its rotund stomach. They huddled inside, brushing a sprinkling of raindrops from their clothes.

'Bidefield Green,' she instructed the driver. 'Seven hundred and thirty-two.'

'Seven hundred and thirty-two?' Jamie repeated incredulously.

'I think the Council must have had a particularly heavy lunch the day that Bidefield Green came up for naming, and found it far too tiresome to think up individual and original road names – hence half of Leighton Buzzard is called Bidefield Green. It starts at number one and goes up to about four million and twenty-seven, I think.'

'Four million and twenty-seven?' Jamie echoed.

'At least,' she confirmed.

The driver swung out of the station road and headed up the hill towards the Linslade side of town and Bidefield Green. Leighton Buzzard and Linslade had once been two separate towns, but had grown together over the years to make one endless sprawl of commuter housing. Teri liked living in Linslade – until she had to order something over the phone and then it was a pain, because she had to spell out every line of her address to the operator.

She turned to Jamie again, who was peering out of the rain-streaked and steamed-up window trying to see where he was going in the darkness. 'The numbers follow no logical sequence either,' she said. 'Odds and evens meander randomly round the estate – it must have been a very good lunch. Still, looking on the bright side, it means that unwanted visitors haven't a hope in hell of ever finding you. Unfortunately, neither do the wanted ones.'

There was a grassy knoll as they approached Bidefield Green – halfway up the hill, separating the main road from the first of the houses. Well, it was more a sloping strip of land with a phone box and a post box on it and a couple of smallish oak trees. The post box was totally inadequate to cope with the amount of letters that spewed forth from the occupants of Bidefield Green. If you happened to want to post one yourself, you were invariably greeted by a smiling letter-slit that was crammed full and refused to take anything else – even the slimmest of overdue bill-payments.

Teri always thought of John F. Kennedy when she

passed the grassy knoll. They had learned all about his untimely death in History in the sixth form, and the teacher, Mr Seward, kept going on and on about 'the grassy knoll'. Teri couldn't remember exactly where the grassy knoll had come into it, but it had obviously played some deeply significant role in the assassination. This grassy knoll seemed pointless by comparison, except it was a good place for your dog to poo if you were too lazy to take it for a proper walk.

The taxi driver turned into the estate and threaded his way through the maze of roads. The leopardskin-lined Mercedes slowed to a halt. 'Taxi drivers are infallible though,' Teri said. 'We're here.'

Jamie helped her out. He turned to the taxi driver. 'Can you wait for me, please? I won't be long.'

Teri felt a flash of disappointment. Any thoughts that they might linger over a medicinal glass of Beaujolais had just gone straight out of the window.

'Give me your key,' he instructed. Teri obliged and Jamie opened the door. 'I'll resist the urge to carry you over the threshold, seeing as we've still to be formally introduced.' He ushered her inside.

The house was in darkness – which was a good sign. At least Clare wasn't around to poke her nose in. Jamie led her gently to the sofa and flicked on the light switch. 'Now let me make you a coffee or something.'

'Really, I'm fine. Your meter's running.'

'Black or white?' he insisted.

Teri gave a sigh of resignation. 'Black, no sugar.'

He disappeared into the kitchen and, following the banging of several cupboards, reappeared moments later carrying a tray which he placed beside her.

'Cheese and biscuits – a very fine Camembert – not

exactly a wholesome meal, but filling. One biscuit jar containing only Jaffa Cakes – Madam's weakness, it would appear.'

'Quite.' *That – and tall dark handsome strangers*, Teri added silently.

'One cup of hot coffee, black, no sugar. One large brandy, two painkillers and a bag of frozen peas for reducing the swelling in Madam's ankle.'

'Where did you learn your bedside manner from? Was it *Match of the Day*, *Casualty* or *Animal Hospital*?'

'From your first-aid book on the shelf next to the kettle – a very sensible place to keep it.'

He pulled the footstool towards her, lifted her foot, rolled the peas in a clean tea towel and balanced them on her ankle.

'Comfortable?'

She nodded.

He passed her the remote control for the television and crouched down before her. 'I'm sorry, but I have to go. Is there anything else you need first?'

A lump had risen in her throat. 'No, you've been very kind, thank you. I really appreciate it.'

'Well.' He stood up to go. He really was quite tall. 'Perhaps we'll bump into each other again on the 18.07. Just joking!' He made his way to the door. 'You probably need to stay off that ankle for a few days.' His face was suddenly serious and he looked embarrassed again. 'Are you sure you're going to be all right?'

'Yes, fine. Clare should be back tonight. Your taxi driver will be getting impatient.'

'I'll see you then.'

'Yes, thanks again.' The front door slammed behind him. She watched, stranded on the sofa, as he got into the taxi and it drove away. He really was the nicest man she'd ever met. There weren't many of them left any more, and he was the nicest of them all. No one had been that kind to her since she'd had her tonsils out and the doctor insisted she eat nothing but ice cream for days. So what if the resulting stomach ache had made her feel even worse than having her tonsils out. It was the thought that counted.

She flicked on the television – *Coronation Street*. Not another dose of emotional strain! She sipped her brandy and then, abandoning any sense of decorum, tipped the rest into her coffee and swilled it down with the two painkillers. It was when Jack Duckworth started to pull his first pint of the night in The Rovers Return that she started to cry again. His horn-rimmed glasses repaired with sticky tape always looked particularly pathetic, but never more so than tonight.

Sobbing on to the Camembert, Teri pulled Jamie's handkerchief out of her pocket. It was dirty, bloodied, mascaraed and wet, and still she had an overwhelming urge to use it to wipe away her tears. Damn the bloody man! Fancies himself as a knight in shining armour and he didn't even think to leave a box of man-sized Kleenex to hand. Then again, he might not have imagined her crying quite so uncontrollably when he left. *She* certainly hadn't.

Chapter Two

To hell with the expense. There was no way he was going back to the station to wait for another train now.

Jamie leaned into the taxi window and spoke to the driver. 'Can you take me to Fraughton-next-the-Green, Milton Keynes?'

He always felt stupid, asking for his address. It was like asking for *Poggleswood* or *Tickle-on-the-Tum*. Whoever named the estate in Milton Keynes had a more warped sense of humour than their counterparts in Leighton Buzzard. Mind you, with so many of them to name they must be running out of ideas by now.

The taxi driver looked blank.

'It's near the Open University,' Jamie said helpfully.

He swung into the back of the aging Merc, glad of the warmth after the penetrating dampness of the night. Gratefully, he sank into the worn seat for the drive home to Milton Keynes. He glanced at his watch. It would take about half an hour, providing the driver wasn't intent on breaking the world land-speed record as they so often seemed to be.

The driver turned at the bottom of Teri's road and headed back past her house. Jamie could just make out her outline through the slatted blinds on the window and thought that he should have closed them for her. With any luck, her friend Clare wouldn't be too long in coming home and she could look after her.

Why did he feel so ridiculously deflated, Jamie asked himself, walking away and leaving her like that? He'd done all he could. She wasn't his problem any more. So what *was* his problem? Why had he felt so ridiculously *elated* when she'd said that there was no one waiting at home for her? Why had he, for a brief and shocking moment, wished that he could have said the same thing?

Pamela would be furious. Again. He had promised that he would be home earlier tonight – and he had nearly made it. If he hadn't been rushing quite so much, he might never have rugby-tackled Teri at all. So really, this time, it was Pamela's fault he was late . . . although it wasn't an excuse he was keen to try on her.

Better to stick to the old faithful, he decided – signalling failures at Watford Junction. It was usually true. He certainly couldn't tell her the real truth. Pamela was not an understanding woman. Anyway, why did he feel so guilty about taking Teri back home? He was only doing the Good Samaritan bit, wasn't he? Anyone would have done the same, wouldn't they? Possibly not these days. There might have been a considerable amount of passing by on the other side.

Perhaps he was feeling guilty because it wasn't for entirely altruistic reasons that he had wanted to dally in her company. Hell, she had looked so sexy with her scabby little knee and her wobbly lower lip and her hair that looked as if she had been pulled through a particularly thick hedge backwards *and* forwards. He'd wanted to take her in his arms and cuddle her until all the nasty men went away – except that he had been the nasty man who had knocked her down in the first place. Well, he couldn't just abandon her after that. Could he?

He could hear the closing bars of *Coronation Street* as he turned his key in the lock and wondered briefly whether Pamela had lost her marbles completely while she was waiting for him to come home. She was not a *Coronation Street* person. *Dynasty* might be getting a bit closer, but certainly not the *Street*. Pamela had a terminal fear of all things working-class; she seemed to think that just by watching the programme, serious dropping of the aitches and a liking for black pudding might ensue.

'Hi, I'm home,' Jamie shouted tentatively. There was no reply. Not promising.

MacTavish was cowering under the radiator in the corner of the hall – this was not a good sign either. He wagged his tail tentatively and Jamie patted him. A brief 'Good boy' was all the encouragement he needed to be sent racing upstairs, tail battering the banisters as he went.

Jamie pushed open the lounge door. Next door's fourteen-year-old daughter Melanie was snogging – if that's what they still called it – with her boyfriend on the sofa. His hand was up her skirt and they both shot three feet in the air when Jamie peered over the sofa and said, 'Hello.'

Obviously, the efforts of the *Street*'s best scriptwriters had failed to capture their attention. Jamie rubbed his stubble. 'What *on earth* are you doing?'

They looked at each other for inspiration. Jamie moved up from his stubble and instead rubbed the frown lines on his forehead. 'Forget I said that,' he waved a hand dismissively. 'Where's Pamela?'

'She's gone to Francesca's school. It's parents' night.'

'Oh shit, shit!' Jamie banged the place he had just

23

rubbed. 'I'd completely forgotten about it.' Pamela would do her pieces when she got home. 'Where are the kids?'

'In bed – about an hour ago,' Melanie said sheepishly. 'We're babysitting.'

'We had a different name for it in our day,' Jamie said caustically. They both looked puzzled.

He dropped his briefcase on the sofa. 'Go on, you can clear off home now I'm back.' They shuffled towards the door. 'Did Pamela pay you?'

They shook their heads. He pulled out his wallet and gave them a ten-pound note. 'Go and book yourself a motel room or something,' he muttered.

'Thanks, Mr Duncan.' They departed hastily – Melanie rearranging her Lycra as best she could – presumably before he could change his mind.

He took his coat off, shook the rain from it and hung it over the banister. Pamela hated that too. He would move it before she came home. Tiptoeing up the stairs, he peeped in the children's bedrooms. Jack was curled up with his thumb in his mouth, a tumble of blond hair curling over the duvet. He looked just like Pamela and, more unfortunately, had every sign of having inherited her temperament as well as her looks.

Francesca was stretched out fast asleep on top of her duvet with Barbie. She was like him – tall, the tallest in her class, dark and easygoing – lazy in school terms. He turned away from the doorway.

'Mummy's very cross with you.'

He suppressed a smile and turned back. 'I know. I was late home from work, when I said I wouldn't be. She's gone to see Mrs Rutherford.'

'I bet that'll make her cross too.'

He smoothed her hair and laughed. 'I hope not. Go to sleep.' He kissed her forehead.

'Mummy had to ring Kathy next door so that Melanie could come round to stay with us. She called you an inconsiderate bastard.' It sounded appealing with a faint lisp due to the absence of two front teeth.

'She's probably right. But those are grown-up words that aren't very nice. Don't try them in the playground or you'll upset Mrs Rutherford.'

'Goodnight, Daddy.'

'Goodnight, darling.'

'Daddy.'

'Yes, darling?'

'MacTavish is under the bed.'

'It's probably a good place for him at the moment.'

'Goodnight.'

Pamela had continued the illegitimate offspring theme in the kitchen. He opened the oven door and took out the well-cooked plate with a folded tea towel. On it were three fish fingers that definitely wouldn't have inspired Cap'n Birdseye to cry, 'Yo, ho, me hearties,' some sadly deflated livid green spheres that probably used to be peas, and some reconstituted potato Alphabites spelling the word BASTARD that were arranged in a neat semi-circle around the edge of the plate.

Jamie wondered whether his wife had got all the letters from one bag, or whether she had opened two bags specially. It seemed more vindictive to open two bags, but he fought the urge to search the freezer to check. Jamie popped the B into his mouth with his fingers. It burnt his tongue.

He took his plate through to the conservatory, taking the tomato ketchup from the cupboard on the way. It could be a bit on the chilly side in here in the winter, but at least looking at some of the exotic plants still thriving in there gave him an indication of the warmer days to come, and helped to dispel the misery he felt at spending six months of the year always leaving in the morning and returning home at night in the pitch dark.

It might also help him to digest this dried-up school dinner. His first inclination had been to scrape it into the bin – or into the dog – and make himself a sandwich, but that would have been ungrateful. It was his fault he was late and he would take Pamela's punishment like a man – or a mouse, depending on which way you looked at it.

Jamie spread ketchup over the rest of the -ASTARD and began to work his way through it letter by letter. It was a well-known fact of life that tomato ketchup made even the most unlikely thing edible. That was why the children smeared it on chips, cabbage, curries and cereal, even Coco Pops. It wasn't that Pamela couldn't cook, it was just that recently she had taken it into her head that everything in the house had to be educational. And that obviously included mealtimes.

These days, his wife wasn't happy unless the children could spell with their food, or at the very least make a funny face – which tended to prolong the time spent at the table. Jack could already spell DOG and CAT with Alphabites. Give him a book or a pencil and he was stuffed, but food, that was a different matter altogether. Jamie was under the impression that it was Pamela's aim for him to be the first three-year-old at the nursery to be able to read the baked-bean version of *War and Peace*. He had some way to go yet. But that didn't stop her from trying.

There had been one temporary moment of politically

incorrect madness when Pamela had returned pale-faced from Toys R Us, Francesca triumphantly clutching a Barbie doll – 'because she was the only girl in the entire school who didn't have one'. She omitted the fact that she had a computer complete with Pentium Processor, jigsaws too numerous to mention, a tool kit – non-sexist household – and all manner of mind-expanding playthings. But all had been forsaken in favour of Barbie – the anorexic blonde-haired bimbo who made Pamela Anderson look positively deflated. Pamela – Duncan, not Anderson – feared she was failing in motherhood and to make up for this brief aberration had turned all family meals into tutorials.

At least the awfulness of his meal had distracted him momentarily from thinking about Teri. He should have stayed and tucked into Camembert and cheap brandy with her – at least then he would have felt his punishment justified. Why did he feel so wretched about leaving her alone with nothing but a bag of frozen peas for solace? He pushed his few remaining peas round his plate in sympathy.

And her name – it slipped so casually off his tongue, as if he had been saying it for years. *Teri.* He wondered if it was short for something or whether her parents had been particularly trendy. He would ask her next time he saw her. Grief! What was he thinking of? There would *be* no next time. How many years had he travelled on that line without seeing her before? Still, he knew where she worked. He could casually orchestrate it so that he was walking by City Television offices just as she was going home for the evening – they were only just up the road from Euston Station. But perhaps she didn't go home at that time every night; perhaps she was leaving early to go to the dentist or something. But then she would have mentioned it . . .

He gripped the arms of his wicker chair. This was a train of thought that must stop – no pun intended. Why was he even thinking of wanting to meet her again? He was happily married – well, mostly – with two point two children, if you included Barbie. He and Teri had nothing in common with each other and no need to speak again. Commuting and communicating might begin with the same letters, but that was where the similarity ended. He had knocked her over – crass, but accidental – and he had done his bit and that was the end of it. And the sooner he convinced himself of that the better.

When he finally heard Pamela's key turn in the lock, Jamie let out a heartfelt sigh. With any luck, Francesca would have done the business and would have sucked up to Mrs Rutherford enough at the last minute to get straight gold stars for everything. That could come close to letting him off the hook.

The only thing that would massage Pamela's ego further was if Francesca's inspirational painting of 'My Mummy' looked vaguely like her rather than the abstract Picasso-style monster she usually managed to produce. Pamela would not be happy if she had green hair, white high-heeled shoes and was smoking a cigarette like she was last year.

'Hello, darling,' she shouted from the hall.

Jamie shrugged and raised his eyebrows. Things were looking up. Then he remembered that his coat was still draped over the banister rail. That could well mean the end of the *entente cordiale* as we know it and the start of another Cold War.

He heard his wife clip, clop across the parquet floor until she paused by the stairs. It was a technique the SS used in old films to menace prisoners of war who had thought to escape by rather overtly digging a tunnel while whistling loudly to cover the noise. The soldiers clicked along the corridors just before they were about to torture them without the benefit of modern anaesthetics.

After a sufficiently significant and nerve-wracking pause, Pamela clipped into the kitchen. 'I'm going to bed,' she announced in clipped tones and promptly clipped out again. She obviously needed time to think up a particularly hideous torture.

Jamie ate the last of his BASTARD with a heavy heart. It seemed he could look forward to facetious Alphabite messages for the rest of the week.

Chapter Three

'So what else did he say?'

'Nothing.' Teri lifted her hands in the air and gestured meaningfully. 'He just got in the taxi and went.'

'Just like that,' Clare said in disgust.

'Just like that.'

'I thought it was only Tommy Cooper who went "just like that!".' Clare did a passable impression. She waited for Teri to laugh.

Teri glared at her instead.

Clare carried on regardless. 'You must be losing your touch.' She flopped down on the sofa next to Teri, dislodging the carefully placed bag of once-frozen, now dripping peas. 'You, the same person who in her time has dated Billy Bunter and the Frog Prince – the one who turned from a prince into a *frog* – have freely admitted that you let the fittest man you have seen this century disappear in a taxi without so much as waving your Filofax at him!'

'He said he had to go.' Teri was getting irritable.

'He might have been waiting for you to ask him not to,' Clare pointed out. 'Men like that sort of thing these days.'

'He had me at a physical disadvantage. I wasn't thinking straight.' She kicked the peas off her ankle on to the floor.

'Besides – asking him not to go didn't keep your dearly beloved David in the marital bed.'

Clare looked stung. 'That was below the belt, Therese Carter.' She pronounced her name with the harshness of a scouser – rather than the softness her mother had sought to inject into it against all the Liverpudlian odds. To Clare, particularly in moments of sublime irritation such as this, she was Tereeza – a bit like *Malteser*. Teri had hated her name at school and wished desperately that she had been called Dawn – which was surprising considering how awful she was at getting up in the mornings.

'I know, I'm sorry.' Teri hugged a cushion forcefully. 'It's just that I could kick myself.'

'I could kick you too.'

Teri scowled. 'That's no consolation.'

'So you don't know where he lives or works or anything?'

'He said he was in insurance.'

'Riveting.' Clare rolled her eyes. 'You could crash your car,' she said helpfully, after giving it some thought.

'I think I'll just stick to hanging round Euston Station looking nonchalant.'

'Your intentions could be mistaken.' Clare picked at the remains of the Camembert. 'Still, you might earn a few bob while you're waiting.'

Teri thumped her with the cushion. 'He's not like all the others. He's nice.'

'Nice? Nice! *Nice* is a banned word! Surely you can't have forgotten the hours spent in Mrs Bagshaw's class discussing nice. "Nothing is *naice*, Clare".' She mimicked her teacher's cut-glass tones. 'She could reel off a thousand other adjectives that were better than dear old nice. And I still can't bring myself to write in red pen because of that woman.'

'He is nice. He's *very* nice! He's the only man I've met who doesn't act like Jean-Claude Van Damme on amphetamines. He's sensitive and intelligent.'

Clare continued unabashed, 'He can't be that intelligent if he walked out of here without fixing himself a hot date.'

'He may not have fancied me,' Teri mumbled.

'What does that matter? You were still panting after him like the Andrex puppy when I came home. Surely he was bright enough to know he was on to a sure thing?'

Teri glared at her. 'I'm glad you think so highly of my morals.'

'You never did know how to play hard to get, Therese. Look at Christopher Parry. You were all over him like a rash.'

'I only went out with him twice and I did have a rash!'

'It just goes to prove my point.' Clare smiled superciliously at her victory. 'So you didn't ask him anything else?'

Teri tutted. 'I couldn't really.'

'Why not?'

'I was embarrassed.' Teri flushed.

'Embarrassed!'

'He kept looking at me – like *looking*.'

'It's a good job you're not a private detective or an investigative journalist – you'd starve to death. You could learn a lot from paying attention to Kate Adie.' Clare wagged her finger. 'For goodness sake, you're a woman of the nineties! You carry rainbow-coloured condoms in your handbag! What are you planning to do with them – blow them up and twist them into cute little poodles or giraffes once they're past their sell-by date?'

'Be sympathetic! I'm supposed to be your best friend. I have opened my home to you in your hour of need; the least you could do is pretend to listen to me in mine.' Teri poured herself some more brandy from the bottle Clare had retrieved from the kitchen. 'And, anyway, you seem to have fewer admirers than Fergie at the moment, so don't give me a hard time.'

Clare groaned. 'Working for an airline isn't the best place for checking out talent. They're all either married or gay.'

'And what about David?'

'Still terminally ensconced with the nubile Anthea. Still declaring that it's me he really loves, but would I be prepared to accept the fact that he can love two women at the same time – and probably in the same bed, knowing David.'

'Bastard.' Teri threw back her brandy.

'Bastard.' Clare joined her.

Teri refilled their glasses. 'Here's to nice men!' The brandy was making her eyes water.

'To nice men,' Clare agreed. 'Wherever they are!'

They both drained their glasses. The brandy was giving Teri a warm glow that made her feel slightly blurred round the edges like a bad photocopy. Amazingly, she couldn't feel the pain in her ankle at all! It had gone clean away – just like Jamie.

The thought was enough to make her reach for the bottle again. She had found her nice man and she had let him go by mistake. Perhaps another drink would help. If she wasn't careful she could become very depressed about it.

Chapter Four

'I'm just amazed that you happened to be walking past the office exactly when I was leaving,' Teri said breathlessly. 'Isn't that amazing?'

'Yes, a coincidence,' Jamie shouted animatedly. 'How's the ankle?'

'What?'

'Ankle!' Jamie bawled, and pointed helpfully.

'Better!' she yelled back and gestured at her ear. 'It's the traffic.'

She pulled her coat around her and they leaned into the chill wind that gusted a few tired and dirty leaves across Euston Road, walking along in an uneasy silence enforced by the noise of the rush-hour.

Teri put her head down to stop the swirling dust blowing in her eyes. Her heart was pitter-pattering like stiletto heels clicking on a concrete pavement. She was keeping pace with Jamie – just about, he took long, easy strides that covered twice as much ground as she could. From the beat of her heart it sounded as if she was running a marathon.

She had been stunned to see him draped casually against the wall outside her office. In fact, she thought it was the closest she had come to suffering a cardiac arrest.

Despite trying to engineer it to bump into him at Euston she hadn't managed it at all and, apart from the physical evidence of a still green and purple ankle, was beginning to think that he had been a hallucination brought on by the stresses and strains of daily commuting. She had been about to give up hope of ever seeing him again. Clare had given up all hope on her unequivocally.

He was gorgeous. More gorgeous than she remembered – possibly because he didn't look quite so harried this time. She risked a sideways glance at him and he smiled in return. He looked suave and sophisticated. He was dark-suited under his light-coloured cashmere coat – brave for a commuter – and looked every inch the success-ful insurance company executive. His dress was immaculate – classic and traditional – but with a rakish cut to the clothes that spoke of a slight rebellious streak pushing against the bounds of staid conformity. The sort of man who wouldn't look out of place modelling designer clothes for *Esquire* magazine. Executives at City Television wore jeans with loud Hawaiian shirts and had bald heads and long ponytails.

They looked at each other and smiled occasionally along the route and did their best to ignore the entreaties of the hopeful homeless selling the *Big Issue* and the hopeless homeless already huddled down for the night in their sleeping bags.

The stark concourse of Euston Station always seemed relatively peaceful in comparison to Euston Road, despite the hordes of miserable-looking people. At least you could hear yourself speak in there. It was a functional station building – that was the best that could be said about it – square, austere, but functional. Its architecture made no effort to mimic the ornate, gothic romanticism of St Pancras or King's Cross. Euston, it appeared, had been styled along the lines of a Lego brick – seemingly a popular style of architecture in the early sixties.

Years ago it had been fronted by a small, scruffy park full of dossers and drunks and day-trippers. In its place there was now a bare plaza with half a dozen struggling trees, half a dozen concrete benches and a browning oblong of grass, banked on three sides by black-glassed office buildings.

In the centre was a modern sculpture – a sort of wigwam of crossed drainpipes bearing cheery colourful metal flags – which looked deep and meaningfully significant. There were two brass plaques at the bottom of the poles. One said: *Euston Banners 1994*, the other: *Smoke Extractor Basement Level Six*.

At the corner of the square next to William Hill bookies, stood a statue of Robert Stephenson, who died on 12 October 1859 – and who must be gyrating in his grave at the current state of the railways.

Once inside, Teri and Jamie crossed the main concourse dotted with small and colourful merchandise kiosks and stood beneath the black departure display board which towered above them. It was doing more clattering than a demented pinball machine.

'This looks ominous,' Jamie stated flatly.

Their train disappeared off the board – all stations to Milton Keynes being replaced by suspiciously permanent-looking blanks. A passenger announcement began in the usual mix of English, double Dutch and mumble. 'The late-running 18.07 for all stations to Milton Keynes has been cancelled. This will now become the late-running 19.07 for all stations to Milton Keynes, departing from

Platform Eight at approximately 19.37 for all stations to Milton Keynes. This unavoidable delay is due to signalling failures at Watford Junction.'

Jamie's shoulders sagged visibly and he looked at his watch. 'This is going to be another free-for-all fight. Do you fancy giving the scrum a miss and going for a drink instead?'

So what if she missed her 'Calligraphy for Beginners' at Vanwall Upper School? She'd long given up hope of ever needing it to write beautifully scripted wedding invitations. The best she could hope for now would be writing labels for jam jars when she eventually succumbed to her bath-chair and joined the WI.

Besides, Mrs Jessop made the ancient craft of illegible writing seem so utterly unenthralling and tedious that you could actually find yourself wishing for death during her lessons. The fact that the class had dwindled from a relatively healthy nineteen to start with, to a sickly four just after the start of the second term was possibly an indication that other students shared the same view.

Mrs Jessop had been teaching calligraphy for twenty-five years, she proudly told them every week. Perhaps twenty-five years ago she had made it sound interesting. Teri wondered how many hapless souls had in previous years signed their twenty-nine quid away to be subjected to torture by italics and half-uncials without any in-tervention from the local education authority – who were presumably supposed to monitor the standard of teaching. The stoic remaining students were all of the same if-you-start-something-you-see-it-out-to-the-end-no-matter-what-the-personal-cost school of thinking. It was now a matter of honour that she should keep this lifelong vow no matter how hard Mrs Jessop and her badly behaved waterproof ink bottle and interchangeable nibs tried to persuade her otherwise.

Teri was sure the other three stalwarts could manage without her for one week. Her low-fat chicken Tikka Masala for One wasn't going to come to any harm languishing in the fridge for a little bit longer either. The decision was made.

Teri nodded. 'I'd love a drink.'

The only pub at Euston hovered high over one corner of the concourse, jutting out over the bookshop and the burger bar beneath it. It was faced in the same flat grey-coloured tiles as the rest of the concourse and, as such, was virtually indistinguishable from the public toilets.

If you managed to get a window seat – a bit of a misnomer because there wasn't actually any glass, just a window-shaped hole through which a constant draught blew – you could watch the disappointed sagging of the shoulders as the swarming commuters ground to a halt beneath the display boards. This was the point where they recognised that it was going to be a long night and any hopes of an early dinner and a night in front of the telly were once again dashed.

The pub was called 'Steamers', presumably through some clever marketing man's bright idea of an allusion to the Golden Age of Railways, rather than to the fact that the only reason most people went to such an awful place was to get steaming drunk. Anyway, they could hardly call it 'Diesel Electrics' or 'Commuter Cattle Trucks', could they? Where was the romanticism in that?

The inside was an illusion of a bygone age, too. A sort of mock-Victorian fantasy had been forced to merge seamlessly with *Star Wars*. The stools were of the finest imitation tapestry, the lampshades crimson and fringed.

Even the toilet doors continued the theme, respectively adorned with silhouetted ladies in crinolines and gentlemen sporting top hats and canes. Somehow the bank of fruit machines, the juke box and the television screens detracted from the overall effect slightly. The prices made no attempt at nostalgia either – they were firmly fixed in the future.

Teri and Jamie joined the throng of other deflated commuters who had decided that battling against British Rail's best efforts to prevent them from getting home was something that couldn't be faced without a seriously topped-up alcohol reservoir. Sitting for two hours in a stone-cold carriage on a red signal while INTERCITY trains whistled past you wasn't something that was easy to endure while still entirely stone-cold sober.

'What would you like?' Jamie was already taking his wallet from his coat.

'A gin and tonic, please.' She really wanted a Beck's but that seemed so unsophisticated. A gin and tonic was so much more of a timeless classic – she didn't like it much, but nevertheless it was a timeless classic.

'Grab some seats,' he shouted over the noise as he pushed his way to the bar.

A table was just being vacated by two exceedingly blowsy women wearing particularly see-through blouses and ridiculously short skirts. As they pulled on their jackets and tottered out of the bar in totally unsuitable high-heeled shoes, giggling and patting overtly at their straw-blonde hair, probably wigs, no one else in the bar gave them a second glance. In the once-quaint market town of Leighton Buzzard they would have stuck out like Richard Branson in a dole queue, yet thirty-five minutes down the line in the great metropolis they were just two more weird-looking people having a drink. It was only slightly more weird that the drinks had been pints of bitter . . . That was feminism for you.

Teri pushed their abandoned glasses to one side, swept the puddles of spilt beer to the floor with the beer mat, and waited for Jamie.

He returned clutching two drinks and two bags of crisps, flushed-faced and obviously sweating inside his coat. He clanked the drinks on to the table and tossed the crisps after them. 'Thought these might keep us going.'

He took his coat off, rolled it into a ball and tossed it on the floor as casually as he had tossed the crisps on to the table. Teri didn't think it was a wise move but said nothing. She sipped gratefully at her drink. It was a dry Martini and lemonade, and the shock of the unexpected sweetness made her wrinkle her nose – but again she said nothing.

'Cheers.' Jamie held up his glass. Some sort of beer. 'I just wanted to apologise again for last week.'

'Were you waiting for me, then – outside work?' Teri swallowed the dry Martini again. It really wasn't so bad once you got used to it. Better than gin and tonic, actually.

Jamie shook his head vigorously and wiped a smear of froth from his top lip. 'Oh no, of course not.'

Teri's heart sank quicker than her vain attempts at making soufflés had.

'Well, when I say no, I mean not exactly,' he corrected. 'It was just that I thought I might see you – on the train – and when a few days had gone by and I didn't, well, I happened to remember where you said you worked and I just thought I'd see if you were around. Sort of.'

'Oh,' Teri said. Her throat had gone tight.

They both took a swig of their drinks. 'Yes, I actually

hung around outside your office waiting for you,' he admitted. 'Sorry.'

She smiled. 'No, that's okay. That's nice.'

'Well, I just wanted to check the ankle was okay, really.' He shrugged with a nonchalance that he didn't really feel. The sort of shrug that says, 'I won't lose any sleep over it' when in fact he had lost lots of sleep. The varying troubles of database management – which were the usual cause of his nocturnal insomnia – had paled into insignificance faced with the turned ankle of a fragile beauty on his conscience. He had been bleary-eyed and bad-tempered every morning after a night spent lying awake thinking about nothing but Teri Carter.

It was ridiculous; he felt like a fifteen-year-old sitting here, suddenly nervous and gawky again. Like a puppy still coming to terms with its oversize paws. She was just as he remembered her, though why he thought she would have changed in a week was uncertain. In fact, he wished she *had* changed, or that his memory of her had been too vivid and overblown, like a movie shown in Technicolor Cinemascope. But no, she was still beautiful. She was still elfin and dainty like one of the flower fairies in the book that Francesca was so keen on him reading at least three times every bedtime – when he was home in time.

Teri looked at him above her glass; her eyes were unnaturally blue and she had eyelashes like Daisy the Cow. He wasn't absolutely sure that she wasn't wearing coloured contact lenses. No one had eyes *that* blue . . . except possibly Paul Newman. Pamela always commented on Paul Newman's eyes. That was why she'd started to buy Paul Newman's Own Salad Dressing, because of his eyes. Teri's eyes could sell salad dressing. They could probably sell ice to Eskimos, too.

He was aware that she was speaking. 'Sorry?'

'I said it's fine, thanks.'

'The drink?'

'The ankle. You asked about my ankle.'

God, he wished she was ugly, he might be able to pay more attention to what she was saying. Her face kept distracting him. She had a tiny, rosebud mouth that pursed and pouted when she talked, and little perfect teeth that showed she wasn't one to neglect her dental appointments.

'Clare and I shared a medicinal bottle of brandy and got rather too carried away.'

Perhaps he should suggest putting a paper bag over her head, then he might listen to her rather than just wanting to sit and look at her. Then again, she could take it the wrong way.

'I had such a bad headache the next day, it made my ankle seem trivial by comparison. They say that the body can only cope with one type of pain at a time, don't they?'

Jamie snapped his attention back to her. 'Do they?'

'I don't know. Anyway, there'll be no more sherry trifle in our house for a while.' She abandoned her low-fat, healthfood kick and split the packet of Roast Beef-flavoured crisps open. All this talk of food, even if it was sherry trifle, was making her hungry.

'You put brandy in your sherry trifle?' he said inanely. 'Isn't there a hint there in the title somewhere?'

She hated sherry trifle and only made it when her mother came to stay. She used brandy in it to make her mother forget to ask her the usual irritating questions about the men in her life, the life in her men and the imminent possibility of grandchildren.

Sometimes the trifle was so strong that it resembled a

Madeira cake floating in half a bottle of Courvoisier, with a pint of Ambrosia ready-made custard precariously balanced on top. That was when it was getting towards the end of her mother's week-long visit. The dish might not be all that attractive or even that edible, but it kept Mrs Carter in a soporific state for a few hours so it certainly did the trick. Desperate times require desperate measures. 'I hate sherry,' she said, by way of simplified explanation.

It was Pamela's favourite drink, dry sherry – a small one on high days and holidays. That, and dry Martini and lemonade.

'Oh hell – I can't believe it! I bought you the wrong drink.' What was he doing? He was here on an illicit . . . an illicit *what*? An illicit drinking session with a girl he didn't know and he glibly bought her his wife's favourite drink. What a prize prat! 'You wanted a G and T, didn't you? Grief, you must think I'm an idiot.'

'I do, but it doesn't matter.'

'Let me get you another one.' He was already on his feet.

'No really, it doesn't matter.' Teri downed the Martini and lemonade in one. 'Oh, to hell with it, why not. Forget the gin, though. I'll have a Beck's and I'll drink it straight out of the bottle.' She smiled wanly at Jamie's startled face. 'Thanks.'

Two hours and several Beck's later they were finally jerking past the graffitied walls and out of Euston. Conversation had been difficult in the bar, partly due to the decibel level of the animated chatter of stranded commuters, and thanks also to the fruit machines, which bleeped and chimed above it all and then clank-clank-*clanked* their hoard of treasure out every few minutes. It was also partly due to the fact that Jamie seemed to go into a trance every time she spoke to him. Teri was beginning to wonder if she was boring him at one point, but he seemed to get over it as the evening wore on. Perhaps he was just tired.

It was difficult to talk now, too. The train was still crowded despite their diversionary delaying tactics of a dalliance in Steamers Bar. Jamie was sitting silently next to her and they exchanged the occasional smile, but neither of them seemed to think it appropriate either to chat or to get their newspapers out. The signals at Watford Junction, it appeared, still couldn't decide whether they wanted to function or not, so the train inched slowly from station to station while the evening sped rapidly by.

Although the term 'cry wolf' lodged itself firmly in Jamie's brain, he was feeling quite mellow. As mellow as a newt probably. But who cared? It only took him a moment to come up with the answer: Pamela would care. Pamela would care deeply. If you ate more than three wine gums in a row, Pamela thought you were on the rocky road to alcoholism. He would have to get a taxi back from the station and risk leaving the car to the tender mercies of the overnight car park. He would be lucky to have any wing mirrors or windows or stereo left by morning or, indeed, a car at all.

As soon as she saw the taxi turning into their drive she would know he'd been drinking. That in Pamela's vocabulary was drunk. As a skunk. Okay, so he'd had more than the local constabulary would find excusable, but he was still a long way off what George Best would consider a good night out. Still, it was worth it. He'd managed in his quest to bump into Teri again – even though it had meant leaving work early and hanging around the windswept wasteland of Euston Road until she appeared. But what had it achieved? he mused. They had spent a very pleasant couple of hours getting sociably inebriated with the perfectly viable excuse of signal failures at Watford Junction, and now what? The urge to see her again was stronger than ever before and she hadn't even got off the train yet! Teri wasn't just pretty, she was feisty and funny and could probably drink most rugby players under the table without looking even slightly the worse for wear.

Why did she seem to come right into the centre of him and fill a gap that he hadn't even realised was there? He wasn't unhappy with Pamela. Okay, they had their moments – sometimes it was like living with Princess Michael of Kent with the added bonus of premenstrual tension – but on the whole they had a reasonable marriage, certainly no worse than anyone else's these days.

All right, so he was bored utterly witless by his job; it was only the sheer volume of work and playing political pat-a-cake that gave him sleepless nights – the actual job he could do standing on his head and sometimes felt like doing so just to prove a point. Still, they paid him a barrow-load of cash just for turning up, so it could be considerably worse. He absolutely adored the kids – even when they vomited in the Volvo on long car journeys. They were the best thing that had ever happened to him. That, and winning the Club Championship at Melbrose Golf Club when he was eighteen . . .

So why was he doing this? Doing what? He wasn't *doing* anything! But if he wasn't doing anything, why did he feel so guilty about not doing it? Why couldn't he say to Pamela: 'I was late last week because I clumsily bumped into a woman and sprained her ankle for her in the process, and I'm late tonight because we happened to meet up at the display board' (slight alteration of the truth admittedly) 'and I took her for a drink to enquire about the well-being of the aforementioned ankle.'

Simple enough? Simple, but deadly. If there was one thing you had to understand about Pamela it was that she couldn't cope with glitches in her daily domestic harmony, and her husband taking a strange woman, however injured, for a drink would definitely be considered a glitch.

He could just see it now – it would mean tears, tantrums, a temporary but inconvenient banishment to the spare room, and an upgrading in the vile atrocities of Alphabite combat. So signal failures it was and signal failures it would remain and he would avoid the endearing charms of Teri Carter – named Therese after a genteel and elderly maiden aunt, but reappraised to Teri on account of the amount of time she spent shinning up trees and playing football as a wee schoolgirl rather than doing cross-stitch – as if they were a deadly plague.

'We're coming into Leighton Buzzard.' Teri stood up and smoothed her skirt, which didn't really need smoothing. He was aware that a few newspapers in the vicinity dipped noticeably.

'It's been great,' Jamie said lightly. She had picked up a thread of cotton on the arm of her jacket from the back of the train seat, which was split at the seam and oozing stuffing. He longed to reach out and take it from her, grooming her so that she looked perfect again. This was ridiculous. He locked his fingers together, just in case they had the urge to disobey his brain. 'Perhaps we'll bump into each other again.'

'I'd like that.'

The train stopped at the platform and the man in front of Teri jumped out. She hesitated, only slightly, but Jamie knew a hesitation when he saw one. Why couldn't she still have a sprained ankle, one that would keep her limping for months, then he could gallantly sweep her off the train and have a watertight excuse for escorting her home? He wanted to go with her to her little seventies box on the hideous sprawling housing estate and close the door behind them for ever.

'What time train do you catch in the morning?' she asked.

'The 6.25,' he answered, his heart pounding like a Bon Jovi bass line in his chest. 'It stops at Leighton Buzzard.'

She smiled. 'Perhaps I'll see you then.'

The door slammed behind her and he watched her picked out in the darkness by the platform lights as she ran nimbly up the stairs of the red metal footbridge. That was how it started. As simple as that.

Chapter Five

'Can't you come up with something more original than that?' Pamela clanged the spoon on the plate as she dished out some Alphabetti Spaghetti. 'Do the signals *ever* work at Watford Junction?'

'It would appear not,' Jamie said resignedly. 'Look, I've had a verra long day and I don't want to argue with you.' His accent always got stronger when he was cross – and he knew it annoyed Pamela. 'Would it make you happier if I told you it was vampire bats hanging from the overhead wires that had caused the delay?' And when Pamela snorted, 'I thought not.'

'British Rail have a much larger catalogue of excuses than the pathetic ones you resort to.' She banged the grill-pan into the dishwasher. 'Whatever happened to the wrong-type-of-snow or the feeble leaves-on-the-line routine?'

'Those are seasonal phenomena which can only be used for a paltry few weeks. The rest of the time they have to use more vague, catch-all excuses. There'd be no point in saying the wrong type of snow was causing delays when there'd been no snow at all.' Jamie rested his head in his hands. 'Commuters might be a pretty stupid bunch, but even we'd spot that one a mile off.'

Pamela tutted. It was an unconvinced *tut!* and she banged the drawer shut to underline it. He looked at his wife from between the hammock his hands made under his chin. She was tall, cool and classy, with great hair. It was long, straight and reddy-blonde like a lion's mane, although she had recently taken to having it surgically enhanced with highlights – unlike his own hair which was seeing the beginnings of genetically programmed highlights. Her eyes were the colour of chocolate buttons and she sort of blended in with autumn. The word which most suited her was 'aloof'. Definitely aloof – and perfect – and socially aware. Pamela was as different from Teri as *I Can't Believe It's Not Butter* is from, well, butter.

'You take no interest in the children.' She obviously had no intention of letting this drop.

'I take lots of interest in the children. It's just that it can't often be on a week night at the moment. They won't always be in bed by seven o'clock.'

'That's still not much use if you can't get home before nine o'clock.' The plate of Alphabetti Spaghetti and two burnt sausages was crashed down on the table in front of him. 'They could be eighteen by the time you get to see them on a Wednesday.'

Still surveying her he could see that Pamela was pale and her face looked strained. She must be tired because she had failed to spell anything vitriolic with the Alphabetti Spaghetti. That could also be because it was much more slippery to deal with than Alphabites. Creative caustic comments with unco-operative carbohydrates required a certain level of concentration – he knew this because he had tried it once to see how long it must take her. Admittedly, a novice at tinned-pasta abuse, he had spent ten minutes trying to find the right letters to spell bloody cow before he gave up. By which time the bright-orange-coloured tomato sauce had gone cold. There was definitely an art to it.

'You don't see them at the weekends either,' she went on tersely. 'You're always out on that damned golf course!'

Jamie put down the knife and fork he had just picked up. 'It's my only form of relaxation – and exercise, come to that. And it's certainly the only exercise MacTavish gets.' The dog slinked guiltily out of the kitchen before he was incriminated further.

Jamie picked up his knife and fork again. 'And despite getting up at five-thirty every morning to go to work, on Saturday I still get up at just after six so that I can play a few holes and be back here by lunchtime to see what word of the day is. Then we have all afternoon to do family things.'

'But we don't, do we? You usually fall asleep in front of the television in the afternoon while purporting to watch motor racing.'

'That's only if you haven't got anything specific planned – and besides, I'm so bloody exhausted at the weekends I can only just manage to sit upright after three o'clock.' He stuck his fork into a sausage and belligerently bit the end off it.

Pamela winced but didn't comment. Obviously, his eating habits would wait until another time.

'I take them to the playground at Willen Lake,' he munched. 'Occasionally.'

Pamela refused to be easily placated. 'It's not fair, Jamie. It's not fair on me, and it's not fair on the kids.'

'Look on the bright side, it's only a matter of time before they'll be big enough to play golf with me.'

Pamela's face darkened ominously.

'It was meant to be funny,' he said, putting his sausage down. 'It was a joke. Remember jokes? They come in Christmas crackers along with paper hats that don't fit and rubbishy bits of plastic that are broken by Boxing Day.'

'I don't think it's funny at all.'

'I don't think it's funny either. And if we're going to discuss not being fair – I hardly think you're being fair.' He pushed the plate away from him and massaged his temples. 'I work five long days each week in a mind-numbing job. I don't need this when I come home. I don't get in at this hour every night out of choice.'

It was horrifying to find out how easy lying became, once you started. The lies took on a life of their own and one little lie built on top of another until you had a huge shaky column of lies and you had to build another even bigger column next to it to support it. It was the same basic principle he was trying to teach Jack with Duplo and with considerably less success – except that with big, brightly coloured building bricks rather than people's lives it was infinitely more simple and didn't hurt so much when they all inevitably came tumbling down.

'Then leave your job.'

'You know I can't do that. I'm handcuffed there.' Jamie rubbed his eyes. 'They pay twice as much as anyone else would for the equivalent post.'

'You could take a pay cut. We could manage.'

'Don't be ridiculous. We certainly couldn't manage. There's the *Alien* mortgage on this house, the car, the *de rigueur* and consequently extortionate school that our offspring attend and are likely to for the foreseeable future.'

'You wouldn't want them to grow up to be vandals

with pierced noses and hair like hedgehogs?'

'No, I wouldn't – no more than you would want to drive round in a clapped-out Metro and shop at KwikSave.'

'And there are your golf-club fees to consider.' It was said in a tone that was sharper than was absolutely essential.

Jamie nodded hesitantly. 'Point taken.' It wasn't exactly the price of tee pegs to belong to the most prestigious golf club in the area. 'But then you wouldn't want me playing golf on a municipal course with apprentice electricians with pierced noses and hair like hedgehogs, would you?'

Jamie walked to the fridge and poured himself a beer. He saw Pamela stiffen and ignored it. 'Besides, there's no guarantee that another job would require any fewer hours or that the trains would be any more reliable. We're talking about something here that is totally out of my control.' More lies. See? Easy.

'Couldn't you drive in?'

'Is that what you want for me – spending two hours each way in a traffic jam? At least on the train I can read the paper.' *And see Teri*.

They had been meeting every morning for a few weeks now. He caught the 6.25 from Milton Keynes, stopping at Bletchley, Leighton Buzzard (6.37) and then only the briefest pause at Watford Junction before arriving at Euston at 7.16 – given a bit of luck and a following wind – and no signal failures at Watford Junction.

It got Teri into work far too early as she only had a five-minute walk from Euston, but she said she didn't mind because she enjoyed their chats together. Yes, they had actually broken the unwritten First Commandment of commuting – Thou Shalt Not Chatter Animatedly To Thy Fellow Commuter – particularly on trains before eight o'clock.

To prolong the agony of parting for a few extra minutes, they had a quick bland coffee together at the End of the Line Buffet before Jamie left to do battle with the Northern Line. Well, more precisely the Northern Line to Leicester Square and then change to the Piccadilly Line for Covent Garden.

The tube was a nightmare at the best of times, but after eight o'clock in the morning it was enough to make a grown man weep – hence the early start which sometimes caught the larks on the hop. It didn't seem so bad to be squashed against sweaty bodies at the end of the day – besides, he didn't have much choice. But to start the morning like that was more than one human being should be asked to bear.

Jamie worked on the far side of Covent Garden, away from the tube, behind the trendy bijou shops and craft stalls that sold clothes no one would ever dream of wearing, scented candles in dubious shapes and clocks made out of scratched sixties records that had failed to become hits. The office was one of those impressive-looking Victorian buildings that are nothing more than glorified rabbit warrens in which you freeze from October to April and swelter from May through to September.

In the summer, the walk to the tube from the office involved doing battle with forty million Japanese tourists and sundry jugglers, fire-eaters, buskers of infinitely variable quality, break-dancing robots, living sculptures of Hollywood legends and Simon the Oracle – a pleasant chap who told you exactly what he thought of you for a small donation. At this time of the year it was relatively free from enterprising hazards and as a result the journey was five minutes shorter. These things matter when you are a commuter.

These things mattered more when he had started to arrange to meet Teri in the evenings too. Not every night. That would be ridiculous – and difficult to organise. Just a quick drink to fortify the heart and gird the loins before subjecting oneself to the mercy of British Rail. Nothing more. Perfectly innocent and understandable. Unless you were Pamela.

Jamie pushed back from the table. 'I'm going to bed.'

'What about MacTavish's walk?'

'I'm giving us both a night off. He can go and pee on the bushes in the garden. He does it when we're not looking anyway.'

'I'll be up soon. I'll just clear away first.'

She was quieter with the pans now that there was no one to make a point to. Which was just as well, because she had given herself a headache with all that purposeful clattering. If it had been the children making all that noise she would have shouted at them.

MacTavish skulked back in warily and, as Jamie suggested, she let him out into the garden. He took the opportunity to chew on his punctured ball and run round the garden with it clamped between his teeth like the frisky young puppy he wasn't. Pamela stood at the back door and watched him scampering carefree across the lawn, growling under his breath as the fronds of the pampas grass – an unwanted leftover from the last occupants that they hadn't got round to digging up – wafted in the gathering wind. It was times like these when she wished wholeheartedly that she was a dog. All you had to worry about was where the next Bonio was coming from and hope that someone would remember to give you your Bob Martin's conditioning tablets regularly.

She didn't know what was wrong with her just lately. The necessity to do the right thing weighed on her like the heavy constricting blankets of a bed that hadn't been updated to the liberating joy of duvets. It was such a hard job bringing up children the right way these days. When she was young, the pinnacle of creative stimulus was piano lessons. Now, if you wanted them to be socially rounded and properly integrated human beings, they had to have a fuller social programme than Ivana Trump.

Jack wasn't yet three and he attended two 'Mother and Toddler' swimming sessions per week at the local leisure centre, one session of 'Tumbling Terrors', two hours of 'Mini Musicians' – which was always a frightful experience resulting in severe Nurofen abuse – and three mornings a week at nursery. Add to that Francesca's dance classes, baton twirling, Brownies, horse-riding, ice-skating, music and swimming lessons, and there was precious little time left to do anything for herself.

And that was without all the birthday parties – 'jelly-flinging affairs' Jamie called them – of which there seemed to be at least one each week. Last Christmas he had bought her a sticker for the car saying *Mum's Taxi Service*, which showed a cartoon car slumped on its front end with its wheels falling off. She hadn't found that the slightest bit amusing, perhaps because it was she who was on her knees, rather than the car . . . and her wheels were in grave danger of falling off.

Taking a part-time job had been Pamela's way of reasserting herself as a human being with a life of her own. It was hardly demanding, but it gave her some extra money and she liked the work. Jamie had been all for it – but then he would be. It had meant not the slightest alteration to *his* daily routine. She was the one who raced around like Damon Hill on a good day, charging from one appointment to another with military precision. If she ever dared to complain, all he said was that if she was finding it too difficult to manage she should give up her job. This made her all the more determined to cope. Work was the only sanctuary she had. He just didn't understand.

She whistled to MacTavish, who came in reluctantly, looking back longingly at his ball and wearing the same expression Jamie did when he came through the door. She could be so hard on Jamie sometimes – it must seem as though she never had a good word for him. Which she rarely did. It was just that he was a typical man. He worked hard, but other than that he took his family responsibilities all too lightly. He didn't worry if Francesca only got silver stars instead of gold, although Mrs Rutherford could be very moody sometimes and had her favourites . . . Pamela sighed deeply. No, he left all the worrying to her.

Pamela spent a long time in the bathroom and when she got into bed she curled against him in a position of penitence. She was warm and soft and smelled of tooth-paste and soap. It made him feel terribly guilty and ashamed.

'I don't mean for us to argue,' she said.

He patted her thigh the way men do when they've been married for ten years. 'I know.'

'Couldn't you look for a job locally? There are lots of big firms moving out of London to Milton Keynes.'

'I'll think about it.' He pecked her cheek. 'Goodnight.'

She pecked him back. 'Goodnight.' They turned off

their matching frilled Laura Ashley bedside lights in unison.

'Jamie.' Pamela spoke softly into the darkness.

'Mmm?'

'What is an *Alien* mortgage?'

Jamie sighed. 'It's a huge unseen monster that is completely indestructible and kills the occupants of the house very slowly from the inside out.'

He turned away from her and moulded his pillow to his face. 'In the building society no one can hear you scream,' he muttered under his breath.

Chapter Six

They had been on the train for nearly half an hour and the doors were still open. Jamie checked his watch for the third time in as many minutes. 'This isn't going anywhere in a hurry.'

It was a rather obvious statement, Teri thought, given the situation. 'A fire causing signals failure at Watford Junction' the muffled announcement had said. It was the third train they had been on so far, running from platform to platform like worried sheep, and none of them had moved. Because of the fire, the staff who were due to drive the trains were stuck on trains themselves – somewhere in that Never-Never land of 'further down the line'.

'Why don't we go and grab something to eat?' Jamie suggested.

Teri nodded her agreement, hiding her surprise. They'd only known each other a few weeks – a month or so at the most – but it was the first time he had suggested going to eat together. Most men she had known would have wanted you in bed within two days and then, equally quickly, would have dumped you. She hadn't had the slow smoulder build-up experience before; most of her exes had been from the crash-and-burn school of courtship. This was taking some getting used to.

Their relationship – and the term should be applied loosely – consisted so far of a quick coffee in the morning – nearly every morning – and an equally quick something more alcoholic at night. It wasn't nearly enough. Even the mornings probably wouldn't happen if she didn't make the supreme effort of getting a train nearly an hour earlier than she needed to, just to spend some time with him.

Clare told her that she was insane and that no man was worth missing an hour's precious beauty sleep for. Mind you, she was a fine one to talk; she was usually up in the middle of the night to get to the airport on time for an early-morning flight. She insisted that it was merely devotion to duty rather than mindless devotion to someone else which made all the difference. And she was probably right. The things we do for love!

Was it love, though? It was certainly deep and lustful infatuation, and that would do for starters! But were the feelings returned, or was this likely to be her forty-second bout of unrequited love since leaving The Sacred Heart of Jesus primary school? She had carried a torch for Michael Lacey that burned steadfastly despite his continued rejections and refused – until she was twenty-three and saw him again in Safeway's with a wife, two children and a not inconsiderable beer-belly – to be quenched.

Once she was in love it was hard for her to remain objective. This was a difficult one. He seemed keen to see her on the train etc., but that was about it. The only benefit to this dawn reveille – apart from the obvious one of seeing Jamie – was that it was gaining her an enormous amount of brownie points with her boss, the difficult-to-impress Richard Wellbeloved, who was stunned that she was not only in before him in the mornings now, but that she was also quite cheerful too.

'There's not a bad little pasta place just outside the station. I can't remember what it's called. It's next to the transvestite shop and that, well . . .' he paused. 'I suppose it tends to overshadow everything else.'

She wondered briefly for the second time whether he might not be a pervert. He had seemed very at home buying tights. Perhaps this would explain his reticence at becoming involved. Perhaps he was just using her as a cure? A bit of therapy as he decided whether to go through with a Gender Reassessment Programme. Both she and Clare had dated people with worse problems in the past.

In the event, the restaurant was imaginatively called 'The Pasta Place' – a nice little haven of minimalist monochrome, an oasis in a bleak and dirty street that had nothing else to offer but its proximity to Euston Station. Unless, of course, you were a transvestite – in which case next door with its array of size twelve stilettos, falsie bras festooned across the window like bunting and the promise of *He to She* transformations in under two hours, would be infinitely more appealing.

There were two men eating alone, faces buried alternately in pasta or the *Evening Standard*, and a young couple giggling and holding hands while they spooned food into each other's mouths. Jamie and Teri ordered quickly – Penne Carbonara for Jamie and Spaghetti Bolognese for her – less cream, less cheese, less fat, less than interesting. A cheapish, goodish bottle of Valpolicella and some garlic bread helped to stave off hunger pangs until the real food arrived.

They talked aimlessly of the weather and the state of the world in general before the waiter – a man with the strongest Italian accent she had ever heard, who had probably lived in Bethnal Green for the last twenty years

– placed two steaming bowls of pasta in front of them.

'Bliss.' Jamie inhaled deeply. He picked up his fork and lunged at his food.

'Enjoya!' the waiter instructed.

'This is wonderful.' He smacked his lips and spooned in some more.

Teri tried hers more daintily, but agreed that it was, indeed, wonderful.

'You don't know what it's like,' Jamie pushed some more Carbonara into his mouth appreciatively, 'to eat food that you can't spell your name with.'

Teri paused with her fork to her mouth and frowned. 'What?'

'I said,' Jamie repeated between chews, 'you don't know what it's like—' He stopped mid-sentence.

She put her fork back in her bowl. 'To eat food that you can't spell your name with,' she finished for him.

Jamie waved his hand. 'It's a long story. You had to be there to get it.' He drank his wine self-consciously.

'I bet you did.' Teri leaned across and pressed her face as close to his as two intervening bowls of pasta would allow. She tapped her fingernails on the table menacingly. 'Are you going to explain, or would you like me to guess?' she hissed.

Jamie's face had gone red, and it wasn't just the steam from the bowls of pasta. Guiltily, he looked round at the other diners, who were eating their pasta and pizzas blissfully unaware of their confrontation. He lowered his voice. 'Like I said – it's a long story.'

She took a swig of her wine and clanked the glass on the table. 'You're married, aren't you?'

Now they were aware. They all sat bolt upright and most of them turned so they could hear better.

'Yes,' said Jamie.

'I knew it! I bloody knew! Why didn't you tell me?'

'It never seemed to crop up.'

'We've been chatting away for the last few weeks discussing everything under the sun! We've even progressed from talking about the extortionate cost of our season tickets and the soul-destroying inequities of commuting with British Rail to black holes and EU directives on BSE – and all the time I've been the one with the mad cow disease.' She didn't know if it was the red wine or the anger, but something was making her cheeks feel very pink. 'Didn't it seem worthwhile mentioning somewhere along the line that you had a wife?'

The waiter from Bethnal Green leaned on the bar and started polishing a glass that already gleamed in the overhead spotlight.

'I didn't think I needed to.' Jamie raked his fringe back from his forehead. 'I just assumed I looked like a married man.'

'And what do married men look like? Do you think you've got *Keep Off – Married Man* stamped on your forehead in invisible ink that only single women can see?'

'I don't know,' Jamie admitted. 'It's not something I've thought about.'

Teri was in full flow now. She took a swig of wine to lubricate her throat. The man on the table next to them slunk down in his seat and raised his newspaper higher.

'I never go out with married men! It's an unwritten policy of mine. I'm a very principled woman.' She thought guiltily of her one illicit date with Clare's ex-husband Dave when he wasn't her ex-husband. It had been a disaster. He had tried to man-handle her in the car park at the isolated country pub he had taken her to before they had even got near the artificial beams and the horse brasses. It was shortly after that that she had become very principled. She vowed to be nicer to Clare when she got home.

'Well, I hate to be a stickler for the *actualité*, but we're not exactly going out, are we?' Jamie said, a mild expression of exasperation making him look even younger and even more appealing.

'What *are* we doing here then?' Teri jabbed meaningfully with her fork. 'Just filling in time until the next train comes along?'

'Well actually,' Jamie looked longingly at his Carbonara, 'that's exactly what we are doing.'

Teri opened her mouth and closed it again. He did have a point. 'So I'm just a better option than the *Daily Telegraph*, a can of lukewarm Coke and twiddling your thumbs for the next two hours while the fire brigade sort out Watford Junction?'

'You're a considerably better option than the *Daily Telegraph*, warm Coke and two hours of thumb twiddling.'

Teri smiled reluctantly. 'Well, I suppose I should be thankful for small mercies.'

'What would you rather I say? That I'm an incorrigible, habitual seducer who wants nothing more than to coerce you into an adulterous relationship?' By now the young couple had stopped spooning food into each other's mouths and were listening intently.

'Is that what you want?'

Jamie sagged visibly. 'I don't know.' He twiddled his fork in the middle of his penne, making a space in the sauce which showed the design on the bottom of his plate – a smiling stereotyped gondolier wearing his stripy jersey and obligatory red-ribboned boater inscribed with that old Italian saying *Hava Nisa Day!* When Teri had visited

Venice, all the gondoliers wore jeans and sulked and charged extortionate prices for the privilege of racing you round their dirty, stinking canals while screeching obscenities at anyone who got in their way. 'The truth is that I'm not an habitual seducer,' Jamie went on. 'And I've never been in this situation before. I just wanted to spend time with you.'

'Why? Why me?' Teri asked. The young couple exchanged a quick spoonful.

'For the last few weeks I've had something to look forward to, something to give my life at least a bit of purpose, rather than sitting on a train for nearly three hours a day and going home to an argument and food designed for five-year-olds. It's been months since anyone has taken an interest in *me*. I haven't talked to anyone for years like we've talked. I mean, *really* talked.'

'But we haven't *really* talked. We might have got on to the subject of your wife a bit earlier if we'd *really* talked.'

'I know. I was going to tell you.' Jamie dabbed at his sauceless mouth with his napkin. The man in the far corner of the restaurant folded his newspaper and the waiter was about to wear a hole in the glass he was still polishing intently. 'It just seemed easier to avoid it and pretend that you must know.'

'If you're a married man, why don't you wear a wedding ring? I'm a stickler for that – I always check.'

The man on the table next to them leaned closer to hear Jamie's reply. 'I lost it, months ago. I take Francesca swimming on Sunday mornings – "Parents and Pests". I haven't got round to replacing it yet. I did harbour the vain hope that someone might hand it in, but you just can't trust people these days.'

Teri narrowed her eyes at this, but her silent sarcasm

was lost on him. 'So Francesca is the five-year-old with educational food?' Teri found her throat had tightened.

'She's six.'

'No wonder you were at home buying tights. You're a regular family guy. I bet you don't baulk at buying Tampax either.'

Jamie shook his head. 'Or Pampers.'

Teri let out a heavy and unhappy breath, that said, 'I really don't want to hear this.'

'Jack's just three.'

'Are there any more?' she snapped. 'This isn't going to turn out to be the bloody Waltons, is it? There's no Jim-Bob, Mary Ellen, Fanny Anne and Uncle Tom Cobleigh as well, is there?'

'No, that's all. That's La Famille Duncan – Frankie, Jack and—'

Teri held up her hand. 'Don't! Don't tell me! I have no desire to know your wife's name. If she hasn't got a name then I can pretend she doesn't really exist.'

'Look.' Jamie lowered his voice further. The other diners in the restaurant and the waiter leaned closer. 'I didn't mean for this to happen – if anything *has* happened. I just wanted us to be friends.'

'And have you told your wife you've found a new friend – or are you leaving her to guess, too?'

'No, I haven't told her.' Jamie turned and glared at the diners who had abandoned all pretence of eating and were straining to hear. 'She wouldn't understand.'

'I don't believe it!' Teri's flabber had never been more gasted. 'My wife doesn't understand me. That's the oldest line in the book!'

Jamie bristled. 'It just so happens to be true. We've drifted apart recently. I can't tell her about you because she wouldn't understand that we can be just friends. Anyway, I'm a hopeless liar, it's best just to tell her nothing.' Admittedly, he was getting better at lying. Practice certainly does make imperfect.

'So that's what we are – just friends?'

Jamie shrugged. 'I don't know.'

'There's a lot you don't know, isn't there?'

Jamie smiled and showed his toothpaste smile. He'd got a piece of parsley from his Carbonara stuck between his teeth and his gum, and she had the most overwhelming urge to reach over and tenderly pick it out.

'From where I'm sitting, it looks like we've got a problem.' Her throat was dry and her voice was tight and even a swig of her rapidly dwindling Valpolicella didn't help. There was a virus going round at work and she hoped fervently that she hadn't got it. Sore throat, nausea, gippy tummy, chest pains, palpitations. Nasty. A lot like love really. 'We're more than friends, otherwise we wouldn't be meeting in secret, but we're not going out and we're definitely not having an affair. So what are we?'

'Hungry?' Jamie ventured.

'Starving,' Teri agreed.

Jamie reached out and laid his hand on top of hers. He chose the one in which she was holding her fork and it started to go sweaty in her palm. 'Besides,' his voice had suddenly gone all sincere and it worried her, 'if we are having an affair or simply going out or were even more than just friends, I could tell you that I thought you had the most beautiful eyes I had ever seen – that they're as striking as two lone cornflowers in a sea of golden wheat. If we were going out I could reach across the table and kiss your hand casually and think that later I could be kissing your neck and smelling your hair. And that for the last few weeks commuting with you has made me feel more alive than I ever thought possible.'

Teri pulled her hand away. 'Yes, yes. All right, I get the picture. So we're not going out and we're not having an affair. We're just friends. Let's get that clear. With no cornflowers and wheat and all that business about smelly hair and the joys of commuting. Well, fine, pour me another glass of wine and we'll continue not going out together and just being friends before our food gets cold.' Teri turned in her chair and gesticulated with her fork. 'And you lot can go back to your food, too!'

They finished their meal hurriedly, partly because they were now awkward with each other and partly because the pasta was unappetisingly lukewarm by the time they got round to eating it. Teri had baulked from asking them to reheat it in the microwave.

They sat on the train back from Euston in silence. Teri stared out of the window, pretending to be fascinated by the empty blackness and listening to the irritating squeak of her seat. How do you talk to a married man who has just declared undying friendship for you? What do you say? Would they be able to carry on meeting, now that things between them had irrevocably changed?

If she had thought only a tiny bit harder she would have realised he was married and would have said no thanks to the emotional Elastoplast he had been providing her with for the last few weeks. Perhaps she had chosen purposefully to ignore the nagging doubts that prodded her painfully in the ribs and pointed to the fact that he was unavailable.

It was like the two blowsy women she had seen in Steamers a few weeks before, swigging pints and wearing stilettos the size of boats. They were men; it was obvious when you looked at them – not even too closely. They must have been customers from the transvestite shop on a day out with the boys – or the girls – or whatever cross-dressers preferred to call themselves. All the clues were there – if only you wanted to see them.

But there is a certain blissfulness about ignorance, that only being hit round the face with the truth like a piece of wet fish can shatter.

Eventually, the train pulled into Leighton Buzzard. Teri stood up slowly. 'Thanks for the meal.'

Jamie was leaning against the window, his cashmere-covered elbow sitting in a puddle of condensation. 'I don't think we should part like this.' He didn't look at her, but stared out of the window at the empty platform. 'There's a lot more to say.'

'I don't know if I want to hear it, Jamie.' She swung the door open. The guard blew his whistle.

'Will I see you tomorrow?' His voice sounded husky.

'I don't know.' They spoke in unison and made each other laugh. It was a sad and strained sound.

'Take care,' Teri said, biting her lip, and slammed the carriage door.

Chapter Seven

'At Secure Home Limited we absolutely guarantee that all homes fitted with our advanced security systems are highly likely to be burgled within ten days of installation. Full stop. We carefully select a scurrilous – I think you'll find that's two r's – a scurrilous band of workmen with dubious criminal records as our employees to ensure that you have no peace of mind whatsoever. Yours, etc.' Tom Pearson sat back from his desk and leaned at a precarious angle in his favourite deep-buttoned leather swivel chair – the most expensive in the executive office furniture catalogue – arms resting behind his head. 'Did you get all that?'

'Yes, fine.' Pamela chewed the end of her pencil.

'I'd like four thousand copies sent out within the next half-hour,' he said with a smile. 'You weren't planning to go to lunch, were you?'

'Yes. I mean no,' she agreed.

'You're not actually listening to me at all, are you?' He sat back upright, elbows on his desk.

Pamela looked up, a frown creasing her brow. 'Oh, sorry, Tom.' She flicked her hair back from her face like a horse flicking an irritating fly away with its tail. 'What did you say?'

'Just read me back that last paragraph. If you'd be so kind.'

Pamela's finger trailed up her notebook. 'Er, from "At Secure Home"?'

Tom nodded.

Pamela continued. 'Er – "At Secure Home Limited we absolutely guarantee that all homes fitted with our advanced security systems are highly likely to be burgled within ten days of installation".' She looked up at him and winced. ' "We carefully select a scurrilous – two r's – band of workmen with dubious criminal records—" ' She let her notebook drop to her lap. 'Oh, Tom! I am sorry.'

'Please continue.' A smile spread across Tom's face and he cupped his chin.

Pamela cringed. 'Workmen with dubious criminal records as our employees to ensure that you have no peace of mind whatsoever. Yours, etc. Oh hell!'

'Your mind's not exactly on the job today, is it?'

'I'm sorry, I'm sorry!' She shook herself like a bird settling its ruffled feathers. 'I'm all right now – go back to where we left off.'

Tom walked from behind his desk and perched on the front edge directly in line with her. 'Give me that page.'

Pamela tore it out of her notebook. He shredded it like confetti and threw it in the air, scattering it on the brown shagpile carpet. Pamela looked horrified. 'Now close your book and tell me what's wrong.'

'There's nothing wrong.' She was perilously close to tears. It was ridiculous. Hot, spiking needles jabbed behind her eyeballs and threatened to shatter what little composure she could muster. 'I'm fine.'

'No, you're not fine. There is something terribly wrong when Secretary of the Year gives me a cup of black coffee with no sugar, when for the last eighteen months she has faultlessly brought me a cup of white with two sugars every morning.'

Pamela put her hands over her face. 'Gosh, did I? Why didn't you say something?'

'Because you looked exactly like you do now. As if you're about to burst into tears at any minute should anyone be cruel enough to say boo to you.'

One traitorous tear slid from under her eyelashes. 'Oh.'

'Come on, get your coat. We can leave the security of Milton Keynes hanging in the balance for a few more hours. I'm taking you to lunch.'

She allowed herself to be led quietly to the luxurious Mercedes that stood waiting in the car park. Tom whisked her at breakneck speed along the dual carriageway, while she stared out of the window at the featureless scenery that whizzed past too fast. If he was trying to impress her it didn't work. By the time they got there she simply felt sick.

They went to a pub aptly named The Windmill. It was at the end of the A5, a harsh new red-brick monstrosity. Its middle section had been constructed to look like an old windmill minus its sails, and it stuck up obtrusively from the barrack-like block of the rest of the building. Inside it didn't look like a windmill at all, but like every other brand-new, old-fashioned pub.

Tom ordered the food which they had chosen from glorious Technicolor replications on a huge laminated plastic menu – just in case anyone was unsure exactly what lasagne or steak pie and chips should look like. When Tom commented on this to the waitress she told them that they had exactly the same pictures hanging in the kitchens, so that the chefs knew exactly what they had to produce – even down to the quarter-slice of lemon, half a tomato and two sachets of tartare sauce that came with every plate of scampi and chips. Original flourishes were obviously not encouraged at The Windmill.

Tom and Pamela perched on uncomfortable stools in an alcove overlooking the artificial lake – which at least had real ducks – while they waited for their number to be called.

Pamela appraised her boss while she sipped her mineral water. Tom Pearson was swarthy-looking – a twinkly-eyed rogue, a gypsy out of place in a well-cut business suit. An Eastender by birth – a barrow-boy made good – he had found out at an early age that the streets of London weren't paved with gold, so at the inception of the new city, had tried his luck in Milton Keynes instead. It had proved to be a good move.

Tom had set up Secure Home Limited on a shoe-string, but with the burgeoning growth in crime that befits a new city cobbled together with the disillusioned from all walks of life, he was now making a not inconsiderable profit, and was living in the style that he always felt he should be accustomed to.

His hair was dark and wavy, and though there was no sign of thinning, there was a distinct snowstorm of grey. Pamela noticed that he still turned heads when he went to the bar to order some drinks, and wondered if her husband was viewed by more dispassionate females in the same light. It was hard to think of your own husband as a headturner, but there was no accounting for taste. And Jamie had managed to turn her head – once upon a time . . .

Tom was fifty-five but you would give him a good ten years off that, despite the greying hair. His figure was athletic, but with a definite softening of the waistline that spoke of too many business lunches under his belt. He dressed quite classily – a tribute to his wife Shirley rather than to his own sartorial tastes – and had a style that conjured up Ian McShane meets Man at Marks & Spencer – the shop where Shirley bought all his suits because someone had told her they were really made by Armani.

'So.' Tom looked at her levelly, one eyebrow raised in query. 'Are you going to tell me voluntarily what's wrong or am I going to have to drag it out of you?'

Her eyes welled up again and she stared sightlessly out of the window in the general direction of the ducks until she had the tears more or less under control. She cleared her throat. 'Things haven't been too good at home lately.'

'You've got two kids, what do you expect?' Tom teased.

She smiled and wiped her index finger under her eye, smearing a stray tear across her cheek. The food arrived, which did look every bit as Technicolor and as plastic as the photograph had suggested. They sat in silence until the waitress left. 'It's Jamie,' she continued. 'I think he's got a friend.'

Tom shrugged. 'We all need friends.'

Pamela tutted. 'I mean a *friend*. A special friend.'

Tom rubbed the side of his nose. 'Ah.'

'He's been singing in the shower.' Pamela held her throat as she felt it tighten. 'At five-thirty in the morning before he goes to work.'

'He might just be happy.'

'He's singing *Knock three times on the ceiling if you want me*.'

Tom stroked his chin thoughtfully. 'Then it's serious.'

Pamela pushed the plate of Technicolor food away from

her and fished a handkerchief out of her suit pocket. 'I don't know what to do.'

Tom swigged his beer and pushed the plate of food back towards her. 'Well, giving up eating won't help.'

Obediently, she picked up the fork.

'Does he know that you know?'

'I don't think so.' She sighed and pushed the plate of food away again. 'Oh damn,' she brushed across her eyes with the palms of her hands. 'I don't know if I'm imagining it all. There's nothing concrete for me to be suspicious about – apart from the uncharacteristic shower singing. It's just a feeling. He seems different. Eager to get out of the house in the morning and less than keen to come back at night.' She gave another heartfelt sigh. 'There's been no lipstick on his collars, no phones going dead when I answer them – nothing like that at all. And yet. And yet . . .' She spread her hands expansively. 'I just know. Don't ask me how.'

'How long has it been going on?'

Every sentence was accompanied by a sigh. 'A few weeks, a few months, a year. Or not at all. I have no idea. But I suppose I started sensing something a month or so ago.'

Tom folded his arms. 'Look, I'll be honest with you. I have to admit that over the years I haven't exactly been a role model for Mary Whitehouse. There have been times when, as a brash and callow youth, I've deviated from the straight and narrow course of marital constraints. But you know that Shirley and I have been married now for coming up thirty years. Only twenty of them happy, mind you.'

Pamela twisted her mouth in a reluctant smile.

'I mean that seriously,' he continued, wagging his fork. 'There have been a few distinctly unhappy years among them too. Most of them my fault.' He took another drink of his beer. 'I don't know what it is with men, but we can't control what lurks in our underwear. One bit of glad eye from a pretty girl and we're off like a dog after a rabbit. It's pathetic really. I've had four affairs during my marriage.' Tom sucked at his lips. 'Four. You'd think I'd have learned before then.' He shook his head. 'Shirley knew about them all. I didn't let on that I knew she knew, and she didn't let on she knew either. She just waited patiently until I came home, tail between my legs. There were no accusations, no recriminations and life went on as normal, me vowing never to stray again – until the next time.'

'So that's what you think I should do? Just ignore it and hope that like a nasty little itch it will go away?'

'It worked for me and Shirl.'

'But it took four times before you came to your senses.'

Tom looked wounded. 'I didn't say it was a perfect solution.'

Pamela shook her head. 'I don't think it's what Relate would advise.'

'What do that bunch of interfering buggers know? A load of psychobabble and claptrap that blames everything on your parents.'

'But they encourage you to talk things through. Didn't you and Shirley ever talk about what had happened?'

'We didn't need to. I've spent the last ten years making it up to her. I treat her like a duchess now, not the duchess of York, of course – it's not good for anyone to be that spoilt. But Shirley only has to ask and she can have whatever she wants.'

Pamela looked uncertain. 'I don't know, Tom. I feel I ought to do something. I can't just sit there and wait to see if he comes back. I've got the children to think about.'

'Can I be really honest with you?' Tom drained his glass. 'Do you know what you should do?' He tilted his chin. 'You should loosen up a bit. You might be a brilliant secretary, Pamela, or assistant or whatever the hell the politically correct term is these days, but sometimes you look like you're chewing a toffee up your arse.' His brown eyes creased at the corners and they were twinkling mischievously. 'And do you know what I want to do?'

Pamela gulped and shook her head. He fixed her with his eyes and continued in a lowered voice that sounded distinctly threatening. 'I want to sweep you in my arms, push all the bloody paperwork on the floor and make love to you on my desk. I want to smear your flawless lipstick all over your face with kisses, tousle your immaculate hair and crease your perfect suit to hell.'

'Oh,' she said quietly, but it came out as a squeak. Her mouth had suddenly gone dry and her teeth were sticking to her lips. It had become very hot in the pub and her hand trembled as she sipped her mineral water. 'And you were just telling me you were a reformed character.' Her voice sounded considerably higher than it should have been.

'I *am* a reformed character.' He laughed easily and she could see why four women other than his wife had found him attractive enough to risk an affair with him. 'Fortunately, these days I not only have Shirley to consider, but also my back.'

'So you're a reformed character out of incapacity rather than inclination?' Her own vocal incapacity had, thankfully, been temporary.

'No. It's just that now I know which side my bread is buttered on. I still have the inclination, but I've also developed a bit of nous too.' He tapped the side of his head, showing that he did, indeed, know where nous was kept. 'Shirley comes first before everything else. It's about time she did.'

Pamela chewed her top lip. Hell, if she wasn't careful she was going to cry again.

'Besides,' Tom continued, unabashed, 'if I put my back out now I wouldn't be able to play in the medal on Saturday at the golf club. And although my urges are still governed by my balls, it's the small white variety rather than the other kind.'

'Your wife is a very long-suffering woman, Tom Pearson,' Pamela stated flatly.

'I know, I couldn't imagine life without her.' He was starting to get maudlin. 'But that's how it happens, Pamela. Men and women can't be just friends. Two minutes ago we were talking just like friends and the next minute I'd stepped over the boundary and we were discussing things that friends shouldn't. It's only another small step for mankind for us to be doing things that friends shouldn't either. And by tomorrow I'll have forgotten what I said and we'll be back to boss and secretary again. Yet you'll think of it every time you see my desk piled high with paperwork. That's the difference between men and women.'

'Well, let's hope that Jamie gets some sense into his head long before you did.'

'Don't be too harsh on him. If you're stand-offish you'll drive him away. Make him want to come home to you.'

'Haven't you ever heard of feminism, Tom?'

'It's bullshit. Why do women want to behave like blokes when we already make a bad-enough job of it ourselves?'

'Put like that it's hard to explain.'

'Act like a woman, not a wife – and least of all not like a mother.'

'If you ever get fed up of fitting burglar alarms, you could always go into counselling.'

'Now you're taking the piss – you must be feeling better.' He looked at his watch.

'Thanks.' She nodded and smiled gratefully. 'I am.'

He passed her coat to her. 'It's time for you to go and collect those angelic-looking brats of yours. Go home first and take that lovely suit off before Jack throws up on it.'

Pamela slipped her coat on. 'He's past that stage now.'

Tom smiled. 'They're never past that stage. My youngest son's just turned eighteen – he's tall, strapping and would make two of me. And he's still testing his limits with a bottle – only at his age it's with more interesting contents than milk. Shirley lies awake half the night until he deigns to come home and then after half an hour's kip she lies awake again for the rest of the night listening to him throw up in the bathroom.'

Pamela wrinkled her nose. 'What do you do?'

'I lie awake with her. The only difference is in the morning I shout at him and she gives him Alka-Seltzer.'

'That's another difference between men and women,' she said wryly.

'There are lots of them – not all of them good.'

'So you think I should take the Tom Pearson Route to Deeply Wedded Bliss and just sit at home like a good little wife, nurture his children and wait for him to realise that he's a complete bastard.'

'What's the other option? Confronting him while he may still be in the throes of passion, blasting off ultimatums like bullets? You might get him to wave a white flag, but he might wave it at you from the other trenches.

It could frighten him into thinking that he's actually in love with her.'

He took her arm and they headed towards the door. She could feel the heat of his hand even through her coat.

'You've said yourself you've got no evidence, that it's only a hunch – and look where that got Quasimodo.' Deep lines appeared at the corners of his eyes as he crinkled them.

Pamela looked at him sideways. 'You are silly.'

She ignored Tom's advice about going home and changing, and instead went straight to collect Jack from nursery. Would she ignore the rest of his advice just as easily? Tom might be a nice-enough man – and well-meaning – but he was hopelessly out of date with the way things were done these days.

People liked to talk, to discuss things openly, to air any problems and analyse them. But if they'd done that successfully, why were they in this situation now? Why was her husband doing strange and interesting things with another woman if talking had done any good?

Perhaps Tom was right. She was too uptight, too motherly and not womanly enough. She knew she had been neglecting Jamie recently, but then he was a grown man and perfectly capable of looking after himself. The children were small, vulnerable and totally dependent on her – it was only natural to put them first. Jamie should know that. He should appreciate how hard it was for her.

Then again, perhaps she should appreciate how hard it was for him, too. Was she the sort of woman who could stand at the door in a basque and stockings with the smell of *coq au vin* wafting from the kitchen? Was it the sort of thing that Jamie would want? She hadn't a clue. It seemed highly unlikely on both counts, but maybe she should give it a try. Perhaps it was asking too much for a man to live by char-grilled pork sausages and Alphabetti Spaghetti alone.

Chapter Eight

It was like *Wuthering Heights* meets *Brief Encounter*. Heathcliff and Cathy meet thingy and whatsit. She couldn't remember the exact details of *Brief Encounter* – except that it was black and white and her mother cried a lot at the end. But it was all about the train causing the strain rather than taking it. That much she knew. Something *she* could certainly empathise with. She was pretty sure that Trevor Howard was in it. After all, he seemed to be in most black and white films. Except she didn't think he was in *Wuthering Heights*. That was definitely Larry – but Trev might have had a bit-part.

The tension was twisting her stomach so much that it was almost like waiting to do her first bungee jump. In fact, it was very much the same situation – she was about to dive over the precipice into a deep and dangerous abyss with no idea what would be waiting for her when eventually she hit the bottom. If it all went horribly wrong, would she be able to bounce back – or would she simply splat in a broken heap and need a bigger budget than the Bionic Man to have any hope of ever being rebuilt?

At least with a bungee jump you had an elastic band for safety and the back-up of a gung-ho, spotty youth called Tarquin to tell you that everything would be all right, he had checked all the gear and they'd never had a fatality yet. *She* was going into this without the benefit of safety equipment. This could warrant a slot on *How Do They Do That?* – a programme featuring deeds of infinite danger enacted by death-defying daredevils – and a tribute to man's enduring stupidity. She always felt it should be more appropriately retitled *Why Do They Do That?*

As the train pulled in she was sure she was going to be sick. Was the mere thought of seeing Jamie again making her nauseous – or was it simply because she hadn't eaten any breakfast again? She had managed to stay away for two whole weeks. Every morning she'd got up early enough to catch the 6.37 and every morning she'd paced the lounge floor, like an addict talking herself out of her next fix, until it was too late – even if she had really rushed – to catch Jamie's train. Every morning she'd pushed her bowl of Weetabix and warm milk away from her untouched. And every morning she'd gone to work feeling unloved, unhappy and undernourished.

Sometimes she'd seen him in the evenings lingering by the End of the Line Buffet where they'd shared their putrid coffee each morning. She had waited outside the concourse, peering furtively through the grimy windows from behind a pillar until he finally got bored and headed for the train. It made her stomach ache watching him there alone with only his briefcase and a polystyrene cup for company, but she had resisted him.

Clare had helped too – not that she knew. There was no way that Teri could tell her in her present predicament that the new love of her life was actually a married man. It was listening to her on the phone with David – the tears, the begging, the pleading, the trying to fit together again the shreds of her life that made Teri feel incredibly guilty. Could she really even consider doing this to another woman? Another woman with children . . .

In other ways, Clare had been no help at all. To deflect attention from her own misery, she had pumped Teri constantly for updated information about this new mystery man. Teri had been reluctant to tell her anything, let alone *the* thing. Perhaps because she had this awful sense of foreboding that if she told her, she wouldn't be able to last out. It was a shame they didn't make patches that could break your addiction to men like they could to cigarettes. But then men were considerably more hazardous to your health than any carcinogenic substance was ever likely to be. And why was it when you finally met the man of your dreams you invariably found yourself in the middle of your worst nightmare?

Jamie always chose a seat in the front carriage – nearest the ticket barrier on arrival at Euston. It was a favourite habit of lazy commuters. She had waited on the platform at the exact spot. As soon as she got on the train she saw him. Her heart lurched at the same time as the train did. He was sitting in the middle section of the carriage, foot up on his knee – black lace-up brogue and fine-knit black sock – his newspaper strewn casually across his balanced leg. There was no one sitting in the seats around him – one of the few benefits of travelling so early.

'Hi, how are you?' she said, as the train pulled out of Leighton Buzzard.

He looked up, startled. 'Teri! It's you!'

'Still at our sparkling best first thing in the morning then?' She sat down opposite him.

He cast his newspaper aside. 'Have you been okay? I've been worried. I haven't seen you for weeks.'

The fact that he had worried about her was touching.

She didn't think she'd been worried about before. Except by her mother who worried about her, and everything else, constantly. 'I've been trying to avoid you.'

His face clouded over. 'Why?'

She looked round to see if they had an audience, but the few other people close to them in the carriage were either buried in their newspapers or asleep. 'You know perfectly well why.'

'I waited at the End of the Line nearly every night.'

'I know, I hung around outside until you'd gone. You made me miss two weeks' worth of calligraphy classes.' Teri put her briefcase on the seat next to her. 'I'll never be able to write jam-jar labels for the WI now.'

Jamie smiled ruefully. 'I'm sorry, I didn't realise my actions would have such far-reaching consequences. I only wanted to talk to you.'

'Why didn't you wait outside my office?' It had struck her over the last two weeks that he hadn't really tried very hard to see her at all. A bit of loitering round Euston Station hardly seemed the height of inventiveness. 'I seem to remember you engineered that quite successfully before.'

'I did wait one night, but it smacked of desperation. At least at the End of the Line, I could pretend I just wanted a cup of coffee.'

'You could have phoned.'

He fixed her with one of his deadly smiles. 'You'd have hung up on me.'

'True,' she said. 'But you could have tried.'

He had tried. Not *to* ring her, but to *not* ring her. How many times had he dialled the City Television number only to hang up when the switchboard answered? He had tried not to think about her, not to doodle her name on his telephone pad, not to see her face in his computer screen, not to loiter outside her office like a lovesick schoolboy. He had tried not to pursue her. If he had bumped into her accidentally then that would have been a different matter. He was a married man – it was too cruel, too calculating, too bloody unfair of him to pursue her in cold blood.

'You're here and that's all that matters.' He looked round to see that they weren't being listened to. 'I don't know why, but I need to touch you.'

He did know why. He wanted to make sure that she was real and that this wasn't just a dream and he wasn't still in bed with the alarm clock about to go crazy in his left ear. His dreams had consisted of nothing but this situation. It had played over and over in his head like a record stuck on a juke box and no one around with any loose change to put a different one on.

He had rehearsed this moment while he was awake, too. Waiting for his coffee to drop out of the vending machine at the office, he had thought up clever and witty things to say to impress her and to make her realise what a good guy he was, and to show her that he had taken her absence in his stride.

However, instead of taking it in his stride, he had stumbled around like a man lost in the empty wilderness without even an Ordnance Survey map to hand. And the clever, witty things? Of course, he had forgotten them all now that she was actually sitting here in front of him.

'Gosh, I've missed you so much.' His eyes were sincere and searching. 'Come and sit next to me.'

'Do you think this is a good idea?'

He shook his head. 'No.'

She slid on to the seat next to him and he took her

hand. 'This is ridiculous. I feel like a naughty sixteen-year-old,' she said.

'I don't think it's wise to try anything else on the train, the ticket collector might have us thrown off.'

'You mean the Revenue Protection Operative,' she corrected. 'Anyway,' she lowered her voice to a hiss, 'you're a *married* man!'

'I could have told you that!' he hissed back.

'But you didn't, did you – and now what are we going to do?'

'I don't know!' they said together.

In the event, it was decided for them. At Watford Junction the door swung open and several people shuffled reluctantly on to the train. They had that haunted, grey look reserved for prisoners awaiting execution on Death Row and Monday-morning commuters. Among them was Jamie's best friend, Charles Perry.

Charles was thirty-one going on forty with a mental age fast approaching nineteen. He was robust, roundish and cheekily attractive and had a more unkempt style of dress than Columbo. Despite these social setbacks he always managed to sport a pretty blonde, of distinctly uncertain age, on his arm when it came to company do's. It could have been the fact that there was old money lurking in the background, which Charles was unfortunately condemned to see only in dribs and drabs until the unhappy day his parents departed from this mortal coil and he copped for the entire wedge.

For this and other reasons that were fairly obvious to all after a few moments of partying in his company, his nickname was Champagne Charlie. He was Jamie's assistant manager at the Mutual and Providential – a job he did simply to fill in his days while he waited impatiently for his inheritance to arrive, whereupon he could dedicate himself totally to wine, women and a certain amount of song.

Charlie had a shock of fair, curly hair and a ruddy complexion that owed nothing to fresh air and clean living, but stated quite clearly that his favourite tipple was something stronger than lemonade. He stood out in a crowd like a Belisha Beacon in a cornfield, yet Jamie failed to notice him at all until he was standing right in front of them.

'Hello, hello, hello!' said Charlie.

Jamie dropped Teri's hand as if it had scalded him. 'For goodness sake, Charlie, what are you doing here? Sit down,' he snapped irritably. 'You sound like bloody Dixon of Dock Green.'

Charlie obediently sat down. 'Someone got out of the wrong side of bed this morning, dear boy – or was it just the wrong bed?' He winked theatrically.

'Don't be so damned rude, Charlie.' Jamie picked up his newspaper and shook it out crossly. Although he loved the bloke dearly, he'd picked a fine time to come barging in. 'This happens to be a good friend of mine, Miss Teri Carter.'

Charlie held out his hand and Teri shook it reluctantly. 'The pleasure's all mine,' he said breezily. That was something Teri could definitely empathise with.

'And this lazy good-for-nothing . . .' Jamie gestured at Charlie dismissively '. . . is supposed to be my assistant.'

Charlie looked suitably offended. 'Now who's being rude?'

'I didn't expect to see you here.' Jamie was still tetchy.

'You've made that quite plain, old thing.' Charlie went from offended to hurt.

'So, what *are* you doing on the train so early? Couldn't you sleep?'

'Haven't been to sleep, old boy. Came straight from the casino. Went home, had a bit of a wash and brush-up, and back out again. I've got lots to do in the office.'

'Don't make me laugh! No one has got *anything* to do in the office – it's like a morgue in there. I keep expecting to pull out one of the filing-cabinet drawers and find a dead body in there with a tag round its toe.'

'My, you are being spiteful today, James.' He sat forward and spoke conspiratorially. 'Look, there's no need to worry about me. Mum's the word.' He imitated a zip closing across his mouth and Teri fervently wished that there really was one there. 'Don't let me interrupt.' He opened his copy of the *Financial Times* and started to read. 'Just pretend I'm not here.' He waved his hand dismissively. It might have looked more convincing if the newspaper had been the right way up.

Jamie was flushed, either with anger or embarrassment or both – Teri wasn't sure. 'Sorry,' he mouthed to her silently.

She shrugged in return – there was little else she could do. It was a morose, mist-shrouded morning and she stared out of the window watching the McVities' factory whizz past just after Wembley Central, with its undeniable legend *You have to go a long, long way to bake a better biscuit* and an attractive, if slightly unnecessary, picture of a digestive biscuit. It failed to cheer her, particularly as you couldn't smell the biscuits baking in the morning. Did it mean that McVities' workers enjoyed a long lie-in, or was it just that her nose wasn't entirely functional until noon? Another question without an answer.

The three sat in uncomfortable silence – Jamie skulking

behind his newspaper. She stared at him and he failed to meet her eyes, so she focused instead on the electric blue and purple zig-zag fabric of the British Rail seats that matched nothing and was hard on the eyes at any time, let alone seven o'clock in the morning. In staring at the seats, she forgot to look for the man who lived in the soulless block of flats next to the sign that said *One Mile to Euston Station*, who vigorously towelled dry his important little places in front of the window each morning.

Another disappointment. Teri could feel the edges of her mouth settling into a downward pout. Three ornate pink lamp-posts loomed optimistically from the grime, and the tangle of tracks increased to spaghetti-like proportions, signalling their arrival at Euston. Whatever had happened to Heathcliff and Cathy and thingy and whatsit – she was pretty sure that a Charlie hadn't turned up in the middle to blight their reunion!

He left Teri awkwardly and reluctantly with a brisk goodbye at the mouth of the underground station and headed off with Charlie towards the Northern Line.

'I must say I'm disappointed in you, old chap,' Charlie said as they pushed through the automatic ticket barriers. Keeping up with the fast pace of seasoned commuters, they descended at a brisk walk down the escalator, which groaned in complaint, to the tube. 'I had you down for Mr Happily Married.'

In the subterranean tunnel, a young student-type played the love theme from *Dr Zhivago*, picking the strings of his battered guitar with the touch of a lover. On the floor next to him, his guitar case was filling steadily with coins. Further along the curving corridor of cracked tiles sat a young mother with a strong Irish accent and a toddler with an equally strong pair of lungs. She proffered the child in the face of passing commuters and said, 'Change, please!' The chipped china cup at her feet was empty.

'I *am* happily married,' Jamie snapped above the rushing noise of the wind on the platform. 'I told you, she's a good friend.'

'Do you always hold hands with your good friends on the train in the morning?'

'I hadn't seen her for ages and she was upset and needed comforting.' Lies, lies, lies. 'It was all going very well until you came along and put your size ten in.'

'I must say she didn't look very upset. She looked positively radiant to me.'

The train arrived and they got on, saving Jamie the need to explain himself further. All the seats were taken, but it wasn't overcrowded, so they stood with their backs against the side panels near the door facing each other.

'Does Pamela know that you meet good friends on the train and hold their hands?' Charlie continued as the train rattled its way to Leicester Square.

'I don't think that's any of your business, Charlie.'

'Look, I may be approaching the brink of alcoholism and the descent into early senility, but I'm not a complete idiot.' Charlie paused. 'You could disagree with me.'

'You *are* a complete idiot.'

'No, it's you, dear boy – *you* are the complete idiot,' Charlie said soberly, concern evident in his voice. 'This is a very dangerous game you're playing, Jamie.'

'It's not a game, Charlie.' Jamie was tight-lipped. 'Whatever you think this is, it's certainly not a game.'

'But it *is*! It's a game with people's lives. The rules aren't fair and I wouldn't mind betting that some of the players don't even know they're on the pitch.' He raised an eyebrow in query. Jamie looked the other way. 'That simply isn't cricket.'

They changed at Leicester Square – which was always heaving with bodies at any time of the day or night – to the Piccadilly Line for the one stop to Covent Garden. Hostility crackled between them like warning lightning before a thunderstorm breaks. A Japanese lady pushed on the train between them and they glared at each other openly. She shuffled uncomfortably and held the two cameras and the video recorder she had slung round her neck closer to her chest. When the train stopped she hurried off in front of them, casting wary glances over her shoulder, assuming that these were the pickpockets so many of her friends had told her to watch out for.

As they marched along behind her, Charlie continued, 'Finish it, Jamie, before people get hurt.'

'Nothing has started, Charlie.'

They waited for the lift to come to take them up to street level. 'You don't hold hands with people unless there's something going on.' He held his own hand up to stop Jamie's protests, which was a mistake. They crowded into the lift like very large sardines in a very small, very tight tin and Charlie's hand was trapped in a truncated wave against his chest.

Jamie glowered at him. 'If you're so ruddy disapproving, what was that camp, nudge nudge, wink wink, routine on the train for?'

'What could I say, dear chap? I was in an embarrassing predicament. I could see I was about as welcome as a fart in spacesuit – but I had to say something. It seemed apparent that polite conversation about Pamela and the kids was out of the question.'

'Okay,' Jamie said as they emerged into the grey drizzle that had started to fall. 'I'll come clean. There might have been the odd illicit drink and one meal. One meal, for goodness sake! That doesn't make me an adulterer. I haven't even given her so much as a peck on the cheek.' He turned and faced his old friend. 'I haven't seen her for two weeks and I've been like a lovesick teenager,' he confessed in a low voice. 'I can't eat, I can't sleep and I certainly can't make love to my wife. Today was the first time I'd held her hand – and look where that got me.' They continued walking. 'A bloody morality lecture from Oliver Reed's soulmate.'

'Nip it in the bud, Jamie,' Charlie said quietly.

He stopped and batted his palm against his forehead. 'You're like a broken record!'

'It's going nowhere, Jamie. Stop it now.'

He swallowed hard. His mouth was dry; he could have done with his usual cup of coffee with Teri at the End of the Line Buffet. He wished he could have talked to Teri properly, to have told her how he felt when he hadn't been able to see her. He wished Charlie hadn't turned up like the proverbial bad penny and spoilt their precious little time together. And most of all he wished he wasn't having this conversation.

The rain was heavier now and it was running down his forehead and on to his nose. He had an umbrella in his briefcase – a fold-up one that Pámela had bought him in Harrods. He deliberately didn't use it. He wanted to be wet and cold and miserable – and he didn't wish to be reminded of Pamela. Although he already had been.

'I don't know if I can stop it, Charlie,' he admitted at last. 'I feel like I'm on a runaway train that's gathering speed. It's out of my control.'

'That's complete bollocks, Jamie – and you know it. You can blow the whistle at any time you like. And the sooner you do it, the less painful it will be. Don't wait until you crash into the buffers and there's a mangled wreck around you.'

Chapter Nine

Clare held the soggy man-sized Kleenex to her nose again. 'If he crawled over broken glass to see me and arrived at the door all nasty and bloody with bits of glass sticking out of his knees I wouldn't have him back now.'

Teri handed her another tissue. 'Yes, you would.'

'No, I wouldn't.' Belligerent five-year-olds knew less about sulking than Clare. She had done A-level sulk.

'Not even if he begged?'

Clare blew her nose heartily and cast the tissue on to the ever-growing pile on the sofa. 'Well, I might.'

'I'm going to put these in the bin before they make a damp patch on the Dralon.' Teri scooped the tissues up with a shudder and went into the kitchen to dispose of them.

'Women who go out with married men should be shot.' Clare's voice drifted into the kitchen in between sniffs. Teri stopped in her tracks, foot on the pedal bin, tissues poised. There was a cold prickling feeling up the back of her neck.

'They destroy lives.' Clare was in full swing. 'In fact, shooting's far too good for them. It should be something slow and torturous, like the Black Death. I know – the Plague of Traitorous Women.' Clare was obviously feeling better on this subject and the sniffing had nearly stopped. 'It should start with boils.'

Teri ditched the tissues and tiptoed across the room to stare into the pine-framed mirror over the kitchen-cum-dining-room table.

'Big black ones, all over their faces,' she said stridently.

Teri tentatively gave her skin an exploratory stroke.

'With a particularly big one on the end of their noses so that everyone could see what they had done.'

Teri examined her nose carefully.

'Then their fingernails should drop out.'

Teri swallowed hard. Hers were long and strong and more often than not, painted red. She was very fond of her nails.

'One by one,' Clare added as an afterthought. 'Then the skin on their necks should sag.'

Teri pulled down her polo neck and inspected her neck. There was a fairly deep crease-line across it, but no sagging.

'Mind you, that usually happens anyway,' Clare said philosophically.

Teri tore herself away from the mirror and rushed to the fridge to pull out the half-empty bottle of white wine. She braced herself to go back into the lounge.

'For goodness sake, Clare! I preferred you when you were suicidal to psychotic. Here,' she thrust the wine bottle at her friend, 'drink yourself into oblivion and then we can both have some peace.'

Clare tutted, but took the bottle anyway. 'You're not much of an Agony Aunt, are you? I would have expected a bit more sympathy. You know how upset I've been.'

'I know – I'm sorry. I've had a bad day.' Teri tugged her hair back from her forehead. 'It's just that you deserve better than David. He's always been a complete bastard and he always will be. I hate to see you wasting yourself on him.'

Clare refilled her glass. 'I need to lose some weight.'

'You've lost loads of weight! If you get any thinner you'll look like Kylie Minogue.'

'*She's* only a size eight.'

'Kylie Minogue?' Teri was puzzled.

'No! Her!' Clare tossed her hair back. '*Anthea!*'

'Is that what he rang up to tell you?'

'No. He's wanted me to know he's putting the flat on the market.' Her eyes filled with tears again and she reached for another tissue.

'Oh hell, I'm sorry, Clare.' Teri sat next to her on the sofa and put her arm round her friend's heaving shoulders. 'Look, it's probably for the best. A clean break and then you can get on with your life.'

'I'll never find another man,' Clare wailed.

'Of course you will.' Teri squeezed her shoulder. 'You've got so much going for you. You're young, you're pretty, you're slim – and getting slimmer. Who could resist you?'

'Everyone!' Clare wiped her eyes. 'My husband did. And everyone else over the age of twenty-one is married.'

'No, they're not.' Teri patted her arm.

'I don't want a toyboy. I want a mature man. A Tom Cruise look-alike, but taller with no emotional baggage and no ex-wives or kids.'

'It's a good job you're not picky,' Teri said lightly. She gave her another reassuring squeeze. 'Look, there are still some – a few – very nice men around.'

Clare turned on her. 'So how come it's taken you so long to find one?'

Teri shook her head and picked some imaginary fluff

from her jeans. 'Perhaps I just wasn't looking in the right place.'

'Still, you've found someone nice now and I'm really pleased for you.' She clutched Teri's hand, crushing it to her. 'I know I've been wrapped up in myself lately. I'm sorry. Come on then, tell me all about him. It'll take my mind off that bastard I'm married to.' She giggled and wiped her eyes. 'Dish the dirt, Tez. I could do with cheering up.'

'There's nothing to tell really.' Teri's voice sounded over-casual even to her. This was dangerous territory.

'Oh, don't be so mean. You know we've told each other everything since you confessed that you let Michael Lacey put his hand up your skirt under the coats in the cloak-room in Mrs Whittle's class.'

'Clare!'

Her friend was unperturbed. 'I know it's still on because you went to the Gossard factory shop and bought a load of new knickers last weekend.'

'What's that got to do with anything?'

'Well, it must be getting serious if you're lashing out on new undies.'

'The reason I bought new undies was because all my other knickers are grey.'

'Rubbish!' Clare elbowed her meaningfully in the ribs. 'I know you better than that.'

Teri's jaw tightened. 'The reason all my knickers are grey is that someone, who shall remain nameless, left a black sock in the bottom of the washing machine.'

'Oh.'

They sat in silence for a few moments and to cover the uneasiness Teri poured herself half a glass of wine, even though she didn't want it.

'So is it on or is it off?' Clare continued.

'Let it drop, Clare. Please,' Teri pleaded.

'We-e-ll,' she elongated the word, 'you're so cagey. One minute you're mad about this bloke – he's the best thing since the video shop started selling Häagen Dazs – and then next thing – *schtum*. What's the big secret?'

'There's no big secret.' The words nearly stuck in her throat. Clare was right – she *had* told her everything since the embarrassing and awakening Michael Lacey incident. They had confided in each other since the day they started at The Sacred Heart of Jesus primary school together. More often than not, this was because Clare did a superlative range of Chinese burns – Teri winced at the memory – and it was easier to tell her innermost secrets to her best friend than trying to explain away another bright red and bruised arm to her mother.

The only thing she had ever kept from Clare was her one moment of madness when she had, for reasons which still eluded her, agreed to a clandestine date with Clare's husband. And Jamie. He could still just about be classed as a secret. Mind you, with maturing years Clare had resorted to mental forms of torture rather than purely physical – and with equally profitable results.

'Then what's the latest state of play?' Clare was getting impatient, which was always a bad sign. 'Why does he never ring you or take you out? And more to the point, why haven't I met him yet?'

'It's just difficult, that's all.' Teri was trying to keep her temper. Her friend was under a lot of strain at the moment and the revelation about Jamie's circumstances wasn't likely to help.

'Why is it difficult?'

Clare could be very stupid and stubborn when she

wanted to be, and Teri was beginning to wonder why she had ever offered to share her home with her. They'd had a flat together once before, just after they finished university, and it had been an utter disaster. There was mould in the lounge, silverfish in the bathroom and a wide range of tropical diseases in the fridge. Clare had been blissfully unaware of all of them.

Within weeks, every plate and cup in the house was chipped, and there was more cutlery down the back of the cooker than there was in the kitchen drawer. A Pyrex dish that had been her mother's pride and joy for thirty-seven years had lasted one night with Clare. She had also taken an inordinate amount of interest in all of Teri's boyfriends. Why she thought it would be better second time around, goodness only knows.

'You've gone a very funny colour, Therese Carter. There must be something fishy going on.'

Teri shot her a filthy look. She could tell that somewhere in the convoluted recesses of Clare's brain, pennies were obviously dropping. Sure enough, Clare clapped a hand to her mouth. 'He's married! Oh God, he's married, isn't he!' She leapt off the sofa and began wearing a tormented path across the lounge carpet. 'Tell me, Therese, tell me that he isn't married.'

'He is married,' Teri said quietly.

'Tell me it's not true,' Clare wailed.

'It's true,' she said, equally quietly.

'What are you thinking of?' Clare wheeled on her. 'You've been cooking with that microwave door open again, haven't you? It's turned your brains to scrambled eggs.'

'I have not,' she said emphatically. Teri thought about sulking, but realised she would be competing with an expert.

'How can you do this to me?' Clare was starting to cry again. 'After all I've been through, how can you do this to me?'

Teri held out another man-sized Kleenex. If it looked like a flag of surrender it was meant to. Clare brushed it aside and wiped her nose on her sleeve.

'Clare, I'm not doing anything to you.' Teri spoke softly and calmly. 'Sit down and stop behaving like a drama queen. You were no good as the Virgin Mary in the school nativity play – a part which should rightly have gone to me . . .'

Clare shot her a withering look. Teri realised her mistake and corrected it, '. . . at the time. And theatrical histrionics don't suit you now either. If you want to discuss this like rational human beings then we can. If not, then I'm going to bed.'

Clare put her hands on her hips. 'You couldn't be the Virgin Mary because you were covered in chicken-pox scabs which didn't seem entirely fitting for the Mother of the Baby Jesus.' She could be very caustic when she tried. 'I seem to remember you crying hysterically until they made you one of the Wise Men – a part which doesn't seem highly appropriate now either.'

Teri slumped back on the sofa. 'I agree, it's very unwise, but I love him.' Her voice sounded matter-of-fact, but her heart was pounding uneasily like someone trying to play the bongos for the very first time. Why was she admitting this to Clare? She hadn't even admitted it to herself before now. And why was her pulse racing like this?

Clare snorted derisively. 'What makes you think that you love him?'

Teri twisted the bracelet on her arm distractedly. 'He's the nicest man I've ever met. He's kind, he's caring, he's—'

'Cheating on his wife,' Clare finished abrasively. They stared at each other. 'Does she know about this?'

'I don't know,' Teri admitted. 'We don't talk about her.'

Clare blew down her nose like an irritated horse. 'I bet!'

'He says they've drifted apart,' Teri explained feebly.

'Perhaps he's just been paddling in the wrong direction.' Her tone could be very scathing too. When Teri didn't answer Clare continued, 'Do you know what it feels like to find out that the man you love has been seeing another woman?'

'No,' Teri answered reluctantly.

'Then you are a very lucky person indeed, Therese Carter.' Clare jabbed emphatically at her stomach. 'It makes you feel sick – as if someone is pulling your insides out so that everyone can see them. Every miserable, broken-hearted, weepy, sentimental load of old pap that's played on the radio is aimed just at you. You can't think, you can't *stop* thinking; you can't sleep, you can't eat.' The tears were rolling silently down her face, which was more painful to watch than the dramatic sobs. 'I lost a stone in a week. A stone! Sod Rosemary Conley and her hips and thighs – the adultery diet beats it hands down every time.'

'I'm losing weight too!' Teri could hear herself whining and it was a very unpleasant sound.

'That's not emotional strain!' Clare wasn't in the mood for being swayed. 'There's nothing in the fridge that's over a hundred and fifty calories.' She pointed accusingly at the kitchen door. 'And that's because you want your bum to look like a firm young peach in your new lacy black thong.' Teri opened her mouth to speak. Clare glared at her through slitted eyes. 'Don't deny it – I've seen the Gossard box in the bin.'

'I resent that!' Teri said – mostly because it was true.

'She'll have no idea this is going on,' Clare said, changing tack. 'I didn't. I thought we were deliriously happy. One minute we were bonking away to our hearts' content, swinging from the chandeliers like Tarzan and Jane swinging through the jungle . . .'

'It was Tarzan and Cheetah who swung through the jungle,' Teri interrupted. 'Jane stayed at home and cooked.'

Clare turned on her. 'Now you're splitting hairs because you know you're in the wrong.'

'If you insist on moralising, at least get your story straight,' Teri said petulantly.

Clare continued unabashed. 'The next minute he was gone. No sooner had his feet hit the floor and the Durex was down the loo, than he turned and said: "I've fallen in love with someone else." Just like that!' She wagged her finger threateningly at Teri. 'And don't even think of doing a Tommy Cooper routine. *I* have the monopoly on bad jokes!' She paused for breath. 'Instead of basking in afterglow like *New Woman* says I should, it was "goodnight and thank you" for good.'

'But David *always* had wandering eyes – and hands!' Teri objected. Clare sagged into the chair opposite her. Teri felt horrible hurting her friend like this. It seemed an appropriate time to confess her own near-miss in-discretion with him to prove her point, but she didn't dare. No doubt it would come out in time, Chinese burns or no.

'Jamie isn't like that,' she went on, her voice softening. 'He's never done anything like this before. It's taken us both by surprise. We never intended it to happen. And besides, it's still purely platonic. How can I feel so guilty when we've done absolutely nothing?'

Clare made a strange strangled noise, which Teri took to mean that she doubted the validity of her statement.

'It's true!' she insisted. 'There's been nothing more than a few drinks and a bit of furtive hand-holding.'

It was true she was still a virgin adulterer, and even to her it was beginning to feel slightly as if it was verging on the ridiculous. She wasn't surprised Clare didn't believe her – she could hardly believe it herself.

'If that is true, then stay away from him, Teri. End it now before you ruin everyone's lives.'

'I don't know if I can, Clare.' They were both crying now. 'When I see him my heart lurches, I feel sick, my palms sweat and my tongue grows to twice its size so that I can hardly get my words out.'

'That's a virus – not love!'

They reached for the Kleenex box simultaneously. 'It seems so unfair. I've waited all my life to meet someone like him.'

'The minor snag is, Teri, that he's already got a wife. A small point, but not exactly insignificant.'

'And two children,' Teri sobbed. She waited for the backlash but it didn't come.

Clare rejoined her on the sofa and pulled the Kleenex box closer to them. She poured the dregs of the wine into their glasses. 'I could hit you on the head with this bottle, you know?'

Teri laughed and sobbed at the same time and it made a bubble come out of her nose. 'What am I going to do?'

'End it, Teri. Commute by coach. Change your job. Have facial reconstruction. Whatever the cost, avoid him.' Clare drained her glass and reached for another tissue. 'There'll be a price to pay for this, my love, and I'm not sure that you can afford it.'

'Just tell me one thing,' Teri looked at her squarely. 'How will I ever get over him?'

Clare sighed. 'Love *is* like a virus. It's totally debilitating and it takes a hell of a long time to recover from. And when you're low it'll hit you again.' She slammed her glass on the coffee table with a sobering finality. 'There's no damn medicine they can give you for it either.' She looked ruefully at Teri. 'If there was, I'd take a bloody great dose of it myself.'

Chapter Ten

Out and About had kept Teri constantly busy for the last two hours. It was a news-based programme, transmitted late afternoon just before they lost all their intended viewers to the BBC and the lure of Australian soaps.

Out and About – not exactly a 'totally crucial' title in her opinion – was produced with the emphasis very firmly on 'youff'. Most of the programme – over-enthusiastic reports from teenagers with obviously capped teeth and baseball caps on back to front – was pre-recorded on video tape, VTR, with live links provided in the studio by two odious brats in their early twenties pretending to be sixteen.

They were a total nightmare. Unreliable, unresponsive and unrepentant. Their idea of fun was to present the show sitting behind the desk with no trousers on and mooning to the crew while the VTR was being played. To their surprise, they were the only ones who found it amusing.

Despite the technological advantage of Autocue, they fluffed their lines constantly and the programme was on its third warning from the British Broadcasting Standards Authority about the repeated inadvertent use of the F-word.

The producer was a homosexual alcoholic with an ulcer and, for the latter complaint, Teri could lay the blame solely at the feet of these two individuals. He was called Richard Wellbeloved and was universally despised by everyone at City Television from the cleaning ladies up.

The main anchor man was an ex-art student with a ponytail and a suspicious habit of nipping to the toilet for lengthy periods during moments of stress. He insisted on being called 'Jez'. He was the main F-word offender, and similar F-words had filtered down from on high – television's equivalent to God, the Head of Programming – to let him know that he was on probation. Teri suspected that it wasn't the first time Jez had been on probation. One more deviation from 'Golly' or 'Wow!' and he would be sacked. It couldn't happen soon enough as far as she was concerned.

The producer, unfortunately, relied not on the educational content or on the skilful presentation of a quality programme to attract its rapidly dwindling audience, but on the fact that most kids watched because the whole thing was total chaos and you never knew when the next F-word might pop up. The entire programme needed a complete revamp, a mix of maturity and street cred to stop the programme from careering off the rails. Look at John Craven – what harm had he ever done to *Newsround*? Those were the days – lying on her stomach in front of the television pretending to do her homework while John intoned seriously about the dire state of the world. What would he have to say about it now? Back then, John was everybody's idea of a hero. Neat as a pin, clean cut, unsullied. All right, so the V-necked jumpers *à la* Val Doonican hadn't lent him the air of street credibility that might be deemed essential these days, but you knew where you were with John. No accidental F-words there.

In fact, what the programme *really* needed was Teri Carter at the helm. Her talents were wasted sitting in the dimly lit glass gallery that overlooked the studio, like some pathetic little fish in an aquarium, counting down the seconds to the links and trying to make sure that Richard Wellbeloved didn't tip his coffee – heavily laced with whisky – into the control panel.

She would add that necessary edge of common sense, sweetened by a girlish charm. And she wouldn't bare her bottom to the camera crew. Mind you, considering that her rear was infinitely more attractive than the pimply buttocks of the gormless presenters, this was something that might not go in her favour.

Teri picked up the producer's abandoned coffee cup and threw it in the bin, glaring at his back as he stamped out of the gallery. All she had to do was convince the inappropriately named Richard Wellbeloved.

She rubbed her eyes as she emerged from the gloom of the gallery into the fierce strip lighting of the office, and noticed that outside in the real world it was still snowing. The snow had been falling steadily all afternoon, intermittently distracting her from the programme schedule. Now great swirls of flakes like lacy doilies floated past her window and landed in drifts in Euston Road; if not transforming it instantly into a Winter Wonderland, it certainly made it look marginally less depressing than usual.

She had arranged to meet Jamie tonight too, which always brightened her day no end. If the weather was this atrocious in town, just think what it was going to be like, out in the sticks. The journey home would take an age. They would be stranded in the middle of nowhere for hours, listening to the futile slipping of the wheels on the line. And in the absence of any Boy Scouts to rub together, they would have to look to each other to provide bodily warmth.

It would be absolute hell. Her mouth curled into an involuntary smile.

It *was* hell. There may not have been fire and brimstone and little curly-tailed devils doing obscene things with toasting forks, but it was hell all right. On the departures board there were, predictably, a lot of blanks where once there used to be trains. The concourse was packed with commuters, ranging from the frankly bemused to the red-faced irate, who either stood and screamed into their mobile phones or at any hapless human who happened to pass wearing a British Rail uniform.

It was a perverse twist of fate, and an indication of the state of their relationship, that normally Jamie and Teri were the only ones who enjoyed delays. But this was the mother of all delays, one that made Eternity look like the brief and momentary blinking of an eye.

They stood holding hands. All fetters of embarrassment thrown off for the brief hour before they got home. Except that by the look of things, it was going to be ever-so slightly more than an hour before they reached their respective homes tonight. They listened to the announcement again, hoping that this time it would sound more like the Queen's English rather than one of the Queen's corgis.

'Bugger,' Jamie said. He translated for Teri. 'Stock excuse. Adverse weather causing signal failures at Watford Junction.'

'Typical!' Teri puffed. 'Is this what they call the wrong type of snow?'

'No, it's the right type of snow – there's just too much

of it.' There was a look of extreme exasperation on his face. 'We'll be lucky to get home at all tonight.'

Teri cleared her throat and said tentatively, 'We could try to get a room.'

'You know I can't do that.' His answer was more brisk than she thought was necessary.

'It was only a suggestion,' Teri said irritably. 'I was trying to be practical, not seductive.'

'Oh hell, I know. I'm sorry, I didn't mean to snap. I doubt there'll be any room at the inn tonight anyway. You know what it's like when one solitary flake falls in the capital, all the big companies phone round and block-book the rooms.'

'Ours doesn't,' she pointed out unhelpfully.

He sighed. 'Neither does ours.' He squeezed her hand. His hands were always warm. Always. Warm and soft. Hers were always like blocks of ice, winter or summer, but particularly in winter when she left her best thermal gloves at home next to the telephone on the one day when it decided to snow. That was another thing she could blame on Clare. It was she Teri had been speaking to on the phone. If you could call it speaking.

Clare was doing nothing to hide her disapproval of Teri's relationship with Jamie. To say that Clare wore her heart on her sleeve was an understatement of the third kind – she wore her spleen there, too. And vented it with a glory that was both Technicolor and alarmingly regular. In fact, she had taken spleen-venting lessons from Sister Mary Bernadette, former headmistress of The Sacred Heart of Jesus primary school.

Sister Mary Bernadette was known to be a strict disciplinarian with a temper that was never humbled or cowed by the constraints of her black flowing habit or her chosen faith. Today she would have been labelled a sadist, and been crushed under the weight of irate and indignant parents. Back then, no one had the gall to question her tactics or her motives. If she wanted to beat someone to within an inch of their lives for not eating their rice pudding, it was entirely her choice. There were times when Teri had been eternally grateful for a simple, if wholly undeserved, tanned backside, for if Sister Mary Bernadette chose to mentally scar you it was considerably worse.

It was sometimes difficult to have a best friend who still modelled herself on their former headmistress. At six o'clock that morning Clare had phoned to say – in curt, clipped tones – that she was snowbound with the airline in Ireland, and wasn't likely to be home tonight. It was even less likely now. Even if they managed to dig her out of Dublin, Luton International Airport would still be up to its ears in icicles. The weather, like their friendship, looked like remaining distinctly chilly for the foreseeable future.

'Come on.' Jamie broke into her thoughts. 'Let's go and get some food and give this another try later on.'

They went to their usual haunt – The Pasta Place. Tonight they were the only customers. Even the transvestites next door had been cowed by the weather conditions. The strings of coloured lights in the window of 'Terrific Transformations' had been turned off and the falsie bras hung forlornly. Perhaps they had all decided that it was one night when jeans and hobnail boots were decidedly more suitable attire than stilettos and pencil-slim skirts. And who could blame them?

Anyone with a modicum of sense had gone straight home and barricaded themselves in with a mug of hot, beefy Bovril. It would have been a good idea if she and Jamie had done the same. The restaurant was cold, the pasta was cold and, when they reluctantly headed back to Euston, the train they eventually boarded was cold, too. But at least they got a seat. And, after several false starts, they managed to find ones that didn't sound like Whoopee cushions when you sat on them.

It was another half-hour before the train moved, by which time every conceivable inch of floorspace had a disgruntled delayed commuter standing on it. Despite the fact that there was no tangible form of heat supplied by British Rail, the carriage started to steam with the warmth of damp and very squashed and very sweaty bodies trying to dry out.

'Good evening, ladies and gentlemen.' A strangulated voice came through the loudspeakers, sounding suspiciously like Charlie Drake. 'This is the late-running 19.07 to Milton Keynes, calling at Leighton Buzzard and Milton Keynes.' There was a flurry of consternation and several blanching faces before the cartoon-voiced announcer continued: 'This train will call additionally at Harrow and Wealdstone, Bushey, Watford Junction, Kings Langley, Apsley, Hemel Hempstead, Berkhamsted, Tring and Cheddington.'

There was an unappreciative groan from the occupants of the carriage. 'We'll be on here all night,' Jamie said under his breath.

Still the announcer droned on. 'British Rail would like to apologise for the late running of this train. This is due to adverse weather conditions affecting signalling equipment at Watford Junction. This train will terminate at Leighton Buzzard.' There was another louder and even more unappreciative groan from the carriage. 'This is due to adverse weather conditions affecting power lines at Bletchley. Transport in the form of buses will be provided for onward connections to Bletchley and Milton Keynes Stations. British Rail apologise for any inconvenience caused and wish you a pleasant journey.'

There were times when the use of the F-word was entirely justified, Teri felt. Perhaps she would look more kindly on Jez tomorrow. Then again, perhaps not.

Jamie flung himself back in his seat with a sigh. 'So the end of the line is sunny Leighton Buzzard and then buses to Bletchley and Milton Keynes.'

Teri twisted her hair round her finger. 'What chance do they have of getting buses through, if the trains can't make it?'

Jamie's brow furrowed and a look of resigned weariness settled heavily into his features. 'Trust you to spot the deliberate mistake.'

'They obviously have greater faith in the local councils than they do in Railtrack,' Teri observed.

'I think their faith might be somewhat misplaced.' He rubbed his chin thoughtfully. 'At this moment I think I have more faith in crystal therapy, divining rods, copper bracelets for rheumatism and Mystic Meg.'

Teri smiled sympathetically. At the end of the day he had quite a shadow of stubble on his face. In the morning, he was baby-faced and scrubbed. At night he looked paler and the stubble gave him a slightly down-but-not-out look. A bit like Bruce Willis in *Die Hard*. Handsome in an unwholesome sort of way . . . She wanted to reach up and stroke it to see if it was soft or scratchy, but so far she hadn't had either the nerve or the opportunity.

He was still muttering. 'And why do they always announce these things once they've got you trapped on the bloody train and it's already trundling out of the station? There's no way that you can make an impartial decision about whether you want to travel or not. Even if you want to get off, you can't.'

He lapsed into a deep and unhappy silence. It seemed somehow too churlish to point out that sometimes she felt exactly the same way about their relationship.

There was a queue outside Leighton Buzzard Station. A very long one. Made up of a lot of damp, dark people huddled together under dripping black umbrellas. It snaked along the front of the station and round past the empty taxi rank towards the snowbound car park. There was one very small and very full bus parked at the head of it. The driver was trying to start its engine. Unsuccessfully. The snow was still falling.

Teri could tell by the look on Jamie's face that his heart had just sunk to somewhere inside his shoes. 'You're going to be here for ever,' she remarked observantly.

Jamie fixed her with a withering glance. 'You could just be right, Ms Carter.'

'Look.' Teri lowered her lashes. 'I know you've turned me down once tonight, but I'll make the offer again. Why don't you come home with me? It's only up the hill.'

'I have to try and get home,' he stated flatly.

'It's madness to try to get home in this.' She fought an overwhelming urge to stamp her foot.

Jamie tilted her chin and forced her to look at him. 'It's madness not to.'

'Either way it's madness!' Her voice was rising, despite the fact that she was trying not to shout.

The bus driver tried his engine again. It reluctantly chug–chug-*chugged* into black, smoking life. Everyone in the queue shuffled forward one step, before the engine died once more into ominous silence.

'I don't know why you've suddenly turned into Mother Teresa of Calcutta on me,' she said vehemently. 'Are we going to spend the rest of our lives looking longingly at each other and holding hands? Tell me, for goodness sake, Jamie, exactly what are we doing?'

His face looked pained and jaundiced under the yellow glow of the street-lamp. He pulled her away from the stoic queue of ever-hopeful commuters. 'I've got a wife,' he said softly.

'And I've got bloody cold feet!' she said, and stamped off ankle-deep in snow away from the station. In the car park a few optimistic souls were trying to dig their cars out of snowdrifts using the scraper from the top of their de-icer can.

'Wait!' She heard Jamie call, but carried on walking, head down against the relentless flurries that were wet and stingingly cold and sharp on her cheeks. Not only did she have cold feet, but there was a hunger growing deep within her that had nothing to do with food. Two Big Macs, large fries and a thick chocolate milkshake wouldn't even begin to fill this space inside her.

He caught her arm and spun her round, flinging her off-balance on the slippery ground. In surprise, she let go of her briefcase and it sailed low over the snow, catching him squarely below the knees and taking his legs from under him as neatly as any of the Lion's full-backs could have done. He landed on the snow with an inelegant *oouf!*

'Oh, Jamie! I'm sorry.' She slithered towards him and reached out her hand to help him. He lay sprawled and lifeless in the snow. As she neared him she could hear him murmur.

'Speak to me, Jamie! What is it?' She crouched beside him, lowering her face to his lips, straining to hear what he said.

She heard a faint croak and leaned closer.

'That briefcase never liked me,' he whispered. His hand reached out and grabbed her ankle and, with an ear-piercing scream, she joined him in the snow.

'You complete bastard!' She kicked out at him, but only succeeded in sending an ineffective flurry of snow spraying into the air.

He was laughing now and pulling her close to him. The snow was seeping into her back, cold and wet where it had crept up inside her coat. It was in her hair and in her ears.

'I'll get you for this!' she spluttered, and grabbed a handful of snow and flung it towards him.

It scored a direct bulls' eye with his mouth, showering his face and hair with glittering shards of ice. He spat it out, laughing and writhing towards her, inching his face next to hers.

Pinning her to the snow with his arms, he raised himself above her. He shook the snow from his hair and the tiny flakes fluttered over her. She was surprised to find that hot tears were running down the chill of her cheeks despite the fact that she, too, was laughing.

He was still breathless when he started to speak. 'The reason I didn't want to come with you is that I'm terrified by what's happening.' He brushed her fringe back from her face. 'I wasn't looking for this. Do you understand that?'

She nodded silently, scared by the intensity of emotion on his face. His lips brushed hers, as lightly and elusively as the snowflakes that were falling in the darkness. 'So you don't need to tell me about cold feet, Ms Teri Carter.'

He parted her mouth with his tongue. It was hot and moist and disturbingly insistent, and despite the fact that she was soaked through to the skin and lying on a bed of freezing snow, she had never felt warmer.

'I know all about cold feet.' He held her away from him. There were snowflakes on his eyelashes. 'Because that's exactly what I've got, too.'

Chapter Eleven

He was an astonishingly good kisser for someone with cold feet. Teri gazed at her reflection in the bathroom mirror, wondering if she looked any different now that he had finally kissed her. Apart from soaking wet and completely bedraggled, that is. She decided that she probably didn't and set about rubbing her hair vigorously with the towel.

It had taken them ages to trudge back up to Bidefield Green. Normally it was a reasonably quick walk to the station – about fifteen minutes at a brisk pace – a bit longer going home as it was all uphill. With a good six inches of snow it was an entirely different matter. Sherpa Tensing and the odd oxygen canister on tap would have made the journey considerably easier.

There was a tentative knock on the door and Jamie peeped his head round. The Kiss hadn't been mentioned and they'd gone back to embarrassed shyness and tip-toeing round each other.

'I borrowed this,' he said.

'This' was her dressing gown. Navy-blue towelling, so nothing too girlie there. But those in the tailoring profession might have called it a neat fit. Its cross-over bit at the front didn't, and he was revealing a rather alarming amount of chest and thigh and there were bits of dark, curling hair that pointed dangerously to hidden bits of his anatomy.

Teri looked back at the mirror and hoped that Jamie realised it was just the steam in the bathroom that had made her cheeks go red. They had changed out of their wet clothes and had languished under the steaming hot shower separately. It was quite the most chaste love affair Teri had ever had. Well, at least since she was sixteen. It made Jamie seem all the more appealing, the fact that he didn't try to jump on her bones every five minutes. Although she did briefly harbour dark thoughts in the shower of him bursting in and taking her against the tiles . . .

'I hope you don't mind,' he said.

Teri cleared her throat. 'No. It's very fetching. I'll borrow Clare's. She won't be home.' Her voice wobbled. 'Her plane's stuck in a snowdrift in Dublin.' She made sure her towel was attached securely and then pulled a comb through her hair. 'It's pink and flowery and not really your colour.'

Jamie looked bashful and grimaced slightly. 'I need to phone home.'

Their eyes met, and there was an expression in his that obviously meant something deep and meaningful. But what? It didn't seem appropriate to ask. Instead she said, 'You sound like ET.'

'Sorry.'

'The phone's at the bottom of the stairs.'

'Thanks. I won't be long.'

She tried very hard not to listen, but it was impossible. Perhaps if she'd actually been able to make herself close the bathroom door and wrap her towel round her head it would have been easier, but with her ear pressed up against the cold, damp doorframe she could hear every word.

His wife must have answered the phone after the first ring. 'Hi, it's me,' he said. Not exactly lovey-dovey. 'I know, it's hell in town too.' Talking about the weather as the first topic of conversation – a sure sign that they'd been married for too long. 'I'm not going to make it home.' Not the slightest bit of hesitation there. 'I'm going to spend the night with Charlie.' Query by the wife? 'Why do you need his number? It should be by the phone.' Longer pause. 'Okay, okay. I'll get it.' Placating tone, but mild irritation creeping in? Rummaging in his briefcase. 'Watford 99246.' Briefcase clipped shut. Firmly. 'It's only for one night. I'll be home tomorrow.' Then: 'Perhaps Charlie will lend me some.' Underwear? 'Or I'll wear the same ones two days running.' Definitely underwear. 'How are the kids?' Lowered voice. 'Did they?' The first stab of pain. 'Give them a kiss from me.' Second stab. 'Me too.' I love you? Well, she's hardly likely to be saying 'I'm cold' and he's hardly likely to be answering 'me too'. 'Bye.' Phone clicks.

Teri poked her head out of the bathroom door. Jamie was sitting on the bottom step with his head cradled in his hands. She crept down quietly and sat next to him. 'I could rinse them through for you and put them on the radiator. They'd be dry in the morning.'

He turned towards her. His face was sad and tired. 'What?'

'Your underwear.'

'You've been eavesdropping.' A twinkle came back to his eyes.

'Only a little bit.'

'I'm finding this really difficult.' He reached out and took her hand and she could feel the tension in his fingers. 'It's not that I don't want to be here. It's just that I know that I *shouldn't* be here. I've never told so many lies in my life and it's not something I'm proud of.' He let go of her hands and scraped his hair back from his face. It was still damp and curled erratically at the base of his neck. 'I don't know if I can do this.'

'Look, let's get this straight. You don't have to *do* anything. I'm not pressuring you at all.' Teri nudged him in the arm encouragingly. 'This has more to do with survival than seduction. I didn't want you slithering home through Stoke Hammond on a suicide mission – although I don't think that particular bus was going to be slithering anywhere in a hurry.'

'No,' Jamie agreed thoughtfully.

'You could go back down to the station and join the queue if it would help your conscience.'

'No,' Jamie disagreed thoughtfully.

'So this is to do with common sense not sex?'

'Yes,' he admitted reluctantly.

'I think you'd better ring Charlie then and tell him where you really are,' Teri said. 'And give him my phone number – just in case. Will he mind?'

'Yes, but not as much as I do.' Jamie sighed heavily. 'If I feel this way about you – and I do – I should be sweeping you off your feet, throwing you over my shoulder and rushing you up the stairs to ravish you on the bed.'

'I'd be disappointed if you did.' *Liar.*

'I feel as though I'm letting you down. But if I don't let *you* down, then I let myself down.' He shook himself as if he was trying to clear his brain. 'I need to get my head together on this, Teri.'

'I know.' She wondered what would happen if she accidentally-on-purpose let her towel slip to the floor. 'You sort your head out while I go and sort your knickers out.'

'You shouldn't even be thinking of washing underwear for a man you barely know.'

'There are a lot of things I shouldn't be thinking about doing for a man I barely know, but I'm thinking them all the same.' She kissed him on the end of the nose. 'Ring Charlie.' She stood up and walked towards the kitchen.

'Hey!' He grabbed her hand and said softly, 'There's something I need to know.'

'What's that?' She hardly dared to ask.

'What *is* your telephone number?'

It was 01525 473663. Pamela knew because a female voice, which sounded like an old BBC announcer brought out of retirement, had broken the devastating news of her husband's adultery in well-modulated, robotic cut-glass tones: '*This tel-e-phone num-ber called to-day at twent-y-one, twent-y-five hours. To re-turn the call press three.*'

Quite an innocuous statement if you didn't realise the implications. She wondered how many more marriages would be destroyed by the invention of British Telecom's 1471 redial facility. She didn't have to be an idiot – despite the fact that her husband was taking her for one – to find out that 01525 was a Leighton Buzzard dialling code and that, wherever Jamie was, he wasn't in Watford with his alibi Charlie Perry.

Pamela stared out of the patio window into the darkness of the garden. The children had built a snowman when Francesca had come home from school. 'Frosty' had been given two charcoal briquettes, left over from last summer's barbecues, as eyes, and a traditional carrot nose. Jack had generously donated some Smarties, except for the blue ones which were his favourites, to provide his smile. He was also sporting a beige cashmere scarf, which seemed a trifle excessive for a snowman, but the children refused to come indoors for their tea until Frosty's comfort was fully catered for, and it was the only scarf Pamela could find.

At the moment, Frosty was being battered by the relentless snow which seemed even heavier than before; he looked as if he needed every inch of the expensive cashmere. He was a very small snowman, and already the fresh snow was drifting round where his knees would probably be, if snowmen had knees. His edges were becoming blurred and there was a mound of snow build-ing up on his carrot nose that would soon make it drop off. He would probably be gone in the morning, or at the very least unrecognisable as the snowman he once was. Like their marriage. That too would never be the same again.

What would happen to Frosty? Would he melt into the ground, covered by fresh snow, so that no trace of him remained? Very soon, would it be forgotten that he had ever existed, what fun he had been and how he seemed so permanent at the time . . . or would they rebuild him? Perhaps make a bigger and better Frosty, more able to withstand the rigours of the elements.

It was the first time she had caught Jamie out in a lie. All the months of suspicion and wondering and she had finally been proved right by a robotic voice that innocently blurted out lovers' telephone numbers. Had she willed it into fruition? By concentrating all her thoughts and efforts into Jamie's supposed infidelity, had she made it come true? They say you should be careful what you wish for, because you might just get it. Had she wished this on herself?

There was nothing she could do now, either for Frosty or for her marriage. She was stuck here, marooned by the snow, caring for her children while her husband made love to his mistress not fifteen miles away in Leighton Buzzard.

Pamela pulled her cardigan more tightly round her and pressed her burning face against the cold glass. A mournful groan echoed down the chimney and the wind whipped the snow across the garden, splattering it spitefully against the window where it ran in slow, sad rivulets like tears down a frozen cheek.

Her husband wasn't making love to his mistress. He was in the kitchen making hot chocolate while she artistically arranged his washed underpants on the radiator.

'I may not be much good with a Black and Decker, but I'm a demon with a microwave,' he assured her. 'I know all there is to know. Primarily, because everything I've eaten in the last six years has, at some time, gone *ping!* Trust me.' He stirred the milk in the pan, having shunned the modern microwave method of milk heating – insisting that before you knew it, and ages before the thing went *ping!* the bottom of the microwave was invariably swimming in escaped over-boiled milk. He returned to his languid milk-stirring. 'Teri,' he said tentatively. 'Would you mind very much if we slept together?'

Teri put the finishing touches to the underpants and stood back and admired them. 'I thought that was the general idea when you were having an affair.'

'No, I mean actually *sleep* together – rather than, well, stay awake together.'

'Oh.' Teri tried to feel philosophical. 'I see.'

'It's just that I don't much feel up to it tonight. If you'll pardon the expression.' He stirred the hot-chocolate granules into the pan with the milk.

'Is it me?' Teri asked. 'Don't you find me attractive?' She leaned against the work surface behind him. The first person in the house after she had moved in had been the kitchen fitter. He had skilfully replaced the seventies orange melamine cupboards with tasteful limed oak – only affordable because the kitchen had so few cupboards.

'Don't think that, Teri. I wouldn't be here if I wasn't absolutely besotted with you.' He slid his arm round her waist and pulled her to him. 'I just don't think I'm a natural adulterer.'

Reaching behind him, she rescued the milk that was just about to bubble over the top of the pan and, moving away from him, she poured it into two mugs.

'Some people can dive headlong into irresponsible debauchery and hedonism. I think I'm the sort that has to put one toe in at a time until I'm accustomed to the temperature of the water.' Teri laughed. 'Does that make me sound terribly wet?' he asked.

'No, but it makes you sound terribly cautious. Little wonder you ended up in insurance.' Teri put the pan into the sink. 'Why on earth did I end up having an affair with the world's only conscientious objector?'

'Come here.' He pulled her to him again. 'I'm sorry, I really didn't mean for this to happen. You deserve someone far better than me. Someone who is free to give you what you want.'

'If you're going to start getting depressed I'll hit you with the milk pan.'

Jamie turned the tap on and let cold water run into the

pan. 'There's a nasty black mark on the bottom. I think I've burnt it.'

'It doesn't matter.'

'You'll need something abrasive to get it off with.'

Teri sighed. 'What a pity Clare isn't here, she'd do a great job.'

'Is she giving you a hard time?'

'Not as hard as Sister Mary Bernadette.'

'Who?' Jamie looked perplexed.

'It's a long story.' Teri picked up the two steaming mugs of chocolate. 'Come to bed and I'll tell you all about it.'

'I mustn't forget my undies in the morning.'

'Are you likely to?' Teri laughed.

He looked bashful. 'I suppose not.'

'Your hanky's there, too – the one you lent me when I fell over. I washed it *and* ironed it. You're very honoured.' She looked at the hanky distastefully. 'Though I have to say I couldn't get all of the stains out.' There were shadows of blood, and dirt-traces that formed random patterns on the cloth and reminded her of the ink-blot test.

'Perhaps I should frame it to remind us of what started it all?'

'Yes – we should frame it and sell it to the Tate,' Teri suggested. 'That grubby hanky could fetch thousands of pounds' worth of lottery money. It ranks up there along-side a pile of bricks or sheep pickled in formaldehyde any day. We could entitle it *Hankering After An Affair*.'

'We could,' Jamie agreed thoughtfully, then he took her hand and pulled her to him. 'Or we could be minimalist and simply call it *Hanky Panky*.'

While the whole country was covered by a blanket of snow, they huddled under a Laura Ashley duvet cover. They hugged it to their knees and clutched their mugs of hot chocolate which had been made marginally more romantic by the addition of a large slug of brandy and some aerosol whipped cream – half fat – that Teri found in the fridge.

Jamie was naked under the duvet, a fact which Teri found most disconcerting. He might feel inhibited about sharing his body with her, but he had no inhibitions about showing it to her, it seemed. He was long and lean. *All over.*

She had sneaked her pyjamas into the bathroom and had changed there – either as a barrier against temptation or frustration, she wasn't sure which. Torture by platonic adultery was probably worse than having your fingernails pulled out one by one. It wasn't an opinion she would voice too loudly though, as Clare would more than likely be keen to oblige if she ever wanted to carry out a real-life experiment.

Teri lay on her back and sighed. The barrier of Marks & Spencer's imitation silk was proving useless against the ache of desire that buzzed in her veins like caffeine drunk too late at night. Sod Trevor Howard and his *Brief Encounter.* She wanted this to be a distinctly brief*less* encounter – a full-blooded nineties fling, not some soppy, old, romantic movie where the undergarments stayed firmly in place and the nether regions well out of camera shot. They were all knowing eyes and puckering lips, but not one half-decent snog. She wanted to rummage in Jamie's under-wear, fling his knickers to the four corners of the earth, not just have them hanging limply on her radiator. He had a tighter bottom than any Lycra-clad *derrière* she'd ever seen pushed tautly at the television camera in the Tour de France. So often in her dreams her fingernails had fondled his firm bare flesh – leaving her breathless and sweating like someone in their first flush of early menopause. Usually, just as the alarm went off.

Why couldn't they just be like everyone else and get their togs off without all this ensuing guilt? Knowing her luck it would be just like *Brief Encounter* – not a bit of nooky in sight. But it would probably all end in tears just the same. This was one of the few sayings of her mother's that was invariably true. Why couldn't Jamie be playing the part of Michael Douglas in *Fatal Attraction*? The opening credits had barely finished before he had his kit off. She'd hardly had time to eat her Mexican Chilli Nachos and cheese sauce – which looked suspiciously like cold custard – before the woman with the blonde curly hair and the big nose was splashing about in the sink with her bottom bared to the full house at The Point multiplex cinema. Mind you that all ended in tears, slit wrists and boiled rabbit. Very nasty. It probably wasn't a comparison worth pursuing.

Jamie pulled her to him and she nestled into the crook of his arm. She had left the curtains open, and together they watched the snow fall soporifically through the dark window panes. His body was hot and comforting, and considerably more muscular than the Boots hot water bottle that she usually took to bed for warmth. He had a moustache of whipped cream on his lip and she hoped that she didn't.

'What are you thinking about?' Jamie whispered as he stroked her hair.

'Trevor Howard.'

He twisted his head to look at her. 'Who?'

'It doesn't matter.'

'If you won't tell me about Trevor, then tell me about your dreams.'

'My dreams?' she said wryly. 'They're all X-rated these days, Jamie, and you usually play the leading role.'

'Only usually?' He looked hurt. 'Is Trevor a rival for your affections?'

'No.' She nudged him with her elbow. 'It's you in my dreams. Mostly.' He challenged her with his eyebrows and she squirmed against him. 'Okay, then – always. It's always you. Satisfied now?'

He frowned at her, trying to hide the smile that twitched at his lips. 'Anyway, I didn't mean those kind of dreams. I meant *dreams* – life's ambitions, goals, hopes for the future.'

'I've got less hope these days than Bing Crosby has without Bob.' She shook her head. 'I don't know if I believe in dreams anymore. None of them ever come true.'

'What did you used to dream?' He squeezed her. 'Before you became a cynic.'

'I used to dream that one day I'd be a famous television presenter like Valerie Singleton or Angela Rippon.'

'Couldn't that still come true?'

'I still have some hope, but I'm reaching my sell-by date quicker than yesterday's milk. I'm the wrong side of thirty – only just – and I haven't had a single presenting job yet. I'd even be prepared to read the weather.' She tutted sadly. 'The programme I work on – *Out and About* –' she rolled her eyes and shrugged her dismay '– prefers spotty youths with attitude problems, and the producer is a homosexual alcoholic with a chronic ulcer so I can't even sleep my way to the top.'

'I think you're much more attractive than Valerie Singleton.'

'I'm eternally grateful for that compliment.' She sipped her chocolate. 'Although calling someone attractive generally means that they're plug ugly but with a great personality.'

'I think you're very beautiful.' He kissed the top of her head. 'And you've got better legs than Angela Rippon.'

'Wow, that's really saying something.' She snuggled further into him. 'What about you? Did you dream of working for an insurance company?'

'No,' he said pensively. 'I didn't dream it. I really do work for an insurance company.'

She kicked him in the leg. 'You know what I mean!'

'I wanted to be a racing driver. Formula One.'

'That's a little bit different from a database manager for the Mutual and Providential.'

'I'm haunted by unfulfilled dreams,' he said wistfully. Which was closer to the truth than he dared to admit.

'Why a racing driver?'

'Glamour, danger, thrills, chicks and huge pay-cheques.'

'So a lot like the insurance business?'

'Don't mock!' He tickled her rib. 'There are similarities between being a racing driver and working in insurance. I get a pay-cheque, possibly not huge, but not insubstantial. I also get the thrill of leaving the office every night – and there's always the danger of dropping a disk drive on my toe.' He rubbed his chin. 'Admittedly there's not much glamour and there are definitely no chicks. Two industrial tribunals have seen to that. Now we have an egalitarian policy of mutual respect and opportunity in the workplace irrespective of gender, creed, colour and whether you went to a comprehensive school. We have lots of that, but definitely no chicks.'

'What do you dream of now?'

'My dreams are simpler these days. I dream of paying

off my mortgage, of London Weighting keeping pace with the amount my season ticket costs and I dream that one day trains will run on time.'

'They're not very ambitious dreams.'

'No, but they're equally impossible to attain.'

'What do you think makes us such dreamers?' Teri asked dreamily.

'Too many hours spent sitting on trains with too much time to think.'

'Talking of which,' Teri said, 'in a few short hours, we'll be squaring up to do battle again with British Rail. I don't know about you but I need to get some sleep.'

'Do you think I could hold you?'

'Is this wise?'

'If we were talking about wise, I wouldn't be here at all.'

'True,' she agreed. They slid down into the bed together. Teri turned off the bedside lamp. Their bodies fitted together perfectly and Teri resisted the urge to rest her leg across his thighs. His mouth was moist against hers, anxious and searching. Her hand travelled over his chest to the hard lines of his stomach. Jamie let out a low groan.

'If you want to just sleep together and not stay awake together,' Teri reminded him, 'then we need to stop this now.'

'I don't know if I can.'

'You can.' She moved away from him. 'I don't want to be held responsible for leading you astray. If you're going to go astray, you must do it of your own volition.'

'You're a hard woman.'

'And at the moment you're a hard man.'

'It hadn't escaped my attention.' He sighed unhappily.

'Goodnight, Jamie.'

'Goodnight.' There was a pause, just long enough for three little words, which neither of them wanted to be the first to fill.

They lay awake on their backs, a foot apart, holding hands. 'Let's make a wish,' Jamie said into the snowlit blackness.

'We're too old to make wishes. They're like dreams. We know they'll never come true.'

'Well, I'm going to make a wish anyway.' He brought her hand to his lips and kissed it.

'Aren't you supposed to follow a ritual?'

'Not that I know of – unless you happen to have a wishing-well under your bed.'

'No.'

He lay perfectly still and she could hear his breathing shallow and uneven. 'I wish there was another way I could do this. I wish I didn't care about my wife and the kids. I wish I could walk away from you and not give you a second thought and I wish I'd left you sprawled on the platform with your scabby knee and tearstained face and had cold-heartedly caught the train. And more than anything, I wish I could forget who I am and make mad passionate love to you and damn the consequences.'

'That was actually five wishes,' Teri said with a lightness she didn't feel. 'And you had your eyes open, so I don't know if it counts.'

'I thought you weren't interested in wishes?' Jamie twisted on to his elbow to look at her, his face framed by the moonlight.

'It's a woman's prerogative to change her mind.'

'So you do want to make a wish?'

'Yes.'

'Go on then.'
'I wish you'd shut up and go to sleep.'
He flopped on to his back. 'Granted.'
'Goodnight, Jamie.'

Chapter Twelve

'He was out all night. He told me he was staying with a work colleague in Watford, but he wasn't – he was in Leighton Buzzard.' Pamela sat back in her chair.

'There are worse places to be,' Tom Pearson said laconically.

She shot him a withering glare, the one she usually reserved for Jamie. 'I phoned the 1471 redial thing and it gave me her number. Then I rang her house in the morning after I thought they would have left for work. It was her answerphone. She's called Teri.' Pamela wrinkled her nose. 'And she sounds terribly young and terribly beautiful.'

Tom clasped his hands behind his head. 'How does someone sound beautiful on an answerphone?'

'Just the same as you can tell when someone is smiling down the phone – or lying.'

'Any more singing in the shower?'

'*Torn between two lovers.*' They looked at each other and pulled the same face.

'Subtle,' Tom said.

'It was always Jamie's strong point,' she agreed.

'I must say, you're taking this very well.' Tom swung his legs off the desk.

'I'm not, I'm just a good actress. My mother always said I should have been on the stage. My time limit for pretending that everything's all right is two hours. If Jamie stays in the house any longer, I have to go up into the shower room and have a good cry and then I'm all right for another two.'

'Did you take my advice?'

'What – and prance round the house like something out of *Playboy*?'

'That's not what I said.'

'I know, but it's what you meant.'

Tom's face creased into a half-smile. 'Well did you?'

'If I didn't know that your philandering days were over I'd accuse you of being voyeuristic.' Pamela unconsciously pulled her skirt down towards her knees. 'And anyway, I haven't had time to be Playmate of the Month. Jack's had tonsillitis and Francesca's just gone down with a stinking cold.'

'So you're still playing at being a mother.'

'I *am* a bloody mother!'

'What you need is a revenge affair.' Tom stood up and paced the floor, slapping the palm of his hand with his pen. She could tell he had been watching too many American cop films again.

'I probably need a hole in the head more,' she said dismissively.

'I'm serious.' He certainly looked as if he was. 'A pretend revenge affair, that's what you need.'

Pamela's smile twisted sardonically. 'This pretend revenge affair . . . it wouldn't happen to be with *you*, Tom, would it?'

'Well, if you insist.'

'For heaven's sake, Tom, you're more transparent than

138

some of Liz Hurley's dresses.' She walked to the coffee machine and poured herself a cup from the constant supply.

'I bet it's a long time since you've been wined and dined by someone other than your husband.' He wagged his finger at her.

She held up a cup to Tom and he shook his head. 'It's a long time since I've been wined and dined by someone *including* my husband.'

'Give him a taste of his own medicine,' Tom said expansively. 'A few mysterious nights out, a few bits of frilly lingerie, a few phone calls that cut off when he answers.'

'I can't do that to him!'

'Why not? He's doing it to you.'

'I know, but he's a man. Men do this sort of thing. It comes naturally to them.'

'I'll take you for a couple of nice meals out, we'll stay a bit later than we should, you'll have a bit more to drink than a married woman ought to – and Bob's your uncle!'

'Bob might be your uncle, but I'm not sure he's related to me at all.'

'I'll take you to that new Thai restaurant, the one that's in the old James Hunt racing-school building.'

She could feel herself weakening, despite the fact that it was a ridiculous plan; however, no one else had come up with anything better. 'Can't we take Shirley with us?'

'Supposing he follows us? How can you be having an illicit night out with your boss if his wife is coming along too?'

'Jamie isn't the jealous type. He wouldn't suspect anything.' She circled the bottom of her cup thoughtfully with her spoon.

'Then make him suspicious!'

'Oh hell, Tom. I can't stand all this subterfuge. It's not in my nature. Can't I just have it out with him?'

'You'll force him into her arms.'

'He's there already!'

'Then you need to wheedle him out.'

'It's you that's trying to wheedle me out.' She pointed her teaspoon at him knowingly. 'What will Shirley think?'

'I'll explain it all to her. She'll understand.'

'She's a better woman than I am if she does.'

Tom looked hurt. 'It's entirely up to you.' He spread his hands. 'I'm only trying to help.'

'Not too many weeks ago you were advising me to sit there and do nothing but keep my mouth shut and my legs open.'

'You have a very coarse turn of phrase when you want to, Pamela Duncan,' he said accusingly. 'Anyway, that was when you merely suspected. Now you're sure and you need to take action.'

'I'm desperate, Tom!'

'Desperate times call for desperate measures.'

'You've said that before.'

'That's because it's true. I don't mind repeating myself when these things need saying.' He wagged his ballpoint. 'I said I don't mind repeating myself when these things need saying.'

Pamela tutted impatiently. 'I don't know if I should be listening to you. You're too damned persuasive by half.' She drained her coffee cup.

'Well,' he shrugged, 'my offer still stands. You only have to say the word.' He rested his arm along her chair and looked down at her.

Pamela swallowed hard. He really was quite muscular when he was at such close proximity.

'But right now. . .' His voice was so sweet and sugar-coated it should have come with a tooth-decay warning. He fixed her eyes with his and there was the suggestion of a contented smile on his face, like a cat which has just eaten a mouse with double cream on top of it. 'Right now I need to sell some impenetrable burglar alarms to some very vulnerable properties, otherwise their skimpy defences could be broken open just like – that!' He clicked his fingers.

She felt her skin flush; the room had suddenly gone very warm. All she needed now on top of everything else was to start an early menopause. How on earth did she think she could cope single-handedly with a night out with this man? He was a Lothario of the first order and always would be. She flicked open her notepad irritably. And why did he always manage to make even the most innocent sentence sound like the most tempting invitation to go to bed . . .?

Shortly before noon on that same day, Charlie came and sat on the edge of Jamie's desk. 'I've arranged for us to go to lunch with Gordy.'

'Charlie!'

'I know he's a crashing bore, but he's got a very salutary tale to tell.' Charlie rummaged aimlessly through the papers in Jamie's in-tray. 'One I think you should listen to very carefully, considering your current predicament.'

'What are you trying to do to me?'

Charlie, for once, lowered his voice. 'I'm trying to knock some sense into that very thick skull of yours before it's too late.'

'Look, I've apologised about the other night. I didn't mean to get you involved – it's just that the opportunity arose what with that business with the trains.' Jamie held up his hands. 'Anyway, I'm not going through that again. You know the story. I'm sorry. It's done. It won't happen again.'

'I can't just stand by and watch you do this. I like Pamela.'

'*I* like Pamela!' Jamie protested.

'You bloody ought to. She's your wife.' Charlie tugged fretfully at his unruly mop of curls. He looked as if he hadn't been to bed again and hadn't shaved. But then that was how he normally looked. 'If you still have any feelings for her at all, why are you doing this?'

'I don't have a choice any more.' Jamie looked round to check that no one else was listening. The worst thing about working in an office that was an ex-rabbit warren was that there were plenty of places for people with big ears to lurk. 'Being without Teri now would be like being without breath – a fairly vital component to human life, I think you'll agree.'

Charlie fished in Jamie's desk tidy and started joining all the paper clips together to form a chain. 'And what about Pamela – and the kids? What would life be like without them?'

'I'm not planning on leaving them.' Jamie's tone was becoming insistent.

'What exactly *are* you planning to do, then? Lead this double life for ever?' Charlie swung the paper-clip chain in front of him.

'I don't think that's any of your business.'

'You didn't go to boarding school, did you?' Charlie raised one eyebrow.

'You know I didn't.' Jamie looked puzzled. 'I am a product of Queen Elizabeth's Grammar School, Melbrose in the Borders of Sunny Scotland.'

'I went to boarding school,' Charlie said flatly. 'I was sent away by my parents when I was seven.'

'Now you're breaking my heart.' It came out more sarcastically than he had intended.

Charlie stared out of the office window. 'Did you go home every night to a loving family with your tea waiting on the table and your mother in her apron?'

Jamie frowned and said impatiently, 'Something like that. Why?'

'I cried myself to sleep every night for two years.' He looked back at Jamie. 'I know what it's like to be without parents. And mine thought they were doing the best for me – giving me a good start in life, making a man out of me.' Charlie pulled a wry face. 'If you can't think of Pamela, think of the kids.'

'I told you,' Jamie repeated tightly. 'I'm not about to abandon them.'

'Emotionally, you're already out of the door.'

'And when did you turn into Claire Rayner?' Jamie snapped. Teri was infiltrating his life so much he was even starting to use her phrases. But then she did have quite a good repertoire of cutting repartee.

Charlie ignored him. 'Supposing Pamela finds out?'

'She won't.' Jamie grabbed the paper-clip chain from Charlie's hands and flung it on to the desk.

'I bet Hugh Grant thought that too.'

'This is entirely different.'

'You're right, it is. You're not famous – you won't have an agent turning it into good publicity. It won't get you plum parts in new movies. And no one's going to pat you on the back and say what a good bloke you are, even though you're a bit laddish and ever so slightly careless.' Charlie stood up from Jamie's desk and stretched like a contented cat. 'Still, at least you're not paying for it like old Hugh.'

Charlie hadn't realised how strong Jamie was until his fist hit his face. It knocked him straight off his feet and on to the floor. But then the element of surprise probably had something to do with it as well. He realised he weighed a lot too, because he was sprawled on top of him punching at his body with a random ferocity that was quite alarming.

'You bastard!' hissed Jamie, showering spittle into Charlie's face. It sounded as if there were two secretaries screaming, but they only had one in the office so she must have been making that frightful din all by herself. Mercifully, someone hoisted Jamie off Charlie's inert and breathless body. He was holding Jamie by the scruff of the neck when Charlie recovered sufficiently to open his eyes. Unfortunately, it was Jamie's boss who had come to the rescue, the merciless Director of Information Technology, John 'Joyless' Lovejoy. Jamie's face was suffused purple with anger and he was still throwing half-hearted punches at the air.

'This isn't the flaming playground!' Joyless shouted. 'Get out of my sight and settle whatever this is about in an adult and dignified manner.' He pointed a finger at Charlie, who was still flat on his back and breathing heavily. 'I want you back in here by two o'clock acting like the best of friends, otherwise don't come back at all.'

Joyless released his hold on Jamie, who stopped flailing and straightened his tie. 'Help him up!' he ordered, and marched out of the room.

Jamie sat sullenly nursing his pint of lager. It was weak and flat and tasted of cleaning fluid. Charlie sat nursing a gin and tonic – a double – and his face. There was a bright red swollen splotch just under his right eye, which would eventually turn purple, and a slight cut – well, more of a slight graze really – along his cheekbone. He was gingerly holding an ice cube against it that he had fished out of his gin. All three of them were crowded round a beer-stained table that was only intended for two, and Gordy was holding court. Jamie and Charlie intermittently glowered at each other.

'We've been together two years, me and Tina,' Gordy said in response to Charlie's attempt at subtle questioning. 'It feels like a bloody lifetime.' His face sank deeper into its usual hangdog expression.

'What went wrong?' Charlie said. He sounded as if he had developed a slight lisp, but Jamie couldn't be sure that he wasn't putting it on in order to catch the sympathy vote. 'I thought she was a right little goer?'

Jamie narrowed his eyes at him menacingly. Charlie looked the other way.

' "Martini" they used to call her when she worked in the office. You know, "any time, any place, anywhere",' he sang tunelessly. 'And by God, she was, too. Over the desk, behind the filing cabinet, in the stationery cupboard – we tried 'em all.'

Charlie swallowed his gin and pursed his lips. 'What happened?'

Gordy raised his pint to his mouth and shrugged. 'She went teetotal on me as soon as we got married. Now it's "I haven't got the time", "we can't do it here" and "no way, Jose".'

'Surely it can't be all that bad.'

Gordy smacked his lips and returned his beer to the table. 'She hates my kids.' He had a line of froth settled on his top lip. '*I* hate my kids.' He sat back and folded his arms. 'I see them every other weekend and the only place they want to go – after McDonald's – is shopping. They've turned into Toys R Us vultures. They swoop in there and won't come out until they've picked the shelves clean. First it was Ninja Turtles, then poofy-looking Wrestlers and now they've got every Power Ranger in the frigging set. If their clothes haven't got a designer label on them, they've "Pocohontas" scrawled all over them instead. I'm dreading what comes next. I blame their mother,' he said sagely. 'She's encouraged them to see me as nothing but a bottomless bank account.'

'That's terrible.' Charlie looked pointedly at Jamie, who remained silent.

'No, Charlie, you know what's really terrible?' He was warming to his subject now. 'I pay for them all – the whole bloody shebang. One ex-wife and three ex-kids. Of course, she's got a lover. Surprising really, but she found one the minute I left. Young chap, too.' He stopped momentarily to contemplate the strange ways of the world. 'But will she marry him? Will she hell! She'd rather see me paying up until the day I die. It puts a terrible strain on our relationship, me and Tina. Of course, that's why she does it. And the courts back her up. There's no justice in this world. What can a chap do?'

Jamie thought that he looked as if he wasn't really open to suggestions.

'Absolute nightmare,' Charlie commiserated. He sat back in his chair, twirling the stem of his glass between his fingers. 'So really, you would say that having an affair was the worst mistake you ever made?' He sounded like the counsel for the prosecution summing up for the jury. Charlie smiled superciliously at Jamie.

'Having an affair? Bollocks!' Gordy said loudly. 'The worst mistake I ever made was marrying Tina. I should have left things as they were. Set her up in a little flat, saucy nooky on tap twice a week, no strings attached. Best thing I ever did was have an affair.'

There was a look of utmost consternation on Charlie's battered face. It was Jamie's turn to wear the supercilious smile.

'In fact,' Gordy leaned forward conspiratorially, 'I'm looking round for a nice young filly at the moment. If you know a good mount who wouldn't mind going over a few jumps with me, you give me the nod.' He winked theatrically.

Charlie's mouth was hanging open. 'You could park a bus in there,' Jamie observed lightly.

Charlie snapped it shut. He looked at his watch. 'We ought to be going, James. I have a mountain of work to be getting on with, even if you don't. We'd better go back together otherwise Joyless will want our resignations.'

Jamie stood up. 'So soon?' Gordy protested. 'I haven't even had a chance to ask you about that.' He nodded at Charlie's eye. 'What was it? Lovers' tiff?'

Charlie threw the rest of his gin down his throat. 'Naff off, Gordy,' he said shortly, and flounced out of the pub.

They walked to the end of the block in an uneasy silence. 'So what was the moral of that little tale?' Jamie said eventually.

Charlie shook his head. 'I'm buggered if I know.' They crossed over the road and then fell in step beside each other again. 'I suppose it just goes to show,' Charlie continued, 'that we never learn by our mistakes. We just keep on making them. And whatever anyone else says to persuade us otherwise counts for bugger all.'

Jamie touched the sleeve of his raincoat. 'Thanks for trying though, Charlie.'

His friend shrugged.

Jamie laughed and tried to lighten the mood. 'Do you think he sussed which one of us is having the affair, or is Gordy too wrapped up in his own troubles to notice anyone else's?'

'Was I that obvious?' Charlie looked concerned.

'Dolly Parton's breasts are less obvious than you, Charles.'

Charlie tutted. 'I thought I was being so discreet.' They walked along in silence again until Charlie said hesitantly, 'I'm sorry for saying what I did earlier, about, you know, about Hugh Grant and all that.'

'That's okay. I'm too touchy at the moment. I shouldn't have hit you.'

Charlie patted his face carefully. 'No, you shouldn't.'

'Not so hard anyway,' Jamie countered. 'I don't know what's got into me, Charlie. I'm sorry. You're not going to believe this,' Jamie dodged two drunks who were lying asleep across the pavement, 'but we haven't even . . . you know. Nothing. So why am I feeling so guilty?'

Charlie's eyebrows pulled together in a crease. 'Not a thing? What about the other night?'

'We slept together – as in asleep.'

'Non-consummated adultery? Now there's a novel concept.'

'It isn't through lack of inclination,' Jamie elaborated hurriedly.

'Mmm,' Charlie said. 'I see.'

'How can you see, if I don't see?' Jamie said crossly.

'You feel guilty, because you are guilty,' Charlie explained.

Jamie's face darkened. 'I don't want to have to hit you again, Charlie.'

'Well, I suppose I should be thankful for that.' Charlie looked sideways at him. 'It's because it's premeditated, dear boy. You can't plead diminished responsibility, because your responsibility isn't diminished. This isn't a flash in the pan, is it? This isn't carnal manslaughter – one moment of madness and you're left with a body that you don't know what to do with, and blood on your hands. This is inching step-by-step to its ultimate conclusion, every move precisely planned. This is first-degree adultery that you're planning to commit. Every jury in the land would find you guilty. If there was still capital punishment, you'd swing.'

Jamie looked stricken. 'If you're trying to cheer me up, Charlie, I have to say it isn't working.'

'I'm merely trying to point out the facts of the case.'

'Not only do you look like Columbo, you're starting to sound like him too,' Jamie said tersely. 'Anyway, I don't know why I'm telling you all this.'

'Because I'm your best friend.' They stopped at the office door. 'Because I'm your *only* friend. And because, even though I think you're a prize prat, you know I'll be there to help you pick up the pieces when it all goes horribly wrong.'

Jamie punched him playfully on the shoulder. 'And don't hit me again,' Charlie said tetchily. 'I mark easily.'

Chapter Thirteen

Teri was sitting on the toilet seat. Clare was in the bath surrounded by an over-indulgence of bubbles which bobbed rhythmically round her chin and showed a blatant disregard for the economies of a water meter. There was a bright yellow duck with an orange beak at the taps end which was struggling to keep its head above the froth.

The bathroom was the only room that Teri hadn't yet tackled. The suite was yellow – primrose yellow rather than duck yellow – and someone had gone overboard, covering every conceivable remaining surface with three-inch white tiles erratically veined with the same yellow. It was truly nauseating and would be hellishly expensive to put right. The bathroom needed a new suite and new tiles – albeit not on the scale of the current acreage. She'd tried sponging and stippling and Artexing, and she could put up a shelf that actually stayed up, but tiling was something that Teri felt was beyond her limited Do-It-Yourself ability. That was definitely a job for someone else.

Teri twisted the top on and off the foaming bath gel. It was an aromatherapy one, optimistically called 'The Source of Life' and the blurb on the back assured her it was enriched with oils of ylang ylang and sandalwood to relax troubled spirits and soothe the tired mind. She'd used gallons of it since Clare arrived. It had made not the slightest bit of difference. Her 'troubled spirit' was still about as relaxed as a poltergeist and her 'tired mind' rather than being soothed felt perilously close to exploding. Clare had also used a gallon of it and it hadn't done anything to make her easier to live with either.

Teri glanced at her friend. She was resting with her eyes closed, a dreamy look on her upturned face, curiously decapitated by the froth. Teri went back to twisting the cap. 'Look, this is going to be really hard for me to say.'

Clare opened her eyes. 'It's about the milk, isn't it? I know I used it all yesterday morning. I'm really sorry, but I think you ought to get some more delivered. There's just not enough, and dry Weetabix is no one's idea of a fun breakfast.'

Teri sighed and counted very quickly to ten. 'It isn't about the milk.'

Clare's brow crinkled. 'It's the ironing board, then.' A hand appeared from beneath the water and she cleared a path in the bubbles just in front of her mouth. 'I can tell you exactly how it happened.' Clare's gabbling was legendary. 'David rang just as I was pressing my jeans and I don't know how but it must have just fallen over. I didn't notice until I could smell the burning.'

'I didn't know you'd burnt your jeans.' A look of concern crossed Teri's face.

'I didn't. It missed my jeans and burnt a hole in the ironing-board cover. I swear I'll buy you a new one though. Just as soon as I get paid.'

Teri closed her eyes. She could feel a headache coming on. A severe one. 'It's not about the ironing-board cover either.'

'I can't think of anything else I've done.' Clare tried to sound innocent and failed.

'I can,' Teri replied tetchily, 'but it isn't anything you've done either.'

'Then what is it?'

Teri took a deep breath. 'I don't think this is working out.'

'What?'

'Us – sharing.'

'Oh really, Teri, it's fine,' she said soothingly. 'You're so considerate. I hardly notice you're here.'

Teri put the bath gel on top of the toilet. 'That's my point, Clare. You hardly notice me and it's my house.'

'But I'm in and out all the time. I'm not exactly under your feet. I'm the perfect lodger.'

'That, unfortunately, is a matter of opinion.' Teri rubbed her temples. 'I never know when you're in or when you're out or when you're likely to be back.'

'You sound like my mother,' Clare said testily. 'And what's more, it isn't attractive.'

'You come in at all hours of the day and night and drink my milk.'

Her friend's eyes narrowed. 'I *knew* this was about the milk!'

'The milk's just one of many irritating little things, none of which add up to the sum of the whole.' Teri sighed heavily. 'I need my privacy back.'

'Oh, I see.' Clare put on her Sister Mary Bernadette look. 'I get it now. You mean you need somewhere to bonk!' A superior expression spread over her face. 'This is about him, isn't it? This Jamie. This *married* man.'

'Partly,' Teri conceded reluctantly.

'How can you do this to me? I thought you were my best friend.'

Teri spoke very quietly and rationally, although it was a struggle to do so. 'We need somewhere to spend some time alone together.' She put her hand on her chest and patted it for emphasis. 'This is my house.'

Clare was indignant. 'I have been abandoned by my husband, but you don't give that a second thought. You want me to move out so that you can move someone else's husband in. Is that what we're talking about here?'

'Pretty much,' Teri admitted. 'Though it sounds much worse when you put it like that.'

'This isn't very nice, Therese Carter, is it? *Is it?*'

'No, it isn't,' she agreed. 'Happy now?'

'Happy! You're kicking me out into the streets with nowhere to go and you ask me if I'm happy.'

'I love him, Clare. I want to be with him. I thought you'd understand, but all you do is make snide comments about him.'

'Don't talk to me about love, Teri. I know all there is to know. It's like a nasty dose of bindweed that spoils the garden of romance – it creeps in innocuously, obliterates everything in sight and is an absolute bastard to get rid of.'

'For a brief moment I thought you were quoting Shakespeare,' Teri said derisively.

'No, this is pure Clare Owen! Educated at the university of life and much better use to you than some poncey old bloke in tights.'

'I can't stand your disapproval any longer.' Teri could feel tears prickling behind her eyes. 'I thought you'd be there for me.'

'I've always been there for you, Teri.' Clare also sounded

close to tears. 'I was there for you when Michael Lacey poured our playtime bottle of milk on your head in Mrs Whittle's class. I told on him for you!'

'It was *you* that dared Michael Lacey to pour it on my head in the first place,' she reminded her.

Clare paused to think about it and then continued, 'I was there for you when Janet Starkey tied you by your plaits to your front gates and left you there.'

'Clare, you came and cut all my hair off! It took months to grow. My mother wouldn't let me out of the house for three weeks.'

Teri waited while Clare sorted through the various files in her brain. She was getting red in the face and Teri was sure it wasn't just the temperature of the bathwater – although she wouldn't mind betting a pound on the fact that she'd probably be washing the dishes in cold water again tonight. Finally Clare said, 'I've been there for you lots of times.'

'I know.' Teri tried pleading, 'And I'm asking you to be there for me now.'

'No, you're not! You're asking me to *not* be there for you. You want me to leave. How much more not being there do you want?'

'I'm sorry.' It was all she could think of to say.

'We could work out time constraints – a rota.' Clare looked completely crestfallen. 'I'll make myself scarce when he's here.'

'It wouldn't work,' Teri said firmly. She had decided on this days ago; it was just a matter of breaking it to Clare. 'I want him to be free to phone me without hearing you tut-tutting in the background.'

'You're wasting yourself on him, Teri,' she warned. 'This will end in tears. The trouble with married men is that they promise you the earth and all you end up with is a handful of poxy little pebbles.'

'He hasn't promised me anything,' she said defensively.

'Then you're an even bigger fool than I thought.'

They looked away from each other. Clare stared at the yellow-veined tiles on the wall by the side of the bath and Teri stared fixedly at the ones in front of the toilet. Several of them were cracked. It was Clare who spoke first. 'I don't know where to go,' she said quietly.

'I've bought the local paper. I thought we could look through it together. You might be able to get somewhere closer to the airport.'

'Shit!' Clare snapped. 'You're all heart!' She kicked the duck out of the bath and it landed with a startled look on its face on the bath mat. 'I don't know if I'll ever forgive you for this, Therese Carter. You're a tart, a harlot and ruthless adulteress. Now get out and let *me* have some privacy.'

Teri stood up and slowly left the bathroom. She leaned with her back against the wall at the top of the stairs and let the tears roll down her cheeks to drip unhindered on the front of her blouse. At this moment, she didn't think that she would ever forgive herself.

'It's me.' His voice was familiar at once.

'Oh Jamie, thank goodness you've called. I've just had a blazing row with Clare. I asked her to leave and she's actually packed her stuff and gone tonight. She's taken it really badly.' Teri sniffed. 'She was in a terrible state when she left. I shouldn't have let her go.'

'Why did you ask her to leave?'

'Oh Jamie, she's been so awful about you. I couldn't stand it any longer. And I wanted my house back to myself so that we could, perhaps, spend some time together.' There was a long pause at the end of the phone. 'Jamie? You do want that, don't you?'

There was a heavy sigh before he said, 'Of course I do.'

'Where are you ringing from?'

'The phone box just down the road from the house. I'm out with MacTavish.'

'MacTavish?'

'The dog.'

'I wish you were here,' Teri blurted out.

'I wish I was there, too.'

Teri's throat was tight and she could feel herself starting to cry again. 'I'm going to do something really silly and take British Telecom's advice. If they think it's good to talk, we'll see how it works.' She took a deep and unsteady breath. 'I think I'm falling in love with you, Jamie,' she said hesitantly.

There was another long silence. Too long. Uncomfortably long. 'I think I love you, too,' Jamie eventually replied. He sounded sad rather than elated, she thought. 'Look, I've got to go,' he said rather too briskly. 'MacTavish has only so much patience and he's starting to do his starving hound impersonation. I'd better get back and feed him. I only phoned to say that I'll see you in the morning.'

They saw each other every morning, so when he managed to phone in the evening it was entirely superfluous and, therefore, all the more welcome.

'I love you,' Teri said. It was easier the second time round.

'I love you, too.' It didn't sound as if it had been any easier for Jamie. The phone went dead.

Teri sat with her head in her hands staring at the wall. Damn, she had blown it! What a stupid thing to say. The guy phones for a few minutes' illicit chat at great personal expense and she comes over all heavy and gives him the complete heebie-jeebies. Why did she never learn to keep her big trap shut when she was tired and emotional? What a berk! Why on earth did she ever think that BT knew what they were talking about? She was going to throw a brick at the television next time that bloody chirpy Bob Hoskins popped up on it.

Jamie pulled MacTavish away from the crisp packet that he had hopefully buried his nose in and started to walk back home. It was a bitterly cold night with a full moon and the crisp whiteness of a hard ground frost, and he pulled his scarf up towards his ears. It was the beige cashmere that had been returned to him on the regretful demise of Frosty the snowman and he was eternally grateful for it – as Frosty had probably been.

His hands were cold and his heart was as heavy as a bowling ball – the heaviest one you could get. In fact, this was much like his first, and last, experience at the Megabowl Alley. It was like slithering down the highly polished lanes in smooth-soled shoes and being totally out of control, unable to get a grip with your feet and being equally unable to let go of the ball, but knowing full well that before long you were going to smash headlong into the waiting row of skittles.

The only difference was that at the Megabowl, with a lot of luck and a following wind, he had eventually managed to chalk up – or log on the computer-aided display – an excruciatingly low score. With Teri he hadn't managed to score at all yet. The really frightening thing was that this unfamiliar out-of-controlness wasn't an entirely unpleasant feeling.

Charlie was right. He had to end it before it became a way of life, before he turned into another Gordy. How could he be doing this to Pamela and the children? What sort of pathetic lech sneaked out of the house on the pretext of walking the dog to phone a beautiful, young, free and single woman who should be out on the town chasing young, free and single men – not sitting at home waiting on the off chance for him to call?

This sort of pathetic lech, whose stomach turned to ice at the thought of Teri with another man, yet who lacked the conviction or the courage to commit to her himself, Jamie concluded bitterly. How could it be possible for him to feel like this about Teri and still profess that he loved his wife? And yet he did. There was nothing inherently wrong with their marriage, they'd just got into a rut, a routine – that happened to everyone. But not everyone went round panting after some young bit of fluff – mental apology to Teri for the political incorrectness – like a lovesick teenager.

It was highly probable that a man could love two women equally – but it just wasn't on in practical terms. Not to mention the slight conflict with the marriage vows: there was nothing in those about 'to love, honour, cherish and to chase skirt' . . . Perhaps he should become a Mormon. They were still allowed a dozen or so wives, weren't they – or was it the Jehovah's Witnesses? Jamie shuddered. Imagine a dozen wives! It was difficult enough trying to juggle two women.

And what kind of monsters were they both turning into? Teri had thrown her best friend out of her house while he had done a totally unreasonable Frank Bruno impersonation and had laid *his* best friend out for some petty little remark. Pamela deserved better than this, Teri deserved better than this, the kids deserved better than this, their friends deserved better than this and even MacTavish deserved better than this.

It would have to end. He would have to call on all his depleted reserves of willpower and walk away from this. It was going to hurt like hell, but it would be for the best in the end. He only hoped Teri would see that, too.

'Come on, doggers,' Jamie said, with a weariness that was embedded deep into his bones. 'Let's get you home, my true and faithful alibi, and give you a nice big bowl of Chum.' MacTavish wagged his tail appreciatively. 'Otherwise we'll both be in the dog-house.'

Chapter Fourteen

'I still don't know why you agreed to work late. You've never worked late before,' Jamie said, labouring the point. He was lying across the bed watching his wife as she got dressed.

Pamela fastened the buttons on her blouse. 'I told you, it's a new contract that's come up. A big oil company's moving into Milton Keynes and they want us to quote. Tom and I need to discuss it.'

' "Tom and I need to discuss it",' Jamie mimicked silently behind Pamela's back. Aloud he said, 'Why can't you discuss it during normal office hours?'

Pamela smiled sardonically. 'Jamie, you're a fine one to talk. If anyone should appreciate that there just aren't enough hours in the day, it's you.'

'Well, I hope he's paying you overtime,' he said petulantly.

'He isn't. That's why he's taking me for a nice meal to make up for it.' She wriggled her skirt over her stockings and smoothing it over her hips, zipped it up.

'Stockings?' Jamie queried. 'You never wear stockings.'

'Don't be silly. Of course I do! It's just that you never look any more.' She slipped her feet into her high heels and hid a smile as she saw Jamie's frown deepen. 'We're

161

going to the new Thai restaurant – the one in the old James Hunt racing-school building.'

'The one with the hideous red and white roof that looks like a bloody circus tent?'

Pamela brushed her hair. 'I believe it's lovely inside.'

'Well, it'd better be. Nice meals don't pay the kids' school fees.'

She turned and looked at him. 'I do believe you're jealous, Jamie Duncan.'

'Bollocks,' he said emphatically. He put the Thomas the Tank Engine he was toying with on the bed. 'It's just that, well, don't you think you're a bit kitted up for a business meeting?'

'I thought you'd be pleased that I'm going out.' She bent to clip her earrings on in the mirror. 'I get precious little chance to dress up these days. The playgroup might be surprised if I turned up in sandwashed pure silk and pearls.'

'You don't think you might give him the wrong idea?'

'I work for him, Jamie; we respect each other.' She fastened her watch on to her wrist.

Jamie snorted. 'Give him an inch and he'd take a mile. I know all about the Tom Pearsons of this world.'

Pamela stifled the urge to say, 'I bet you do.' Instead she said sweetly: 'Tom's all right if you know how to handle him.'

'I'd rather you didn't handle him at all!' He picked up Thomas again. 'Don't you think I should come with you?'

'No, I don't.' Pamela turned to him. 'For goodness sake, Jamie, it's one night! Who'll look after the children?'

'I'll get Melanie in from next door.'

'It won't kill you to look after your own children for one night,' she said, exasperation making her voice sound harsh. 'Jack's already asleep and Frankie will be too, as soon as you read her a story. I don't know why you're making such a fuss. I thought you came home early for me especially.'

'I did.' A scowl settled into his features. 'I just don't like you going out. You never go out.'

'All the more reason for you to be pleased for me and give in gracefully.' She kissed him lightly on the cheek. The sound of crunching gravel heralded a car pulling into their drive. Pamela peeped out of the window. 'He's here.'

Jamie got off the bed and strode to the window. 'Typical. Why do all British businessmen drive German cars? Where's their sense of patriotism?'

'It's very comfortable. Lovely and smooth and quiet,' Pamela said, admiring herself in the mirror.

'How do you know?'

'He took me out to lunch in it last week.' Jamie stood open-mouthed. 'Eternity or Passion?' she said, holding up two bottles of perfume.

'Don't you think that's a bit over the top?' His eyebrows knitted together as he surveyed the perfume bottles.

She chose the Passion and sprayed it liberally over her throat.

'You won't need plates,' Jamie said sarcastically. 'He'll be eating out of your hand.'

'Then perhaps I'll ask for a pay rise,' Pamela quipped. She twirled in front of him. 'Tell me I look nice.'

He hadn't seen her so excited in years. There was a girlish bloom to her face and a pinkness to her cheeks that he didn't entirely approve of. 'You look beautiful,' he said truthfully.

She kissed him on the cheek. 'I won't be late. I should be back by eleven.'

'Have a nice time,' he said reluctantly.

He heard Pamela skip down the stairs – yes, skip – and then the front door slammed, despite the fact that the kids were in bed. Pulling the curtain back, he watched as she slid her elegant legs into Tom Pearson's Mercedes and there was a sick and sinking feeling in his stomach. As he saw his wife kiss her boss on the cheek he let the curtain drop. Slowly, he walked through to Francesca's room, where he could hear her having a loud and exaggerated conversation with Barbie about the untimely demise of Take That.

'How did it go?' Tom said as Pamela settled herself into the luxurious surroundings of his car.

'Like a dream.' Pamela looked totally perplexed. 'If I hadn't seen his face for myself, I would never have believed it. It was a picture.'

'And not a pretty one, I'll bet.' The car crunched out of the driveway. 'What did I tell you? There's nothing like a touch of the green-eyed monster to give a flagging marriage that extra bit of spice.'

'You're a wily old dog, Tom Pearson.' Pamela shook her head and her hair tumbled round her shoulders. 'I know now that I should listen to you more often.'

Francesca had been easily placated with a few pages of her storybook and he had left them both in peace – Francesca sucking her thumb and Barbie looking as wide-eyed and bimbo-ish as always. Jamie eyed Barbie dispassionately. Her proportions would be humanly impossible. Scaled up, she would probably have a forty-eight double-D chest, a ten-inch waist, size two feet and legs like a giraffe. Shopping at Sainsbury's would be hell for her.

He could understand why Pamela objected to Barbie as a plaything. She said the doll encouraged girls to become anorexic. He thought she would probably have the opposite effect. Having seen what Barbie was like, and the fact that she could only pull a gimpish-looking bloke like Ken, he hoped Francesca would eat sensibly and have aspirations to become a brain surgeon. In future, he would try to support Pamela in her quest for more educational and challenging toys. Barbie was totally unrealistic.

But then, who ever wanted to play with things that were realistic? Wasn't that what play was all about – escapism? Perhaps that was why people had affairs . . . the adult version of play, when you reached an age at which escapism could no longer be achieved with wide-eyed, large-breasted dolls and Meccano. When Lego gave way to a leg-over. Was it the only chance adults had to escape from reality? To lose yourself in another person who didn't notice that you were going grey, had more flab than a Sumo wrestler and needed to mainline Phyllosan before you could tackle anything more energetic than mowing the lawn? To have someone think you were Tom Cruise when you actually felt ready to settle for nothing more strenuous than a Caribbean cruise was something that could quicken even the most stagnant heart. Had the fact that Teri obviously saw him as someone interesting and attractive made him forget for a short while that he was a boring, staid insurance executive with unfulfilled dreams, family responsibilities and an insanely high mortgage? To his wife, Jamie was nothing more than a meal ticket, a provider, financial security. That was reality. And reality wasn't all it was cracked up to be these days.

He had gone into the lounge – a tribute to interior

design magazines – where MacTavish had greeted him with a welcoming wag. At least someone wanted to spend the evening with him. Jamie poured himself a whisky and sat on the sofa, staring into the embers of the fire burning in the inglenook fireplace that dominated the room, and wondered where it had all started to go wrong.

He had never seen Pamela looking like that before – well, not for years. She had behaved like a schoolgirl out on her first date and it worried him more than he cared to admit. When she took the time, she scrubbed up very nicely. And she certainly had taken the time tonight. She had looked absolutely beautiful for her date – correction 'business meeting' – with Tom Pearson.

Was that what was irking him, the fact that she never took the time for him, and yet had pulled out all the stops for another man? Was that what Pamela wanted now – a so-called 'open' marriage? Was she really having an affair with that smooth cockney slime-ball? Was Tom her 'plaything'?

The thought made Jamie shudder. He'd never trusted Pearson, not since she'd started working there. And anyway, the chap was a good twenty years older than Pamela. Okay, so he didn't look it – but the age-gap was there nevertheless. He had never been so blatant about Teri; he had been the very soul of discretion. Then again, if Pamela *was* having an affair, would she be quite so transparent? She could be very devious if she put her mind to it. Perhaps it was just a purely innocent business meeting . . .

Jamie tasted his whisky and contemplated the fact. Business meeting, my eye! he thought viciously. She had been so obvious she might as well have said that she was going mountaineering in Holland. And to think he had been going to call a halt to his relationship with Teri!

He had been on the verge of telling her today, but his courage had failed him at the last minute. How could he announce to her in a crowded commuter train or in the sweaty smoke-laden atmosphere of Steamers that their beautiful friendship was destined for the dung heap before it had really started?

By asking Clare to leave, she had cleared the way for them to become more intimate – and what had he done about it so far? Zilch! Was that what he was frightened of? One more step and he would be off the end of the cliff and tumbling through the air into the tempestuous sea of infidelity, without the benefit of a safety net. No more pretending that this wasn't really an affair.

How much longer could he hide behind the nice, safe, secure meetings which they currently indulged in? Travelling together on the train – how quaint – morning coffee at the End of the Line Buffet and a quick drink at Steamers on the way home – no risk of being overcome by an urge to have sex on the table there. Especially not with all those beer stains . . .

He'd been torn for months between his desire to remain loyal – and faithful – to his wife, and his desire to take Teri home, tear her clothes off and ravish her on the Axminster. So far, Pamela had been winning.

He had thought, naively, that she needed him, but he was labouring under a complete misapprehension there. Pamela needed no one. She sailed through life like a stately galleon, while all around were mere jet-bikes – tossed and flipped repeatedly into the sea by little waves and wholly inadequate to deal with the storms of life. Pamela remained unaffected, aloof, unsympathetic and totally upright. His wife could sail life's charted course unaided. All she needed was a generous maintenance allowance.

* * *

Jamie watched television until midnight – or, more accurately, alternated between the clock and the television from eleven o'clock onwards when Pamela had said she would be home.

He had watched *World in Action*, *Take Your Pick* with Des O'Connor – not a patch on Michael Miles (or was it Hughie Green?) – a wildlife programme about predatory animals – very appropriate – some awful chat show hosted by Barbie's big sister that wheeled out equally vacuous celebrities intent on promoting their new film, highlights of a football match between two countries he'd never heard of – still rubbish, but better rubbish – and he'd just finished listening to Jerry Paxman harangue two inept politicians who deserved everything they got.

He went to the phone table in the hall and took out the *Yellow Pages*. There was an appointment card from 'The Hair Cut' by the phone, that showed Pamela had also been to have her hair done today – she was really pushing the boat out. He hadn't noticed and that had probably gone as a black mark against him to be used in later skirmishes of Alphabite warfare.

Jamie looked up the telephone number for the Thai restaurant. Its advert featured a stylised line drawing of an ornate Thai building rather than the re-hash of the old James Hunt racing school that it really was. He spent the next ten minutes vacillating about whether to phone or not.

He didn't want his wife to think that he was checking up on her – which he was. Nor that he was worried – which he also was. Pamela never stayed out late. In fact, she never went out in the evenings at all without him – except to school things and that didn't count.

When he did finally and reluctantly ring, he was told courteously in a strong Oriental accent that Mr Pearson and his companion had left some time ago. Companion! Jamie put the phone down and looked at his watch. It was twelve-fifteen. They were normally in bed hours ago. It would require superhuman effort to get up in time for the 6.25 in the morning. Teri would be in bed too . . .

His fingers ran hesitantly over the number pad of the phone. How could his loyalty to Pamela have been so misplaced? He had held himself back from his baser desires only to find that his wife was having a quick leg-over in a lay-by somewhere in Milton Keynes in the back of a top-of-the-range Mercedes. Well, they both knew where they stood from now on. At least he did. He would phone Teri and to hell with the fact that her number would appear on the Itemised Call bill.

'Hello.' It was obvious from her voice that she had been fast asleep.

'Did I wake you?' It was a stupid thing to say. It was up there along with, 'Are you hurt?' when you come across a car on its roof and the bleeding occupants are hanging upside down by their seat belts. Of course he'd woken her up.

'No,' she yawned. When you asked stupid questions, you invariably got stupid answers.

'You're a liar and I love you,' he said thickly.

'Is anything wrong?' She was wide awake now.

'No, everything's fine. I just wanted to know if you were doing anything tomorrow night?'

'You phone me at . . .' he heard her pulling the clock towards her . . . 'twelve-fifteen just to ask me if I'm busy tomorrow night?'

'Yes,' Jamie answered lamely.

'Of course not,' she sighed. 'You should know that by now.'

'Can I spend the . . . evening with you?'

'Of course you can.' Her voice was puzzled. 'Are you sure everything's okay? You sound peculiar.'

How can you explain to someone sleepy and separated by sixteen miles the quantum leap that his simple proposition held? He wasn't going to attempt to try, he just hoped she would understand tomorrow.

'Perfectly,' he said in answer to her question. 'And you sound sleepy. Go back to bed. I'll see you tomorrow.'

'All right.' She was still unconvinced. 'Goodnight.'

'I love you,' he said hurriedly, but the line had already gone dead.

As he put the receiver down, he heard Pamela's key in the lock. She stumbled over the step and swung into the hall still firmly attached to the door and her key. The way she was giggling gave the impression that Jimmy Tarbuck had just told her his all-time favourite joke.

'You're drunk,' Jamie said. He could well walk away with Stupid Statement of the Year Award tonight.

'I'm not!' Pamela protested, and fell off her shoes. She was obviously a contender too.

'What time do you call this?'

She peered at her watch. There was something wrong with the face. She tried it close up and far away, but she couldn't quite see where the hands had gone. She hoped they hadn't dropped off in her Thai green curry. This thought made her chuckle again.

'It's half-past twelve,' Jamie said crossly.

'Is it?' She was genuinely astonished. 'Doesn't time fun when you're having a fly?'

'I'm going straight to bed and I suggest you do the same.'

'I think you might have to help me,' Pamela slurred. 'I'm feeling a bit too relaxed to climb the stairs all by myself.'

'Humph,' Jamie said. 'Any more relaxed and I'd be sending for the AA and I mean Alcoholics Anonymous rather than the Knights of the Road!'

In response Pamela slithered down the wall and landed in a heap at his feet. 'Oh, for heaven's sake, woman!' He put one hand under her bottom and the other under her shoulders and struggled her into his arms. 'How much damned curry have you eaten tonight? You weigh a ton.'

The fact that she was a dead weight and wasn't co-operating one iota with being carried didn't help matters much.

It reminded Pamela of her honeymoon, being swept into Jamie's arms – perhaps not so much swept as wrestled – but it was a long time since he had carried her over the threshold.

They had taken a cottage in Yorkshire, just outside Hebden Bridge, in a cobbled and impossibly steep village that clung precariously to the side of a hill – the destination dictated by the paltry amount of money they had been left with after paying the deposit on their first house. The rain had fallen constantly for the whole fortnight, leaving the cobbles treacherous, which hardly mattered since they had rarely gone out.

He really was a very handsome man – it was funny how you could sometimes forget that when you saw a person every day. She had stopped looking at how his hair curled neatly into the nape of his neck and the strong line of his throat as it disappeared beneath his shirt. He had wonderful eyes, too – although at the moment he seemed to have more than was entirely good for a person.

It felt wonderful to be pressed against his chest again. He was warm – and getting warmer – and his body held the faint scent of citrus from his aftershave. Perhaps she would try harder to notice him again, to look at the things that she had adored about him, rather than focus on the things that constantly irritated her. She reached out and stroked his cheek.

'Get off,' he said as he panted up the stairs.

'I can't help it.' Pamela was feeling decidedly emotional; she wanted to kiss him for ever and ever. 'I'm in love.' Her voice cracked.

Jamie's voice sounded tight. 'I don't want to hear this, Pamela.'

'But I am, I'm in love,' she whined. 'I can't help how I feel.' And she couldn't. She was overwhelmed by her love for her husband. Perhaps Tom was right – a taste of the green-eyed monster had done her good, too. She didn't want Jamie looking at – and certainly not touching – another woman, and she would have to take measures to ensure that he didn't.

'I'd be grateful if you kept your thoughts to yourself,' Jamie wheezed. 'I've nothing personal against Tom – other than a surging desire to push his teeth down his throat. But this is difficult enough without you regaling me with the gory details.'

She agreed with Jamie. Tom was a nice enough man to work with, but the evening had only been bearable because of the copious amounts of white wine he had plied her with as part of the master plan. In fact, she had drunk more wine tonight than her usual annual quota. If there was one thing she hated – apart from *Coronation Street* – it was a drunk, and she had been starting to feel decidedly squiffy herself. It was good to get home to Jamie. She felt a rush of love tighten her throat and realised too late that it wasn't so much a rush of love as a rush of her Thai green curry and two bottles of particularly good Sancerre making a desperate bid for freedom.

It succeeded and she was sick down the front of Jamie's shirt. He deposited her in a most ungentlemanly fashion on the bed and disappeared into the en-suite to get a facecloth. When he returned he scrubbed Pamela's face with an enthusiasm that he normally kept for the bumpers of the Volvo.

'Get yourself undressed while I go and take a shower,' he instructed before disappearing again.

She lay on the bed trying to remember exactly how buttons came out of buttonholes. Tonight had been quite a success, all things considered. Jamie was in the shower, but he wasn't singing deep and meaningless love songs which had to be a good sign. Perhaps he would make love to her tonight. It was something they hadn't done for a long time. She would try to stay awake long enough to show that she was willing.

Sweeping her hair seductively over the pillow, she tried to arrange herself as seductively as possible with a selection of limbs that ranged from completely numb to totally incapacitated. Pamela smiled contentedly to herself and gave up with her buttons. If only there wasn't a helicopter trying to land in the bedroom, everything would be perfectly all right.

Chapter Fifteen

'She's taken a lover,' Jamie said starkly.

Teri looked up from the cushion on his lap. 'Does that make you feel better?'

'I suppose it should, but somehow it doesn't. What's the quaint old saying about two wrongs not making a right?'

'It's a very old saying.' It was unbelievable that he'd finally suggested spending the evening with her voluntarily. She should have realised that something momentous had happened. 'Is that the only reason you're here?'

Here was in her lounge, straight from work with no obligatory stop at Steamers, a quick takeaway Chinese and now they were sprawled out on the sofa together in quiet companionship. She was vaguely aware that he still had one eye straying towards the clock.

'No, of course not. It's just that it puts a different face on things.'

'You mean it's given you permission?' Teri said cynically.

'I wish that weren't true, but in some ways it has. I've been tying myself in knots over this.'

'I don't know why you worry so much,' Teri said. 'Everyone does it these days.' She tried not to think of the pain 'everyone doing it' had caused Clare, and the fact that to manoeuvre herself into a position of 'doing it' she had kicked her best friend out when she most needed her.

'You make it sound like the latest appliance,' Jamie said bleakly. 'Ranking up there alongside dishwashers, microwaves and mobile phones as the latest must-haves.'

'Lifelong marriage happens to be a very outmoded institution.'

'So is the BBC, but that keeps struggling along.' He shifted position on the sofa. 'Besides, don't knock it until you try it. There's a lot that's good about marriage.'

'That's why you're here?' Teri raised one eyebrow.

'Just because I can mentally analyse the situation, it doesn't mean that I can make my heart or my body fall in line with it. I don't *want* to be here, just like I don't want to take a double bogey on the eighteenth hole at the golf club, but there's a certain inevitability about it and precious little I can do to control it.'

They stared at each other in silence. 'Let's go to bed,' Jamie said.

'I thought you'd never ask,' Teri replied.

He swept her into his arms and tried to push away the image of Pamela in the same position last night, hoping vehemently that Teri wouldn't be sick on him. That would take some explaining away when he was supposed to be stuck in a minor disrailment just outside Watford Junction . . .

It was hard work making these dramatic gestures, he thought as he carried Teri up the stairs. She was lighter than Pamela, but he was definitely getting less fit as he got older. All this was very bad for his heart.

He kicked open the bedroom door. Clint Eastwood had done it once in a film and it had always struck Jamie as terribly impressive. He hoped that Teri would appreciate it and that she hadn't seen the film and wouldn't realise that it wasn't a totally original display. Why was he so nervous about making love to her? Was it because it was a long time since he had been to bed with anyone other than Pamela? Surely, there was nothing to worry about there. It must be like riding a bike; he hadn't been on one for years, but he wouldn't turn down out of hand a cycling holiday.

Perhaps there was a new trend that he wasn't up with – a bit like putting black pepper or balsamic vinegar on strawberries, rather than sugar. He wished that he'd paid closer attention to Pamela's copies of *Cosmopolitan* – which always had such shocking headlines they had to be hidden from the children. There must be a few tips in there. He would have to have a search through the wardrobe to see where she kept the back copies. She swore that she only read it for the recipes. It could well be true, for nothing too inventive had percolated into their love-making . . . but then there had been precious little evidence of it in the kitchen either.

He laid Teri on the bed. She was panting expectantly, like MacTavish did when he reverted occasionally to puppy mode. How would he know if she was enjoying herself, if he was doing the right thing? With Pamela he could tell. It was an unspoken code that had developed over the years; one tone of squeak meant slower, another tone quicker and a final one, which didn't occur very often these days as they always had one ear out for coitus interruptus of the offspring variety, that meant everything was just right.

How would he know that he had hit the spot with Teri? Particularly if it was her G-spot, which was much lauded on the front cover of *Cosmo* – she'd have to give him a map if she wanted him to look for that. He hadn't known there was so much terror involved in adultery, and at this precise moment he was wondering why the hell so many people seemed keen to indulge in it.

Teri wriggled below him and drew him down towards her. He started to open the buttons of her blouse as if in a trance, while she ran her fingers through his hair. The skin inside her blouse was soft and warm, so much softer than Pamela's despite her indulgence in skin-soothing cream that cost more than sixty pounds a pot – he knew that because she had berated him for using it to rub lavishly into his dry hands after playing golf. Perhaps the sensations were simply heightened by unfamiliarity. Her breasts were small and hard and unspoilt by child-bearing and breastfeeding. And he thought guiltily of Pamela for the last time.

He eased the clothes from her body until she lay naked beneath him. Her stomach was firm and flat, her hips narrow – her figure more boyish than womanly. She undid his shirt and eased it from his shoulders. This was something he had forgotten too, the sensual pleasure of undressing someone else. Why the minute you got married did you automatically revert to undressing yourself?

'Have you come prepared?' she whispered breathlessly in his ear.

Jamie propped himself up on his elbow and looked quizzically at her. 'Come prepared?'

She flushed slightly. 'You know. Condoms.' The pink tinge spread over her cheeks – her facial ones.

'No,' he apologised limply. 'I never thought.'

'Are you vasectomised?'

'That makes it sound even more painful than normal,' he winced. 'No, I'm not.'

'Funny, I thought you might be.'

'I never got round to it,' he said pathetically, as if he were talking about returning an overdue library book rather than emasculating his manhood.

'There are some Durex in the bedside drawer,' she said. 'They're probably near their expiry date. I bought a twelve-pack ages ago in the vain hope that I would get seriously lucky at least once a month. You'll probably notice that they're still in their cellophane wrapper,' she added ruefully.

Jamie rummaged through the drawer – even Indiana Jones would have had trouble finding anything in here, he thought. Fighting his way through tubes of cream, lipsticks, headache tablets – hopefully she wouldn't need those tonight – roll-on deodorant – too phallic by half in his opinion – and sundry other cosmetic appliances, he eventually found the box of condoms.

He unwrapped it reluctantly. 'I haven't used one of these since I was at university,' he said, examining one of the small, neat envelopes distastefully under the bedside lamp. 'It always reminded me of having a bath in a plastic mac.'

'Is that something you do often?' Teri smiled.

'What?'

'Have a bath in a plastic mac?'

'No. And this isn't something I do often either,' he added sheepishly.

'Then put those down and come here.' She drew him towards her. 'We won't be needing them just yet.'

Jamie lay back against the pillows and stared at the ceiling.

'It's at times like this that I wish I smoked,' he said wistfully.

Teri snuggled against him. 'If that was what having a bath in a plastic mac feels like, then I'm going to abandon 'The Source of Life' aromatherapy bath gel and go straight down to Millet's to buy a cagoule.'

He squeezed her to him. 'Why does forbidden fruit taste so sweet?'

'For precisely that reason. Because it's forbidden.' She twisted the hairs on his chest between her fingers. 'If you could have it every day, it would be like any other boring old banana.'

'What an interesting analogy.' He kissed her hair.

They relaxed in silence, luxuriating in the nearness of new naked skin until Teri said, 'Tell me about your family.'

'Now?' Jamie was surprised. 'It seems a funny time to talk about my home life. I thought you didn't want to know about it.'

'I didn't,' she admitted, 'before. I feel part of you now and I want to know everything about you.' She trailed her finger lazily over his chest.

Jamie sighed. 'What do you want to know?'

'We could start with something easy,' she said. 'What's your house like?'

He shrugged underneath her. 'Big, expensive and a mixture of architecture that would look totally out of place anywhere other than Milton Keynes – or possibly Savannah.'

Teri draped her leg over his. 'Tell me about the kids.'

'Jack's three and is a little devil.' Jamie stroked her shoulder absently. 'Francesca's six going on thirty-six and she's a little madam.'

'Do they look like you?'

'Francesca does. Jack looks like Pa— my wife.'

'You can tell me her name if you want to,' she said softly.

'If I do that she'll become real, and right now I can pretend for a short while that she doesn't exist.'

'I want to know what she's like.'

Jamie sighed wearily. 'Pamela is Pamela.' He looked at Teri accusingly. 'There – you've made me say it!'

'Go on,' Teri prompted him with a nudge in the ribs. 'In the true tradition of Magnus Magnusson, you've started so you might as well finish.'

'She's self-contained, aloof and distant. And she doesn't understand me one bit.' Jamie held up his hand. 'I know it's a cliché and you did voice that very vociferously on one occasion, I seem to remember,' he said wryly. 'But she doesn't. We've nothing in common any more. She doesn't understand why I find *Men Behaving Badly* the funniest programme on television or how I can even laugh at *Absolutely Fabulous*. She doesn't understand why I weep openly at something like *Toy Story*, and yet can't cry at funerals. She doesn't understand why I find working for an insurance company the most stifling experience in the world. She doesn't understand why I, along with the children, don't like her home-made granary bread and long for shop-bought bleached and chemically adulterated white sliced loaves. She doesn't understand why I find playing golf a relaxing way to unwind. Neither does she understand that although I enjoy watching football I have lost all desire to kick one.'

He turned and buried his face in Teri's neck, tasting the salty sweetness of her flesh. 'And most of all she wouldn't understand why I need you.'

She arched towards him and his body met with hers.

They made love again, without the urgency of the first time and without the judicious intervention of latex. It was a wild and reckless thing to do, he thought as he lay beside her later. Particularly for a man who works in insurance.

Teri was slumbering softly when he stroked her breast to wake her. 'I have to go,' he murmured.

She made an appealing groaning sound and went to get up. 'You stay here, I'll let myself out.' He kissed her shoulders. 'I'll see you tomorrow.'

He crept out of the bed and pulled his clothes on. 'Do you want me to close the curtains?'

'No,' she answered sleepily. 'When I was Francesca's age, I was afraid of my curtains. The patterns on them used to make monsters and give me nightmares. I still sleep with them open.'

He smiled. 'Okay.' He kissed his finger and touched her nose. 'Sleep tight.'

He had driven to Leighton Buzzard Station that morning to meet Teri so, thankfully, the Volvo was now parked conveniently outside her house.

You could tell the sort of man he was from the car he drove. A Volvo – a reliable, roomy family car. Ideal for child car seats, carry cots, pushchairs, picnic hampers, bikes, balls, Barbie and all the other bloody paraphernalia they took with them whenever they moved out of the house. It was engineered for safety and always fared well in traffic accidents. An insurance man's dream. And the most sensible car in the universe.

He wished momentarily that he drove a Ferrari. Red and sexy. Too small for anything else but a chick with a tight skirt and long legs. And certainly no room for his conscience.

It was a cold night, but there was no frost and it was good to think that spring might be just around the corner. He turned the car heater up, so that as soon as the engine warmed it would be blasting out hot air. It was frightening to think that he had reached the age where he also appreciated the fact that the car seats were heated. The night seemed all the more chilly for his having just got out of a warm and comfortable bed . . .

It was late, but not suspiciously so. There would be time for a night-cap and a chat with Pamela before they went to bed. He wondered if he would be different now he had taken this irrevocable step into a life of deception. The actual deceitfulness became easier in practical terms, but the mental side seemed to grow steadily worse. Where was this going to end?

He thought of Francesca asleep at home, blissfully unaware of her father's duplicity. Would it change her life? Was she afraid of her curtains as Teri had been? There seemed nothing scary about fabric with Beatrix Potter characters on it to him – only the price of it – but then he wasn't six. She had nothing else to worry about. There had been no crises in her life other than the inadvertent loss of an idolised hamster called Gazza up the vacuum cleaner. She had a mother who fretted over her every move and a father who catered for all the material needs her mother could ever dream up for her.

And what of Jack? *His* only worry was overcoming the so-far unfathomable joining of Duplo. Jamie hoped to God that nothing would happen to change that.

As he drove back from his lover in Leighton Buzzard to his wife in Milton Keynes, he prayed fervently that his children would always enjoy deep and dreamless sleep. At the moment he was having enough night-time terrors for them all.

Chapter Sixteen

The Tom Pearson Ten-Step Plan for Rehabilitation of Errant Husbands wasn't working. The daily crooning in the Calypso Power Shower was growing even more forceful than the steaming jets of water that coursed over Jamie as he lathered his body. He was stuck on slushy love songs of the seventies and had worked his way through 'How Deep Is Your Love' – the Bee Gees' version, not Take That's, 'Three Times A Lady' – Commodores – 'All Of Me Loves All Of You' – Bay City Rollers (worrying) – most of 'Saturday Night Fever' and several of the more sentimental songs of Gladys Knight and the Pips. An alarming deviation had been 'Great Balls of Fire'. It wasn't only Gladys Knight who had the pip.

Pamela combed her hair and stared at her pale reflection in the mirror. They used to have sex in the shower. Years ago, when they were first married. She couldn't understand why now. It was a tiny shower in their first house and they used to bang their elbows and knees on the tiles and the Perspex cubicle door. Finally, a bottle of Vidal Sassoon's 'Wash and Go' had hit her on the head and that had been an end to it. They had a much bigger shower room now, but the urge to make love in it never seemed to arise.

Tom had suggested another evening out, to solve the current crisis. She thought this excessive, and there was also a faint whiff of ulterior motive about it. But what else was she to do? It had worked so well last time. She could tell that Jamie had been jealous, but since then his zeal for working long hours and sneaking out to make late-night telephone calls with MacTavish had simply increased.

The discovery about the phone calls had come when she had been forced to take MacTavish on his nightly constitutional due to Jamie's lateness. The poor dog had been crossing his legs and howling balefully at his lead and, ever mindful that the future displays of daffodils that were sprouting in tender infancy through their soil wouldn't benefit from a watering with MacTavish's urine, she had reluctantly donned her Barbour and walked him down the road.

It was when he had stopped at the phone box and refused steadfastly to budge until she had gone through the pretence of making a phone call that the penny dropped. It was with a leaden heart and a lump in her throat that she marched him home and rewarded him with a large bowl of Chum for his treachery. And they say a dog is a man's best friend! MacTavish was obviously unfamiliar with that concept.

It was disconcerting that when she told Jamie she was going to the Thai restaurant again on another business meeting with Tom there was a distinct lack of batting of either of his eyelids. 'Fine,' he said – and he sounded as if he meant it.

So here she was, dressed up to the nines again and going out with her boss when she would rather be staying in with her husband on the one night he managed to get home early – although, if Tom's hare-brained plan actually worked Jamie would soon be coming home early every night.

Pamela went slowly downstairs and waited uneasily in the lounge. Jamie didn't flinch as the majestic Mercedes swept into their drive. She was the one that did.

The restaurant was busier than last time. There was a party from one of the large computer companies doing some particularly raucous bonding following a seminar on 'Lateral Thinking in the Nineties'. Bottles of wine were being passed across the table with an intent that was almost savage in its ferocity. The only thing this lot were likely to be doing laterally tonight was sliding under the tables.

As Jamie had pointed out, from the exterior the restaurant looked rather like a circus tent, with the addition of two gold lions – or were they dragons? – placed strategically at the front door to give it an Oriental authenticity. Inside, it had been transformed from a sea of functional chrome and plastic that said 'racing school' into a Far Eastern wonderland of hastily carved rosewood and precarious bamboo canopies.

Tom and Pamela were shown to a table as far away from the inebriated lateral thinkers as possible, on a raised platform towards the back of the restaurant. Two tiny waitresses in traditional costume fluttered round them like exotic butterflies. They ordered a set menu because Tom had forgotten his reading glasses and she was feeling too disinterested to choose.

'So it's not working too well?' he said when the waitresses had left.

'No,' she sighed. 'It seemed to have the desired effect briefly, but then matters sort of escalated. He's staying out late – very late – and coming home smelling of Chinese food and 'Obsession'.'

Their own food arrived. 'Perhaps you're not playing the part convincingly enough,' he suggested, as he dipped a fish cake into one of the sauces which had been placed alongside them.

'I never said I was Dame Judi Dench.'

Tom unwrapped a piece of chicken from some sort of sturdy foliage. 'We might have to take this one stage further.'

'Why do I think I'm not going to like the sound of this.'

Tom shrugged nonchalantly. One thing she had learned early in life was never to trust a salesman when he shrugged nonchalantly. 'Perhaps we need some realism injected into this.'

'Now I *know* I don't like the sound of this.'

The butterflies cleared their plate of starters which had been decimated mainly by Tom and brought the main course. He covered her hand with his. 'You're a very beautiful woman, Pamela.'

'And you're an attractive man.' She moved her hand away. 'A *married* one.'

One of the lateral thinkers crashed to the floor on his chair. Tom moved his closer to her and spooned some noodles languidly on to her plate while not taking his eyes from hers. It was obviously a practised move and, as such, was quite impressive to watch. 'I've always wanted to get to know you better.'

His eyes had taken on the hard-edged glint of a predator. 'Don't do this to me, Tom. Please.'

'What harm could it do?' He was beginning to sound oilier than Italian salad dressing.

'I'm in a deep state of confusion and emotional strain

as it is. If I even consider placing one more card on the top, the whole wobbly pile will collapse.'

'Can I be frank with you?'

'I'd rather you weren't. I'd rather you were just Tom. The Tom I know and *don't* love.'

'I don't think you've been properly fulfilled as a woman.'

Two of the lateral thinkers started singing 'Agadoo' and the restaurant's owner hovered nervously round their table.

'I'm perfectly fulfilled as a woman, Tom,' she said tightly. 'And if I wasn't, I would be looking to my husband to fulfil me. The answer to my current domestic predicament isn't a quick bonk in the back of a well-built German car.'

Tom looked slightly deflated. 'So you don't think a full-blown revenge affair is a good idea?'

'No.'

'Wouldn't it be fun finding out?'

'No.'

'I just—'

'*No.*'

His face took on a look of pained honesty. 'I want to make love to you really badly.' He was sounding desperate.

She didn't have the heart to tell him that she'd rather be made love to really well, and that if anyone could do that it was Jamie. Instead she said, 'Tom, exactly which part of the word *no* is it that you're having trouble with?'

His fixed expression, she guessed, was meant to convey deep and painful longing. It looked instead like he had deep and painfully trapped wind. 'My arms ache for you.'

'I thought it was somewhere lower down the anatomical scale that was supposed to ache.'

'My whole body aches.'

'At your age, Tom, that's just a touch of rheumatism not love – or even lust.'

He fell silent. His face deflated as though he had just had a gaseous release. Perhaps she'd been right about the trapped wind after all.

'I don't know what I'm doing here at all.' She dropped her fork on the plate of untouched food. 'The whole thing has been a catalogue of crassness and stupidity. I should never have listened to you. You didn't want to add a bit of extra spice to my marriage, you wanted to throw the whole damn chilli pot on it and make it totally bloody unpalatable.'

She pushed back from the table. 'I don't want to fall out with you, Tom, I like working with you, but I think if I don't go now we'll both say things that we'll regret.'

'Not so fast, lady.' It was a loud voice for a small restaurant – booming out with a broad and less than chirpy cockney accent. Pamela looked round stunned, but nowhere near as stunned as Tom was. It stopped the lateral thinkers in their tracks and even the Agadoo-ers stopped Agadoo-ing. She hadn't met Tom's wife Shirley before, but she had heard enough about her to know that it was Shirley who stood in front of her now.

'I know your game,' Shirley said menacingly.

'Shirley, sit down,' Tom hissed. 'You're showing yourself up.'

'*I'm* showing myself up?' Her neat, over-made-up face was red with anger. 'You can talk. Business meeting!' Shirley spat the word out and some spittle landed on Pamela's cheek, but she was too terrified to lift her hand and wipe it off. She could feel it glistening in the seductive lighting, obvious to all the lateral thinkers who were staring at them with mouths gaping wider than the Dartford Tunnel.

Tom lowered his voice to a whisper. 'Of course it's a business meeting! You know Pamela's my secretary.'

She put her hands on her hips. 'So this is Pamela?'

'Pleased to meet you,' Pamela said quietly, and offered her hand.

Shirley looked at it as if she had been offered rat poison. Pamela retracted her hand.

'Secretary, personal assistant, typist – they've all had different names and guises – blondes, brunettes and now a redhead,' Shirley continued unabated. 'I don't think you've had a redhead before.'

The restaurant was deathly silent. The reassuring chink of cutlery and glasses had ceased completely. She could hear the faint hum of the heating system and somewhere a chair scraped uncomfortably over the polished wooden floor.

'Mrs Pearson,' Pamela pleaded in hushed tones. 'Shirley. You've made a terrible mistake.'

'The only mistake I made was marrying this mangy old tom cat.' She checked that everyone had heard her. 'Tom by name, tom by nature!'

'Shirley!' Tom was affronted.

The two butterflies had stopped flitting and were frozen to the spot, supporting the restaurant owner who looked perilously close to fainting.

'This is not what it seems,' Pamela said calmly. But what was it? Would it really help to tell Shirley that she was pretending to have an affair with *her* husband to make her own husband jealous and stop him having an affair . . . but that all along Tom had secretly fancied his chances? No, she thought it wouldn't. It all sounded terribly complicated and she wasn't sure she understood it herself. It didn't strike her as very convincing either, once you looked at it closely.

'Well, you can have him.' Shirley was obviously not in the mood to be placated or reasoned with. 'You deserve each other.' She pointed aggressively at them both. Tom winced. Shirley lunged at the table. 'And you deserve this.'

The bowl of Thai green curry was tipped on Pamela's head before she knew it. The delicate fragrance of lemongrass became overpowering as it ran past her nose to drip on her skirt. It was warm and creamy. If she had been eating it she would have been tempted to complain that it wasn't piping hot. As it was, she was grateful that it was only tepid. The noodles were hotter, but they landed in her lap and would only ruin her skirt rather than give her third-degree burns.

Tom was wearing the sweet and sour chicken before the restaurant manager galvanised himself into action and grabbed both of Shirley's arms.

'I call the police!' he shouted.

'Naff off!' Shirley kneed him in the groin and he fell to the floor like a sack of King Edwards. 'You!' She pointed at Tom. 'You don't need to bother coming home. I'm going to the solicitor first thing in the morning and I'm going to have an injunction served on you!' She marched past the restaurant manager who was doubled up in agony and crashed out into the night.

The lateral thinkers hooted and hollered and broke into spontaneous applause. They started a raucous chorus of 'I can't stand losing you' alluding to The Police the pop group, rather than the police the law-enforcement group.

Tom looked perplexed. He stood hands on hips, orange sauce running from his once-pristine white shirt on to the floor. A piece of carrot hung from his gold neck chain like a limp goldfish.

'I think you'd better go after her,' Pamela said, smoothing Thai green curry from her face.

'Do you think . . .' He took three steps towards the door. 'What about you?'

'I'll get a taxi.'

'I could run you home. Another five minutes won't make any difference, will it? I'll square it with Shirley as soon as I get home.'

Pamela looked at him in pure astonishment. The man had skin thicker than a whole herd of rhinoceroses. Or was it rhinoceri? 'Fuck off, Tom,' she said with unconcealed malice. 'Just fuck off.'

Tom, as instructed, did fuck off. Without paying the bill. She settled the account herself stoically, dripping curry on to her chequebook and trying not to cry. The restaurant manager, once he had recovered his dignity, called a taxi for her. For the next twenty minutes, she was forced to endure him ineffectually, but thoughtfully, sponging her down with a damp J-cloth, and the guffaws of the lateral thinkers while she waited for it to arrive.

The lights were still on when she reached home – which wasn't surprising as it was only an hour and a half after she had left. Jamie would gloat. How she wished she could have sneaked past him and cleaned herself in the steaming waters of their shower before he saw her. Unfortunately, the crunch of the gravel heralded her arrival and he stood with the door open as she paid the taxi fare. The driver hadn't taken kindly to her stinking his cab out with Thai green curry and noodles and, shamefacedly, she tipped him heavily to compensate him for his trouble, which he hadn't hesitated to point out.

'You're ear . . . ly,' he said, as she emerged from the darkness into the harsh light of their hallway. His eyes travelled over her, slowly, from head to foot, taking in the white creamy sauce, the shredded basil leaves and sundry bits of chilli that still adorned her. 'I didn't know it was fancy dress,' he said jovially. 'What have you come as?'

Pamela started to cry. 'I don't want to talk about it.'

Jamie's face softened. 'Come here.' He went to put his arms around her, but she pushed him away.

'I don't want you to touch me either.' She stifled a sob. When MacTavish appeared from the lounge and started to lick her legs, she gave him a swift kick and he ran for the sanctuary of the kitchen. It was bad enough to lose one's dignity like this without being mistaken for a doggy treat.

'Is there anything I can do?'

'Stop smirking.'

'I'm not smirking.' Jamie face tightened. 'I'm concerned.'

'Then don't be.'

Jamie leaned against the wall. 'What happened?'

'It's none of your business.'

'I'm your husband!'

Pamela's face tightened. '*That* is a matter for debate,' she said tartly.

Jamie sighed heavily.

'I'm going to bed,' she said wearily, and climbed up the stairs with as much haughtiness as a walking menu can muster.

'Do you want a hot drink?' Jamie shouted after her.

Her heart melted. He could be so sweet when he wanted to be.

'Perhaps some Jasmine tea?' he suggested.

For the third time that night, and the third time in her life, she used the F-word.

Chapter Seventeen

Jamie allowed his body to be buffeted by the movement of the tube train, swaying his weight from foot to foot to keep his balance. He didn't strap-hang, so that people would be able to tell he belonged in London and wasn't just some country bumpkin who was up for a day in The Smoke. Not that you could call it strap-hanging any more – 'rubber-ball-and-spring-hanging' just didn't have the same ring. But what did it matter, anyway. He would soon be with Teri and she would pour oil on the troubled waters at the end of his day. For a short while he would be able to forget he was married, with a mortgage the size of the national debt of a small Third World country.

Pamela was still refusing to discuss what had happened at the Thai restaurant with Tom. There had been several phone calls when she had slammed the phone down with a force that was quite unnecessary, and several answer-phone messages in which a doleful-sounding Tom had begged her to return his calls. As far as Jamie knew she hadn't done so. Nor had she gone into work for the last three days, which was a worrying trend. She assured him that she was using up her holiday, but even he could see that was something of a coincidence following the curry-wearing episode.

To placate Pamela he had tried to be as helpful and cheerful around the house as possible. It had worked to a certain extent in that the Alphabite combat had tailed off to a half-hearted effort in which Pamela limited herself to 'git', 'sod' and 'pig' – words not normally in her vocabulary, but at least brief and to the point.

Tonight he had promised to be home in time to go to Francesca's school concert. She was playing the recorder with the music group from year one. It was destined to be a hideous cacophony of ill-timed shrills and peeps through which Mrs Rutherford wandered with the original melody of the tune on the piano with a level of skill that would provide no obvious threat to Barry Manilow.

Jamie knew this from bitter experience of 'The Christmas Extravaganza' – a two-hour endurance test of lisps and lapses as the school performed, Mrs Rutherford announcing stoutly, 'Favourite Carols, Old and New'. Mothers oooed and aaahed appreciatively at their off-spring's attempts at entertaining, while fathers generally made nuisances of themselves recording the moment for posterity with the latest in video camcorder technology. Tonight it was to be 'Spring into Springtime', and Jamie shuddered at the thought. Francesca was the only one with any talent among them. But then he would think that.

On reflection, Teri wasn't likely to be in oil-pouring mode when he explained that he couldn't spend any time with her tonight before going home. He had tried to call her all day but she was apparently 'in programme rehearsals' – which probably wouldn't help her temper either. It was with a heavy heart that Jamie let himself be swallowed by the crush from the underground, squashed up the escalators and then finally spewed out, battered and broken like a recycled tin can, on to the Euston main line concourse.

She was there, waiting at the End of the Line Buffet. When she saw him she drained her coffee and walked towards him – her small tight walk, confident and vulnerable at the same time. His heart lurched and his stomach turned, and it wasn't the fact that he'd eaten nothing since his pork pie and pint with Charlie in the Clog and Calculator. How long had this been going on for now? And it still didn't feel any more right or any more wrong.

Teri passed him a polystyrene cup of coffee with a lid on it as she greeted him with a light kiss. 'Hi,' she said.

'Shitty day?'

She nodded. 'The worst. And you?'

He shrugged. 'Same as ever.' He noticed the carrier bag bulging with shopping and gave her back the polystyrene cup so he could take the bag from her. 'It's going to get worse.'

'What?'

'Your shitty day.'

'Oh.' Her face darkened. They set off down the slope towards the platform.

'I can't come back with you tonight.'

'Jamie!'

'I know, I know. I've been trying to ring you all day. I promised Pamela that I'd be home in time to go to Francesca's school concert.' They got on the train and found seats opposite each other. He pushed the shopping under his legs hoping that she would forget about it.

She missed nothing. 'You can give that to me.' She pulled the bag from under his legs and pushed it under her own. Glowering, she thrust his coffee back at him.

'Thanks,' he said meekly, and took a swallow of the warm, foul-tasting liquid.

The nights were getting lighter. A true sign – other than Francesca's concert – that spring was on its way. It enabled you to see the full squalor and decay of London as you travelled in and out of Euston, a pleasure that could be forgotten – if only briefly – during the darkness of winter. It enabled you to enjoy the full impact of the mindless psychedelic graffiti that was sprayed over everything that didn't move.

Willesden INTERCITY maintenance depot was a prime target, where all the broken trains bore the indecipherable legends NOS, FIG, SUB and DUNE and something that looked remarkably like SYRINGE. Though why anyone, even of limited intelligence, would want to boast of the tag SYRINGE was totally beyond him.

Once you were past Watford Junction you started to leave behind the depressing scenes of urban decay – the car-breakers' yards, tumbledown workshops, boarded-up factories and the backs of crumbling terraced housing. In fact, once you had hit the Ovaltine factory – which blinked the time and temperature at you in tangerine digital dots – the journey became quite pleasant.

Past the faded station at Hemel Hempstead, things became positively rural. Fields, that did actually roll. Trees, lots of them, dotted about the actually rolling fields. Not the spindly, jam-packed newcomers of Milton Keynes, but old majestic ones with tree trunks like proper tree trunks and room to spread their magnificent branches. Trees that had been there for centuries before anyone thought of railways.

And cows . . . not the concrete ones of Milton Keynes, but real ones. Cows that you could tell the weather by, although he could never remember whether it meant rain if they were sitting down or standing up. He usually stuck to Michael Fish, who was probably no more accurate, but at least these cows had the potential for weather prediction. That was the point.

There was the man-made meandering of the Grand Union Canal, complete with ducks and swans and quaint lockside cottages, and the brightly coloured narrowboats moored along its sides. You could get a quick glimpse of the ruins of Berkhamsted Castle if the train wasn't going too fast and you didn't blink. It was a shame that very often the train windows were so grimy, that everything was viewed through a veil of smeared mud and dirt . . . although so few people ever looked up from their newspapers that it would probably be a waste of water to wash them.

Teri was staring out of the window, jaw set, watching the discarded milk cartons, Tango tins and shopping trolleys as the train clanked slowly out of Euston. Eventually, she announced through gritted teeth: 'I have spent all day listening to temper tantrums from the universally hated Richard Wellbeloved, and non-deleted expletives from Jez, and I am trying very hard at this moment not to start shrieking myself.'

'I can understand that,' Jamie said quickly.

'No, you can't!' she shouted under her breath. 'The few precious minutes I did manage to snatch for lunch I spent *shopping*,' she pointed at the bag between her feet, 'for a meal for us tonight.'

'I tried to call,' Jamie ventured again.

'I bought smoked salmon, tiger prawns,' she counted the items off on her fingers, 'rainbow-trout mousse, a small but nevertheless expensive tin of caviar, a box of cute-shaped biscuits, champagne and, to finish off with, some tiny but highly calorific caramel meringue things with fresh cream and chocolate in them.'

Jamie looked guilty. 'Won't it keep?'

'No, it won't!'

'Would it make you feel better to know that I'll probably be having abusive Alphabites and burnt sausages?'

She smiled reluctantly. 'It might.'

He took her hand and tutted softly. 'You know I can't help this. This is one of the hazards of being involved with a *married*' – he mouthed the word silently – 'man. I wish *you* could come tonight. It would be wonderful.'

Teri's eyes widened. 'Oh yeah, wonderful,' she echoed sarcastically.

She was right. Why on earth would his mistress find it wonderful to sit and watch his child and her valiant attempts to come to terms with the mysteries of the recorder? Sometimes he wondered if he was losing what slender grip he had on reality.

He squeezed her hand comfortingly. 'What will you do tonight?'

'I'll stay at home and eat all this myself and sulk. Then I'll watch numerous repeats on the television and go to bed early still miserable and discontented with life.'

He smiled sadly. 'I'll make it up to you,' he promised.

'How?'

'I don't know.'

Teri settled into her seat. 'Well, start thinking. You've got two stations and it had better be good.'

'You're merciless!'

'I'm hurt,' she said.

It was just outside Cheddington that he finally said, 'What about if I come to stay for a whole weekend?'

Teri leaned forward, excited. 'Friday to Monday?'

Jamie looked unsure. 'Saturday and Sunday.' And when Teri slumped back in her seat, 'I'll come early Saturday morning and stay until as late as possible Sunday night.'

She looked at him warily. 'Promise?'

He crossed his heart. 'Hope to die.'

'This weekend?' Teri asked.

'That only gives me a couple of days.' Jamie fidgeted in his seat. 'It might be difficult to arrange at short notice.'

'This weekend,' she demanded.

'That's unreasonable!'

'This weekend!'

'This weekend,' he agreed. 'You drive a hard bargain, Therese Carter.'

'I'm a hard woman.'

He rubbed his temples. 'What am I going to say?'

'You'll think of something.' They were pulling into Leighton Buzzard Station. 'You're a clever and inventive man.'

Jamie snorted dismally. 'You mean I'm deceitful and an inveterate liar.'

'If you insist.' She stood up and kissed the top of his head. 'Tomorrow?'

'Tomorrow.'

Teri jumped from the train and banged the carriage door. Jamie pulled his newspaper from his briefcase and settled back in the seat, flicking the paper open at the sports page in one deft move. The train moved off.

Out of the corner of his eye, he saw Teri running along the platform keeping pace with the departing train. She was waving and blowing kisses and he could tell that she was shouting, 'I love you'. He smiled and lowered his paper. 'I love you too,' he shouted.

The words froze on his lips and he spun to face the rest of the carriage, realising too late what he had done. Everyone else had lowered their newspapers; there were some smiles and some ill-disguised sneers and most of them looked at him expectantly. He attempted an embarrassed, but light-hearted laugh, but it stuck in his throat and came out like an embarrassed cough.

Reddened and suitably chastised, Jamie huddled behind his newspaper. The muffled announcement for Milton Keynes Central Station couldn't come quick enough.

Her arms were at least a foot longer, having dragged the unnecessary and expensive bag of shopping up the hill. Teri massaged her forearms, which twinged painfully, through her dressing gown. She dipped in the carrier bag and spread the goodies she had bought in for her and Jamie on the coffee table.

Originally, she had thought they might eat them in bed – it was the sort of romantic thing they did in films. As she took the lid off the caviar she realised it was probably as well to eat them downstairs in front of the telly – in films you didn't appreciate the fact that it would leave the bedroom stinking of fish for weeks.

She popped the cork of the champagne and let it fizz over into one of her tall best glasses without spilling too much on the lounge carpet. It was very melancholy, the sound of a cork being popped by one person. Traditionally, it was the signal for celebrations, parties, romantic couples – not commiserations and nights in by yourself.

Perhaps she should have tried to phone Clare. She'd managed to track down one of her friends at the airport who had reluctantly divulged Clare's new number. She could have pretended that all this was part of a peace offering . . .

Teri bit into a heart-shaped biscuit piled with smoked salmon and caviar, cracking the livid green face pack that she had smeared lovingly over her skin. She tutted, swallowed the rest of her biscuit, ate two tiger prawns and swilled them down with a gulp of champagne. Even Clare wasn't that dim. She would have seen through her immediately and would have gone all Sister Mary Bernadette-ish again. No, ultimately, it was better to over-indulge oneself alone.

She used the remote control to switch on the television. Repeats of *Dad's Army*. ITV? Repeats of *Heartbeat*. Channel Four? Repeats of *Cheers*. BBC2? Cricket – England versus Pakistan. Not a repeat, but not exactly a wild night's viewing either. *Dad's Army* it had to be. Rainbow-trout mousse on a fish-shaped biscuit this time. And one tiger prawn.

Teri wound tissues between her toes. She found the bottle of nail polish hiding behind the champagne bottle and filled her glass in passing. Caviar on its own piled on a boring round biscuit. She put her feet on the coffee table and painted each toe bright red, being careful not to paint the coffee table in the process. Caviar topped with smoked salmon on a diamond-shaped biscuit. Three prawns.

She wondered what Jamie was doing now. Was he enjoying playing the dutiful father? Would Mr and Mrs Duncan be arm in arm looking on tenderly and misty-eyed as Francesca did her party piece? Would it make him realise that Teri was superfluous to his life? She was outside his family unit and why did he need her? Or would he be numbed by the drudgery of it all, stupefied by the singing six-year-olds, and realise that he wanted her, only her and his freedom?

But what if he did leave Pamela for her? Wouldn't the whole jolly circus just start all over again? Teri wanted children. She wanted to go to school concerts. She wanted to go home to a house full to the brim of family commitments. What would happen then? Would he meet someone else – another willing, wistful woman on another packed commuter train?

Jamie never talked of the future. He had never promised her anything, except for this weekend. Smoked salmon topped by rainbow-trout mousse topped by a tiger prawn *and* caviar on a frilly-edged biscuit. After burping, Teri excused herself with a swig of champagne.

Dad's Army really was quite hilarious. Fat Captain Mainwaring swaggering about, and all that 'They don't like it up 'em' – it was enough to make even the most depressed and disappointed person in the world laugh. Teri had some more champagne and started on the caramel meringues. Perhaps they were a little too rich on top of half a pound of smoked salmon, a tub of rainbow-trout mousse and two dozen tiger prawns – but it was only one teeny-tiny tin of caviar, and besides . . . they were such a temptation and it was true what she'd said to Jeremy . . . er . . . Jamie. Cream didn't keep!

It was at the end when they started singing the theme tune that Teri began to feel ill. When they sang that they were on the run, Teri had to run, too. She was doing quite well until she reached the bottom of the stairs on her way up to the bathroom and the phone started to ring.

What should she do? Charge upstairs, answer her call of nature and forget about the phone? But it could be Jamie. He would worry if she didn't answer. Or should she answer and face the prospect of redecorating the hall?

Desperately searching her dressing-gown pockets for tissues that didn't resemble Ryvitas, she decided to answer the phone. It was a decision she would live to regret.

Chapter Eighteen

Jamie threw his briefcase into the hall and slammed the door. 'What time does it start tonight?' he shouted.

The house was amazingly quiet. Strains of classical music floated through the hall – Vivaldi's *Four Seasons* – 'Spring'. Perhaps Pamela was getting herself into the mood for tonight. There was no MacTavish trying to whip Jamie's legs from under him. No incessant babbling from Francesca about how horrid Jack had been to her. Instead there was a funny smell. No, not funny, just unusual. It was cheesy – in the nicest sense of the word. And garlicky. It smelt like proper food. Not Alphabites or Alphabetti Spaghetti or even fish fingers. Adult food.

A puzzled look crossed Jamie's face. They couldn't be expecting anyone for dinner – they were going out. He took off his jacket and hung it over the banister – he would risk Pamela's wrath later – and went into the kitchen.

'What time— What the blazes!' Jamie was struck speechless.

Pamela was standing serenely in front of the cooker concentrating on stirring something in a pan. It was a halogen cooker and there were red lights coming on and going off everywhere, indicating a hive of activity on the hob front – either that or an alien spacecraft was about to land in the kitchen. She was wearing a tight black dress – or rather a tight black dress was wearing her – and five-inch black stiletto heels. Her legs, which looked surprisingly long in heels that high and a skirt that short, were encased in fine fishnet and her stocking tops were just visible at the hem of her skirt.

Jamie loosened his tie as it seemed to be making his eyes bulge. The dress had a low-cut neck and her breasts, balanced on top of the neckline, were pale and plump and misted damply from the steam in the kitchen. Jamie gulped. She wore a tiny white frilled apron which obviously wasn't designed to cope with major domestic spillages. Her deep auburn hair was wound in a knot at the back of her head, which made her neck look incredibly long and slender, particularly as there was such a long way from her chin to the start of her dress.

'What are you doing?' It was an inane question, but the best he could manage in the circumstances.

'Cooking dinner.' Pamela smiled sweetly. 'Have you had a good day?'

It certainly wasn't one of his best, but at this rate it would probably count as one of his most memorable. He shrugged. 'Okay.'

'There's a bottle of red wine breathing in the utility room.' He hoped it was doing better than him, Jamie thought. 'Why don't you take a glass up with you? Dinner will be ready as soon as you've showered.'

Jamie's eyebrows met in the middle. 'I thought we were to be entertained by our budding James Galway in "Spring into Springtime" tonight?'

'I lied.' Pamela smiled sweetly again. 'That's next week.'

Jamie was dumbfounded. He looked round perplexed. 'So where is everyone?'

'The children are at my mother's.'

'Your mother's?' Jamie decided he would try the wine. 'What did she think about that?'

'She thought it was time we were alone as man and wife.' Pamela held the spoon to her lips, tasted it delicately then ran her tongue over her lips. They were red and glossy.

Jamie licked his lips.

'Man and woman,' she added seductively.

Jamie swallowed hard. 'And the dog?'

'MacTavish is next door for the night.'

Jamie popped into the utility room and found the bottle of wine. A good bottle, too. The wineglasses were in the cupboard next to the cooker and it meant he would have to go within close proximity of the Lycra creation and the pinny. He didn't know if he was up to it without breaking into a sweat.

Pamela normally wore silk and chiffon – floaty things. They were stylish but shapeless, covered in a profusion of muted flowers that finished somewhere round her ankles just before they reached her flat, sensible shoes that she had worn since she had given birth to Jack – because her back had never been quite the same. He didn't think he would ever be quite the same either. If he had seen his wife's bottom in Lycra before, he didn't remember it – and he was sure that he would have. It was tight and small and very touchable.

He yanked the cupboard open, grabbed two glasses, slammed the door shut and retreated to a safer part of the kitchen to busy himself with the process of pouring out the wine with trembling hands. He noticed that the table in the conservatory had been set for two. There were candles on it, and red roses in a crystal vase they had been given as a wedding present. The festoon blinds had been lowered slightly. He took a hearty swig of his wine and offered Pamela hers, too, in the vain hope that she might break her vow of temperance. She nodded demurely.

'Go and shower,' she said. 'I'll be ready when you come down. Don't be long.'

There was a sardonic twist to his smile as the wine started to relax him. 'May I just ask you exactly what you're cooking up?'

'It's from *Cosmopolitan*.'

'I might have known.'

' "How to liven up your home-cooking by giving it a more continental flavour." '

'Was the outfit *Cosmo*'s idea too?'

'No.' Pamela flushed attractively. 'That was my own idea.'

He took her glass of wine and placed it next to her, then stood behind her taking in the sweet cloying smell of her perfume and the even sweeter and more appetising smell of her cooking. He kissed her neck and felt her tremble. Nipping her earlobe, he whispered, 'Then I'd better go and slip into something more comfortable, too.'

Jamie wasn't sure what the male equivalent of a French maid's outfit was, so he settled on smart casual instead. Fawn trousers. A light silk shirt. Okay, so it had golf-type things all over it, but it was subtle – it didn't scream golf and therefore was less likely to annoy Pamela. He put on black underpants in an attempt to look sexy. They hadn't made love in months, but it was obviously on the menu tonight. He went downstairs with mounting trepidation – no pun intended.

Pamela had lit the array of candles in the conservatory and he had to admit that it looked very romantic. She brought in the steaming *Cosmopolitan* dish of continental delights and he was sure that she bent over further than she absolutely needed to while she was dishing up, given her back complaint. Perhaps it was just those shoes throwing her centre of gravity out?

Cosmo's idea of home meets continental cooking, it turned out, was nothing more threatening than a combination of shepherd's pie and spaghetti bolognese. The mince contained tomatoes, mushrooms, garlic and the other necessary components of bolognese sauce, and the mashed-potato topping was heavily flavoured with Parmesan cheese. It smelt divine and Pamela had taken the trouble to pipe 'I love you' on top of the mashed potatoes.

They ate slowly, watching each other's mouths as they did so. Pamela seemed light-hearted, she laughed when he told a joke, even if it was a bad one, and he realised it must have been an effort for her. He wondered nervously what he had done to deserve this and what the bill, when it eventually came, would be.

Pamela had abandoned *Cosmopolitan* for the dessert and had instead taken the advice of Delia Smith – goddess of calories, cream and cholesterol – and produced tiramisu. As he licked his spoon, Jamie marvelled at how Pamela had managed to fit it all within the constraints of the Lycra.

She cleared the dishes, then returned and took his wine glass from him and placed it alongside hers on the sideboard. Elegantly, in one supple move, she hoisted herself on to the table and laid back seductively on the tablecloth, which was the one his mother had bought them for

Christmas, and pulled her husband towards her by the lapels of his favourite golfing shirt.

Obligingly, he undid her apron, throwing it manfully to the floor – there was going to be no dishwashing tonight – and joined her on the table. She unbuttoned his shirt.

'Supposing the neighbours see us?' he asked tentatively. It wasn't every day that people made love on the breakfast table in the conservatory in full view of Fraughton-next-the-Green.

'You are an old stick-in-the-mud, Jamie Duncan.' She turned and blew out the candles in the candelabra. In the moonlit darkness he watched carefully as his black underpants sailed across the conservatory. His secretary had told him all about *Animal Hospital* again, a few days ago. Rolf had watched enraptured while the vet – the nice smiley one that she liked – had extracted a pair of Thomas the Tank Engine underpants from the stomach of a labrador puppy. Apparently, it was touch and go whether the dog would make it. Jamie's Thomas-free underpants landed on the floor in the corner. His last thought before he surrendered was that he must remember to retrieve them in the morning before MacTavish came home and ate them for his breakfast.

They were in bed, Pamela curled against him. The lights were off, but they were both awake. Jamie cleared his throat. 'I have to go away this weekend on a course. For work. Just Saturday and Sunday.'

Pamela snapped her bedside light on. 'A course?' Her hair was loose on her shoulders. She still had her make-up on, but her red glossy lipstick was gone, kissed away by Delia's tiramisu and his own traitorous lips. 'This weekend? Why didn't you say something earlier?'

Jamie's throat was dry. 'It hardly seemed appropriate.'

'You know what I mean.'

'I know it's short notice, but it really has only just come up.'

She pulled her hair away from her face and stared at him. He could hardly withstand the intensity of her eyes. She was naked and suddenly he couldn't bear to look at her. 'I don't believe you.'

'What?' He could hear his heart pounding. Why was he doing this? They had just had a wonderful evening – flirting, teasing, making love as if they were teenagers again.

'I said I don't believe you,' she repeated.

'Look – what's brought this on? We've just had the best evening together in a long time.'

'Exactly! We should be sharing a moment of intimacy and caring.'

'Is that another one of *Cosmo*'s ideas?' He couldn't believe he was sounding so heartless. Was it his suspicion that this sudden reawakening of sexual interest could have more to do with Tom Pearson than with him? The thought of Pamela doing erotic things on dining-room tables with her boss was making him feel sick.

'No, it's one of my ideas – and I hoped it would be one of yours. I don't know how you can do this.'

How *could* he do this with a ravishing woman, his wife, next to him? He didn't know himself, so how on earth could he expect Pamela to understand? Did adultery lead directly to insanity? It certainly seemed to be doing so in his case.

'What course is it?' she asked tightly.

'Management Ethics.'

'Management Ethics!' Pamela snorted. 'It should be a short course then.'

Jamie remained silent. It was the first thing that had come into his head and he wished it hadn't been.

'Show me the joining instructions.'

'The what?'

'The joining instructions. For this course.'

'I can't.'

'Why not?' Pamela was kneeling in front of him, clutching the duvet.

'I haven't got any.'

'You're a liar, Jamie Duncan. There are no joining instructions because there is no course.' She had started to cry and her sobs wrenched his soul from his body, but he was powerless to move, to comfort her, his limbs frozen by his own culpability. 'I know where you're going and you know I know where you're going.'

'I'm going on a course!' he insisted. What sort of course? A collision course.

She jumped from the bed and pulled her dressing gown round her, hiding her nakedness. 'I'm going to sleep in Francesca's room.'

'You'll be cold,' Jamie warned, unable to think of anything more useful to say.

'No colder than I feel now.' Pamela's eyes narrowed. 'I don't know how I'm ever going to trust you again.'

It was Jamie's turn to shout. 'And how do you think *I* feel, knowing that you're with that cockney oil-slick!'

Pamela looked shocked. She reeled slightly and steadied herself on the doorframe.

'Don't come the goody two-shoes with me, Pamela,' he went on self-righteously. 'It won't wash. I thought you wanted it this way. You can't change the rules whenever it suits you!'

She walked out of the room quietly and sedately. He

flung himself back on the bed, dejected and despising himself. He had ruined Teri's evening, he had ruined Pamela's evening and he had ruined his own evening. How soon would it be before he stooped to the level that Charlie had said he would, and ruin *all* of their lives completely?

Chapter Nineteen

'She's left me,' he said flatly, staring at the view of neat parallel roads interspersed with derelict strips of land waiting expectantly for someone to come along and build another chrome and glass monstrosity on them. 'Shirley's left me.'

Pamela sighed and perched on the end of his desk. 'Would it help if I talked to her?'

'Only through a medium.' Tom's eyes twinkled mischievously.

'This is serious!'

Tom shook his head. 'I've tried everything. I've explained the situation over and over again, but she just won't listen.'

'I thought you said she was understanding.'

'She was. Until she met someone else.' Tom rubbed his eyes. They were reddened and swollen, either from lack of sleep or from crying, she couldn't tell which. 'She's got a lover. What a joke! Can you believe it? After all this time. When I'd finally gone straight.'

'Don't push the point too far, Tom.' They exchanged rueful glances.

'Well, you know what I mean. You were a challenge. I had to give it a go. Don't blame me for that.'

219

Pamela crossed her legs. 'Jamie thought you'd succeeded.' She turned to look out of the window with Tom. 'He thinks you and I are having an affair.'

Tom looked thoughtful. 'I take that as a compliment.'

'I shouldn't if I were you,' Pamela warned. She crossed her arms as well as her legs. 'I did what you suggested. I dressed up like something out of *Allo, Allo*, legs akimbo, breasts heaving. We had a wonderful evening. We weren't exactly conservative in the conservatory. It was a re-enactment of *The Postman Always Rings Twice* in Fraughton-next-the-Green. It worked a treat. I wish you could have seen it.'

'So do I,' Tom said earnestly.

'Then afterwards he announced that he's going on a course this weekend. Saturday and Sunday.' Pamela humphed. 'A course! I couldn't believe it – not after what we'd just done.'

'Bastard,' Tom agreed.

'Then you know what really surprised me? Really took my breath away? He said he thought it was what I wanted, and how could I accuse him when I was having an affair myself? I was stunned, Tom, honestly I was.'

Tom smiled sadly. 'Is it so hard to imagine having an affair with me?'

Pamela flushed. 'It's not that.' She waved her hand dismissively. 'You *are* an attractive man.' She felt herself flush deeper as she said it. 'I thought he'd know it was just a charade, a pantomime, done purely to get him back. Deep down, I thought he knew that. He *must* know that. I was astonished that he actually thought I was capable of having an affair. Doesn't he know me at all, Tom?'

Her boss slid back into his ostentatious leather chair. 'I could ask the same about Shirley. For the first time in my life she's actually accused me of having an affair when I haven't laid so much as a finger on you. And, to top it all, she's now playing away from home. *My* Shirley. What is the world coming to?'

'It feels terrible to be unjustly accused, doesn't it?' Pamela commiserated.

'Disgusting!' Tom crossed his feet on the desk and chewed on the end of his pen.

'Wait there,' she suddenly instructed him – although Tom didn't look as if he was about to go anywhere. 'There's only one way to put this right. I'll be right back.'

Pamela flicked open the address book on her desk and ran her finger down the pages. She put the receiver to her ear and tapped a number into the phone. After speaking she put the phone down again thoughtfully and went slowly back through to Tom's office. His lower lip was pouting and his face bore an expression of utter misery.

She leaned on the doorframe and took a deep breath. 'Do you still want to make love to me badly?'

'Yes,' he said uncertainly.

'Let's go and have a therapeutic tumble then.'

His feet crashed to the floor. 'I can't believe you just said that.'

'I've booked a double room at The Happy Lodge.'

He closed his eyes and opened them again. 'I had to check I wasn't dreaming.'

'If we're being accused of it, we might as well do it. Surely it's better to be hanged for a sheep as a lamb.'

'I still can't believe you're suggesting this.'

'Neither can I.' She picked up her handbag. 'Come on, let's get going quick before I change my mind.'

They drove across Milton Keynes to The Happy Lodge

in stunned silence. Tom kept both eyes fixed firmly on the road, both hands fixed firmly on the steering wheel. The cassette player was strangely silent too, its usual diet of graunching country and western music trapped mutely inside its security coded system.

The reception staff at The Happy Lodge weren't. They were as miserable as sin – or at least as miserable as Tom had been. A blonde-haired girl, chewing gum like a languorous cow chews grass, handed them the key card to their room and looked disdainfully at them for their lack of luggage. It made Pamela feel all the more determined.

'Room four oh five.' She was Irish.

Tom looked puzzled. 'Room Four?'

'No. Four *oh* five. 'Not four *or* five. It's on the second floor.'

They took the lift up to the second floor. The lift was carpeted halfway up the walls, the rest was mirrored and Pamela thought how pale they both looked. Barry Manilow warbled unevenly in the background from a tape that was either badly stretched or was heedlessly being chewed by the distant tape machine.

Pamela followed Tom along the corridor until he found their room, which was bland and innocuous – it would impress no one and offend no one. It was painted in pale blue and beige with a dark blue carpet that would show no stains. The walls displayed two similar paintings of blurred landscapes in blues and beiges that she suspected were also present in every other room. It was a no-smoking room and the air was thick with the artificial sickly-sweet smell of lavender air-freshener.

Not knowing what else to do, they undressed each other briskly and she hid a smile as Tom broke away from their passion to fold his trousers into the trouser press.

'Are you sure you want to do this?' was the only thing he said to her.

'No,' she answered, before they guided each other to the blue and beige bed.

He didn't make love to her badly as he had insisted he wanted to. He made love to her gently, confidently and professionally. Proving he was an expert lover, as somehow she expected he would be. Afterwards, wrapped in a thin white towel with *The Happy Lodge* embossed on it, she made coffee from the little packets provided in the room along with fiddly cartons of long-life milk. They sat up in bed and nursed their cups until it was cold enough to drink and ate the two packs of McVities' Digestives that were also provided, containing two biscuits each. Pamela admired the swirling pattern of the Artex which hung in tiny stalactites from the ceiling.

They slept for an hour curled together like spoons. Tom showered and dressed alone and then sat and watched cricket on the television while she had the bathroom to herself. She luxuriated in the bath, using all the miniature bottles of foaming bath gel that had been provided and twisting her hair into the thin plastic shower cap that was also part of The Happy Lodge complimentary toiletries.

After drying herself, Pamela sat and looked in the mirror. She was surprised that she looked no different. She didn't feel any different either. No older, no wiser, no more wanton. No less in love with Jamie.

Her mouth was full, slightly bruised from the insistence of Tom's kisses, and she ran the tip of her finger over her lips to make sure that it was her mouth that was reflected. There was a flush on her throat that usually rose there as she orgasmed, increased by the heat of the bath. But it could have been someone else's throat that she was looking at. It didn't feel as if it belonged to her.

Was this how Jamie felt after making love with his mistress? There was a vague detachment from reality. She felt no guilt, no pain, no love. There was pleasure, satisfaction, even release. It had been pleasant rather than earth-shattering. But although the earth hadn't exactly moved, it had wobbled a bit. And while they were making love, Jamie hadn't existed. She hadn't thought it was possible to make love to one person without falling out of love with the other. But it was. Responsibilities were forgotten, children, cooking, cleaning, committees – all receded to nothing. No one was hurt. No one was any the wiser.

Except perhaps she was, after all. Was it always so easy to slip effortlessly into adultery? That was the only thing that shocked her. One minute you weren't an adulterer and the next you were. It was quicker than going round Sainsbury's.

Barry Manilow hadn't changed either. He still warbled unevenly in the lift. Tom squeezed her hand as they descended to Reception.

'Do you feel any better?' she asked him.

He bit his lip before he answered. 'No,' he said truthfully. 'Do you?'

'No. But I don't feel any worse.'

The lift doors opened and they strode across the crisscross carpet in Reception to pay their bill to the disinterested girl who was still chewing gum. The cost of an afternoon's adultery was £66.50 plus VAT. Tom insisted on paying and folded the receipt into his wallet. Tax deductible too. Pamela smiled and said thank you.

They drove back to the office in silence too. She needed to pick up her car to go and collect Jack from nursery. Tom twisted towards her as he stopped the car.

'You know it can't happen again,' she said.

'I know,' he answered. 'But thanks anyway.'

'Friends?' she asked.

'Friends,' he agreed. He picked her hand up and lightly kissed her palm.

She sighed. 'You know what you should do now?'

'What?' He looked less tired and drawn than he had before.

'Go and buy the biggest bunch of roses you can find and take them home to Shirley.'

He smiled. 'I think I might just do that.'

'Tell her how much you love her.'

He placed Pamela's hand back in her lap. 'I do love her, you know,' he said quietly.

'I understand that now.' She understood Jamie's situation too. She understood it, but she still didn't like it.

She got out of the car and stood leaning into the open door. 'There's one other thing that you ought to do too, Tom.'

He raised an eyebrow in query.

'This time make an appointment with Relate.' She blew him a kiss and closed the door.

Chapter Twenty

Jamie felt like a complete heel as he drove away from the house to Leighton Buzzard on Saturday morning. Francesca and Barbie were waving wildly. Pamela stood holding Jack on her hip, looking suitably forlorn and abandoned.

He hadn't seen Teri since he had promised to spend the weekend with her. She hadn't been on the train for two days or waiting at the End of the Line Buffet with his usual polystyrene cup of warm battery-acid coffee. And she hadn't been into work.

At night he had sneaked out with MacTavish to the public phone at the end of the road, but the line had been constantly engaged. MacTavish, who wasn't known for his enduring patience, whined incessantly despite all manner of hideous threats, and Jamie had been forced to return home without being able to find out if the weekend was still on.

He had wanted to cancel. Heaven knows, this had gone far enough. Charlie had given him another pep-talk about the ethical and moral responsibilities of marriage and fatherhood, and this time he had listened. Truly listened. It was just so much more difficult to end than it had been to start.

He parked outside Teri's house feeling more like a prisoner on his way to execution than a lover on his way to a secret tryst. He pulled his holdall from the boot of the car. Pamela had remained tight-lipped in the kitchen as he had packed the few paltry things that he needed.

He rang the doorbell and leaned against the wall surveying the row of identical houses, individualised only by the differing colour of their front doors. Even then, white seemed to be the most popular choice.

An elderly woman opened the door, which took Jamie by surprise. She was small and tubby, and had wiry grey hair curled in the same style as the Queen, which made her look older than she probably was – just like the Queen. Someone should get them both a new hairdresser, Jamie thought absently.

'You must be the television repair man,' she said affably, glancing at his holdall. 'Therese said she was expecting you. Come in, dear.' She turned and went inside.

'No, I'm . . .' Jamie looked round to check that she wasn't talking to anyone else and then followed her, perplexed.

Teri was lying on the sofa, covered by a duvet and looking suitably pale. 'Hi,' she said feebly. 'You've come to fix the television.'

Jamie's eyes widened in disbelief.

'Would you like a nice cup of tea, dear?' the Queen's sister said.

He nodded and he wasn't sure why.

'I'll go and put the kettle on then.' She went out into the kitchen and left the door open behind her.

'Be careful what you say,' Teri advised in a whisper. 'She's got ESP.'

Jamie looked impressed. 'ESP?'

'Extra Sticky-beak Power.'

'Oh.' Jamie lowered his voice. 'TV repair man?'

Teri gave a resigned look. 'Sorry,' she mouthed. 'It was the first thing that came into my head.'

He eyed the duvet suspiciously. 'What *is* the matter?'

'My mother,' she mouthed silently.

'I can see that, but what the hell's she doing here?' he whispered. 'Now? *This* weekend?'

Teri sank into her pillow. 'It's a long story.'

He tapped his foot impatiently and watched the kitchen door, whence a badly hummed rendition of *The Archers* theme tune was wafting. 'Well?' he urged, when she seemed reluctant to say any more.

She rolled her eyes and propped herself up on her elbows. 'I came home and ate all the food I bought the other night.'

'All of it?'

'And drank the whole bottle of champagne,' she added regretfully.

'What, you mean *all* the smoked salmon?' he whispered incredulously. Teri nodded. 'And the tiger prawns?' She nodded again. 'The rainbow-trout mousse too?'

'And the caviar and all of the caramel meringue thingies.' Teri had gone green.

'I'm surprised you weren't sick!'

'I *was* sick,' Teri snapped, 'just as my mother happened to phone. I thought it was you and made the fatal mistake of answering it, and it was *her*!'

On cue, Mrs Carter popped her head round the door. She waved a J-cloth like a lace hanky. 'Don't let me keep you from your work, dear. The tea can be brewing while you fix the set. I don't want to miss the omnibus episode of *Brookside*, do I?'

Teri collapsed back on to her pillow.

'What am I supposed to do now?' Jamie hissed.

'Turn the telly on. Look like you're fixing it.'

'I wasn't talking about the television, I was talking about us,' he said, as he obediently turned the television on and it blazed into life. 'Hey – there's nothing wrong with this.'

'I thought you knew nothing about televisions?'

He shot her a withering glare. 'I know a bloody healthy one when I see it. How am I supposed to look as if I'm fixing it?'

'Turn it to the satellite channels and keep flicking through them – they're all ghosting like mad at the moment. There must be a storm brewing.' He treated her to another glare which she ignored. 'Tell her that it's due to atmospheric pressure and that normal viewing of *Brookside* will be totally unaffected. That should do the trick. It's mainly MTV that's squiffy anyway and I don't think she'll want to watch that. Unless Tom Jones is on it,' she added thoughtfully.

'I've been trying to phone you, but it's been permanently engaged,' Jamie said, trying to keep one eye on the door and the other eye on scanning the channels.

'As I was saying, she phoned just as I was being sick. She was on the first train down from Lime Street the next morning and has been phoning all my relatives the length and breadth of the country ever since to tell them how desperately ill I am. She thinks it's food poisoning. She's convinced that you can only get salmonella from smoked salmon. How can I tell her all I had was a ruddy great hangover brought on by my married lover abandoning me with nothing for comfort but a surfeit of fine food and cheap champagne?'

Jamie looked at her reprovingly.

'Don't look at me like that,' she said through her teeth. 'I normally watch my diet very carefully, except when I'm bingeing.'

'You could have phoned.'

'Oh yes – how? What could I say? "Sorry to disturb you, Pamela, but my interfering mother has turned up so could you possibly tell Jamie our weekend love-in is cancelled." 'Teri twitched her head towards the door. 'Old Miss Marple in there doesn't miss a trick.'

'Milk or sugar?' her mother called.

They stared at each other blankly. 'Just milk, please,' Jamie replied.

'She'll be here for days,' Teri said tersely. 'She's harder to get rid of than curry breath.'

Her mother appeared with a tray of tea. 'Haven't you fixed it yet, dear?' she asked Jamie. 'It is taking you a long time.'

'Nearly finished,' he said tightly.

'Can't we offer Jamie a biscuit, Mum?'

'Jamie, is it? My, we're little miss friendly.'

Teri closed her eyes momentarily. 'Jamie is a friend – an *old* friend. I told you. He fixes televisions for a lot of people I know.'

Jamie scowled at her blackly.

'Do you like Jaffa Cakes?' Mrs Carter asked, nose wrinkled. 'All she ever has is Jaffa Cakes.'

Jamie smiled sweetly. 'They're my favourites.'

'I can't stand them myself,' her mother said, and disappeared into the kitchen.

Jamie waited until she had gone. He turned to Teri and asked his original question again. 'And what am I supposed to do now?'

'I don't know.' Teri sounded exasperated. 'Go home.'

'I can't do that. I'm on a course.'

'What sort of course?'

'Management Ethics,' he said reluctantly.

'Management Ethics,' she repeated incredulously.

'That's what Pamela said,' he snapped. 'It was the first thing that came into my head. So that makes us equal for the television repair man.'

'If you can't go home, go to a hotel then.'

'Thanks a bunch!' Jamie punched at the channel buttons.

'Look, I'm really sorry. There's nothing I can do about it.' Teri turned to check the kitchen door. She lowered her voice. 'This is exactly how I feel when you let me down. It can't be helped. We'll have to do it another time.'

'You have no idea what it has cost me to get here for you this weekend, do you?'

'I take it we're talking emotional cost here rather than petrol money?'

'Have you done this to punish me?'

Teri sagged against the pillows. 'Oh Jamie, don't ever think like that – if you do, we're finished.' Her eyes were bright with tears. 'You know I'm as disappointed as you are.'

'Here are your Jaffa Cakes, dear.' Her mother waltzed back into the lounge and put the plate on the coffee table after dusting it with the J-cloth. 'It's nice to see you've put a bit of colour back in her cheeks. She looks all pink and flushed.' A worried look crossed her mother's face. 'You're not going to be sick again, are you, dear? I'll get the plastic bucket if you are.'

Teri's face went from pink to puce. 'No, I'm not going to be sick.'

'Look, I'm finished here.' Jamie picked up his holdall. 'I'll be on my way.'

'No Jaffa Cakes?' The older woman looked hurt.

'No, thank you.' Jamie started to back out of the room.

'I hope it's nothing I've said to put you off.' Her brow was wrinkled. 'I thought they were your favourites?'

'They usually are.' He glared at Teri. 'I'm suddenly not hungry.'

Teri's mother followed him with the plate of biscuits. 'Just one?'

'No, thanks.'

'Just a little one?'

'No, really.'

'There's hardly any calories in them.'

'Well, okay then.' He took a Jaffa Cake, realising that he wasn't going to be let out until he did. 'Thank you.'

Mrs Carter glanced at the television. 'This still doesn't look right to me. There's all wiggly lines and shadows.'

'Ghosting,' Jamie said, confidently pointing at the screen with his Jaffa Cake.

The woman's eyes followed a solitary crumb that fell to the floor. 'It's due to atmospheric tension,' he added meekly.

'Pressure,' Teri snapped.

He grabbed the remote control and switched to Channel Four. 'Look – perfect.' He smiled encouragingly at Teri's mother. 'No problem with *Brookside* now.'

'Good,' she beamed benevolently. 'I can't live without my weekly dose of emotional turmoil, can you, dear?'

'I could give it a try.' He glanced meaningfully at Teri. 'Goodness, is that the time?' He looked at his wrist and realised he wasn't wearing his watch. 'So many televisions to fix and so little time.'

'Well, it was very nice to meet you, young man,' Teri's mother said. 'It was almost worth having a broken television for, wasn't it, dear?'

Teri, blanched against the pillow, had closed her eyes.

'Say goodbye, Therese,' her mother instructed.

'Goodbye Therese,' Teri said without opening her eyes.

Her mother tutted. 'I'll show you to the door.' She ushered Jamie outside, where she whispered conspiratorially, 'You ought to pop round again. We'd like to see you and Therese makes a very nice casserole. Not just stew, casserole. She's a very good cook. She takes after me.'

'Thank you, I'll remember that.'

'Well, goodbye now,' she said loudly and winked.

'Yes,' Jamie said uncertainly. 'Goodbye.'

He was back in the Volvo clutching his holdall and his Jaffa Cake, not knowing what to do with either of them before Teri's mother closed the door. 'Shit,' he said loudly to himself and stuffed the whole Jaffa Cake into his mouth.

Teri's mother peeped out of the curtain as Jamie started the car and drove off down the road. 'He's a very nice young man.' She turned to Teri, who had not yet dared to open her eyes.

'He's not a young man – he's thirty-seven,' she said tartly.

Her mother bristled. 'That's young in my book.'

Teri remained silent.

'Anyway, at least he's not got three earrings in every ear like most of them have these days. And he watches his figure. I had to press him to take one tiny little Jaffa Cake.' Mrs Carter reluctantly let the curtain drop back into place. 'You ought to find yourself someone like that,

Therese. You're not getting any younger.'

'Thank you, Mother.' She would ring Clare as soon as she was better and beg her forgiveness.

Her mother wagged her finger. 'You mark my words, young lady, he'd make someone a very nice husband.'

Teri opened her eyes. 'You had better get that plastic bucket – I think I *am* going to be sick, after all.'

Chapter Twenty-One

Jamie took the scenic route back to Milton Keynes, twisting through Soulbury before crossing over the Grand Union Canal and heading up the hill, past the golf club and through Great Brickhill. It was a sharp, sunny day and groups of golfers pulled their trolleys round the course that bordered the canal – which was probably half-full of their golf balls. Jamie envied them, wishing he'd had the sense to keep a set of clubs in the boot of the Volvo. Bright shoots of green sprouted from the hedges along the tight lanes and spoke of the promises of youthfulness and hope. It depressed Jamie intensely.

He had hit the roundabout at the bottom of the A5 before he decided where he was going to go. Briefly, he considered phoning Charlie Perry and bumming a room for the weekend, but two things had persuaded him against that course of action.

For one, Charlie was unlikely to be up at this hour, given the normal aftermath of his Friday-night entertainment, and secondly, he was bound to give him a lecture – an even longer one than he had dished out last time and Jamie wasn't sure he could stomach that just now.

Teri was right, he had to go to a hotel. How could he

return home now, especially after Pamela had been so scathing about Management Ethics. No way could he simply turn up and announce that the course had been cancelled. She could dine out on that story for the rest of the year. Anyway, she might have organised a wild night in, out or shaking all about with the grease-ball. It was hardly fair of him to pour cold water on that, just because his own extramarital aerobics had failed to get off the ground.

How on earth could Gordy *enjoy* having affairs?

Jamie groaned aloud. It was beginning to feel like a nightmare from which he would never wake up.

Driving through Milton Keynes on a Saturday was like driving through a ghost town. All it lacked was a bit of tumbleweed blowing down the dual carriageway. Most of the activity seemed to be centred round the shopping centre and there were never any traffic jams anyway – except when there was a pop concert on at The Bowl, when the whole of the city became gridlocked.

The city was like a little bit of America plopped down in the middle of a flattened square of Buckinghamshire countryside – a maze of vertical and horizontal roads that looked completely identical. There were no distinguishing features or landmarks, which meant that visitors got hopelessly lost. You couldn't say to someone, 'Turn left at the Dog and Duck,' because all the Dogs and Ducks were secreted away in housing estates. Instead, the roundabouts had been given names to try to help matters, but this had failed miserably.

The sun glinted off the glass slab-sided buildings, which had all been restricted to low-rise elevations; they epitomised the total lack of character of the city. The exception was The Point, an entertainment centre shaped like a pyramid that could be seen for miles around when all of its red neon lights were working.

As a student, Jamie had travelled a bit – it had once been one of his aims in life 'to travel'. He hadn't ever seen himself in a cottage in North Wales playing ball on a wind-lashed beach with two hyperactive children and a depressed wife. He had spent one summer in India, one in Morocco. Lands of gaudy colours, the gaggingly pungent smell of stale spices and unwashed bodies, the deafening babble of incoherent sounds and stomach-churning sights to assault the senses.

There are no snake-charmers in Milton Keynes. Or water-sellers to harass you into buying water that tastes as if it has been produced by themselves. Or amateur dentists pulling teeth out on the streets with nothing more than a pair of pliers. Or hands that clutch at you as you walk, raking you with hard eyes more intimately than is comfortable, dirty un-innocent faces hissing aggressively '*Rupee, rupee*' or '*Dirham, dirham*' – the mantra to part you from your money. In fact, there aren't any people on the streets at all. But there are roundabouts – lots of them – and trees. Millions of them. At one time there were more trees than people. Although Jamie wasn't sure if that was the case any more. So many of the trees had been vandalised.

In Milton Keynes everything is monochromatic, straight and neat and the air smells of nothing. To make up for this absence of environmental stimulus there are the concrete cows. They stand in a field near the main London to Glasgow line and are black and white-splotched – more manic Dalmatian dog than a true representation of a British dairy herd. Stiff-legged and angular, they looked like the sort of painting Francesca would do of a cow.

Jamie drove past them, feeling melancholy for the days when all cows in fields had been real, but they could no longer be seen clearly from the road due to the millions of trees. He followed the V's and H's – vertical and horizontal roads – until he came to The Happy Lodge. It was a sad brick building that resembled an abandoned Tesco's. He took his pathetic-looking holdall and went inside.

The bored blonde on Reception popped her chewing gum in one side of her mouth as he approached.

'Do you have a room vacant? Just for tonight.'

'Four oh five.'

Jamie shrugged. 'Four?'

'No. Four *oh* five.'

'Sorry,' Jamie laughed. 'I thought you said . . .'

She glared at him ferociously.

'Never mind.'

'Second floor.' She handed him the key card and went back to chewing the cud.

Room 405 on the second floor. Shouldn't it be on the fourth floor? Looking at the top of the receptionist's head, he decided not to pass comment. Jamie found it, surprisingly, on the second floor. It was a pleasant room. The same as any hotel room in any hotel in any city, anywhere in the world – but pleasant nevertheless.

After unpacking his holdall to give him something to do, he then wondered how he would fill the next twenty-four hours. He examined the wicker basket in the bathroom filled with minuscule toiletries, checked his nearest fire exit from the diagram on the back of the door, read the hotel directory from front to back, glanced at his watch and still only ten minutes had passed.

He opened the mini-bar and pulled out a cold beer –

despite the fact that the sun was nowhere near over the yard-arm. Kicking off his shoes he lay on the bed and reached for the television remote control, struggling to find the right button to switch it on. So much for the TV repair man in him.

It wasn't the same watching *Grandstand* without Jack bouncing on his lap or Francesca trying to plait his hair. He could actually hear what the commentator was saying – and what a load of old twaddle it was! – and watch the motor racing without two grubby fingers trying to explore his nose. Damon Hill had just spun his car on a practise lap and he had been able to watch all six of the slow-motion action replays without having to read something out of *Thomas the Tank Engine* in a forced Ringo Starr accent. It was altogether too peaceful.

He drained his beer and padded across the room, bringing the entire contents of the mini-bar back with him, cradled in his arms. He dumped all the bottles on the bed. There were three more beers. Two whiskies, two brandies, two vodkas. Two tomato juices, two lemonades and two Dry Gingers. Two ordinary Cokes and two sugar-free, caffeine-free Cokes – which presumably meant two tins of fizzy coloured water and a load of E numbers. Two packets of honey-roasted peanuts, two packets of cashew nuts and two packets of pork scratchings – which looked suspiciously like old toenail cuttings. There was also a bar of expensive Swiss chocolate which was too cold to bite into; when he tried, he decided to leave it until it had warmed up a bit, rather than risk losing a tooth.

Perhaps he should follow the Therese Carter School of Therapy and drink all of the attractive little bottles in front of him as a means of attaining oblivion from his current predicament. He started on another beer.

Suddenly there was a high-pitched giggle from the room next door and the creak of bedsprings as something heavy – and still giggling – was dropped on the bed. These walls were paperthin. Jamie turned Murray Walker up.

A steady, rhythmic banging began in the next room, and the headboard beat a familiar tattoo against the wall behind Jamie's head. He groaned and increased the volume of Murray Walker, who was also winding himself up to a climax of feverish incoherence. The banging became quicker and so did Murray. On the screen Murray shouted ecstatically about Damon Hill. In the next room someone shouted ecstatically, 'Oh yes!'

There was a brief respite during which Jamie's jangled nerves started to recover. He left the television on loud in the hope that the lovers would realise there was someone within earshot and would curb their passion – or at least curb their noise. But there is something about unbridled lust that makes one oblivious to anyone else's discomfort . . .

When the headboard and the earth started to move again, Jamie resignedly drained his beer and reached for the last one. After this it would be on to the hard stuff. What sort of perverts came to The Happy Lodge on a Saturday afternoon and bonked themselves senseless anyway? *Lucky ones*, Jamie thought bitterly.

Chapter Twenty-Two

Pamela answered the telephone. It was a man's voice.

'Could I speak to James Duncan, please?' She didn't recognise the voice. It was refined, clipped.

'I'm afraid he's away for the weekend. On a course,' she added without thinking.

'Oh.' There was a long pause.

'This is his wife. Can I take a message?'

'It's very important that I get hold of him.'

'I haven't got a contact number for him.' It was a lie; she knew exactly where he was. The thought made Pamela feel irritable. 'Who am I speaking to?' she said shortly.

'You don't know me,' the man answered. 'My name's Richard Wellbeloved. I'm a . . . a friend of Charlie Perry's. I'm afraid I have some bad news.'

'There's a woman on the phone for you, Therese,' her mother said. 'Very posh, won't say who she is.'

Teri struggled from beneath the weight of the duvet and stretched like a contented cat before walking to the phone – despite the fact that she was still feeling less than contented.

'Teri Carter,' she said, much more brightly than she felt.

No one spoke for a few seconds, then the woman said: 'This is Pamela Duncan.' Her voice was tight. 'Can I speak to Jamie, please?'

There was another uncomfortable silence as Teri tried to find her voice which, coward that it was, seemed to have deserted her. 'He isn't here,' she said eventually.

'Don't play games with me,' Pamela snapped. 'I need to speak to him urgently.' There was another pause and Jamie's wife sounded as if she was struggling to control her emotions. 'I wouldn't have phoned otherwise. I'm not in the habit of humiliating myself unnecessarily.'

'I'm being serious,' Teri said. She smiled at her mother and kicked the door closed. Her smile died. 'He wasn't able to stay.'

'Where the hell is he then?'

'I don't know. I think he was going to find a hotel.'

'Do you know where?'

'No. No, I'm sorry I don't.'

'Well, if he contacts you, tell him to get his lying backside home as quickly as possible.'

'Is there something wrong?' Of course there was – why else would she phone?

'Nothing that need concern you.' The phone went dead.

Pamela put the phone down with shaking hands. Her stomach was twisted into a tight knot and her mouth was dry. The girl had sounded even younger than she had on the answerphone, but less confident than Pamela had expected.

Why wasn't Jamie there? What had gone wrong? If he hadn't been able to stay, why hadn't he come home?

Even through the unanswered questions there was a

faint hope pushing up like a weed through a pavement. He hadn't spent the weekend with Her.

But where the hell was he? Teri said she thought he had gone to a hotel. Pamela pulled the *Yellow Pages* out of the drawer. She would try the most obvious place first. The place where pain and pleasure met, sin and solace, love and lust. The Happy Lodge. She dialled the number.

They had been at it for more than three hours, virtually non-stop. Jamie was feeling exhausted just listening to them. Murray Walker had given way to another less exuberant commentator, presumably while he refreshed himself in the BBC's hospitality suite. Even Murray couldn't keep going for three hours unabated.

Soon the shred of plasterboard that separated the two rooms was bound to give and spill the copulating couple right on to his bed. Jamie had tried banging back on the wall – although it made him feel like a complete spoilsport – but this had done nothing to quell their ardour.

He was sipping the second of the miniature whiskies straight from the bottle, alternating it with sips from the Dry Ginger bottle in his other hand when the telephone rang. He put the whisky bottle between his teeth, turned down Muddly Talker's counterpart with the remote control and put the receiver to his ear.

'Hello,' he said into the whisky bottle.

'It's Pamela.'

He swung guiltily off the bed and put the whisky down. 'How did you know I was here?'

'I've just spoken to Teri. After that it was an educated guess.' She sounded philosophical rather than annoyed.

'Oh.' Jamie was confused. 'Is everything all right?'

'No.' Now he could hear the strain in her voice.

A lump blocked his throat. 'Is it the kids?' He would never forgive himself if anything happened to them.

'No, they're fine, but you need to come home right away.'

'I can't.'

'What do you mean, you can't?'

Jamie answered sheepishly. 'I've been working my way through the mini-bar. I'm not in a fit state to drive.'

'Oh, for goodness sake, Jamie!'

'I'm sorry.' It seemed an inadequate thing to say in the circumstances.

'Look, I'll come and get you. I'll see if Melanie's around to look after the children.'

'Can't you tell me what's wrong?' There was a feeling of dread rising in him, darkening his mood.

'It's Charlie,' was all she said.

'I'm in room four oh five,' Jamie offered. 'Pamela, are you still there?'

Her voice was barely audible. 'I'll be with you as soon as I can.'

Chapter Twenty-Three

Charlie lay deathly still on the bed. His face was as white as the hospital sheets and there were dark unnatural circles round his closed eyes. His normally effervescent curls were plastered flat to his head with sweat, making it look as if someone had shaved his skull. He looked older and more haggard than he normally did after a night on the tiles – and that was really saying something. Upturned on the bed, his wrists swathed in bandages still seeped tell-tale lines of blood.

'Good grief,' Jamie said. 'You look like Uncle Fester from the Addams Family.' He pulled the nearest plastic chair over to Charlie's bed and sat down heavily.

Charlie opened his eyes and smiled. It was a weak, feeble smile that didn't reach his eyes. 'What are you doing here?'

'I'm here on behalf of the Mutual and Providential management to make sure that you're not just skiving.' Jamie picked some grapes off the bunch from the bedside table next to Charlie's. The occupant was asleep and unaware that his fruit was being pilfered. 'Actually, you asked for me when you were coming round. Richard phoned to tell us.'

Charlie stared at the ceiling, where a whirling fan made

an ineffectual attempt to provide a breeze in the stuffy, disinfectant-scented heat.

'I don't know what to say, Charlie. I had no idea.'

He looked squarely at Jamie. 'What – that I was gay or that my lover had left me?'

'Both, you silly bugger. Oh, sorry.'

Charlie grinned. 'It's all right, dear boy, you can still be politically incorrect with me.'

Jamie sighed. 'So how long have you been . . .'

'Homosexual?'

'If you want to put it like that.'

'Years, dear boy.'

'But I thought we were best friends, Charlie! How come you never told me? I thought you were one of the lads – a man's man and all that sort of macho crap.'

'Some of us are.'

Jamie's brow was furrowed. 'And what about all those busty blondes you brought to the office parties?'

'All front, old chap – me, not them.'

He looked at Charlie's mutilated wrists and twitched his head. 'So what caused this?'

'Richard left me – two weeks ago.' He cleared his throat. 'We'd been together ten years. He came back last night to collect his things. That's when I decided to do a re-enactment of *Psycho* with me playing Norman Bates *and* Marion Crane.'

Jamie looked puzzled. 'Marion Crane?'

'She was the one in the shower,' Charlie explained. 'Janet Leigh. It was her finest moment. Don't tell me you're too young to remember. If I remember, so should you.' Jamie still looked blank.

Charlie shook his head impatiently, then sighed heavily and bit his lower lip. 'I made a terrible mess of the

248

grouting.' His eyes filled with tears. 'Richard's set up home with a twenty-one-year-old television presenter called Jez with pierced nipples and a sperm whale tattooed on his penis. How can I compete with that?'

Jamie shook his head incredulously. 'I'm not sure that you should want to.'

'Perhaps you're right,' he said listlessly.

'Why didn't you say something, damn you! You should have said you were feeling so . . .'

'Suicidal?' Charlie smiled ruefully. 'You can't just drop something like that into the conversation. Besides, you've got problems of your own, love.'

Jamie stole some more grapes. 'Tell me about it.'

'I didn't think you'd take kindly to my moralising if you'd realised that my own life was more tangled and shredded than clothes in a clapped-out washer-dryer.'

'I didn't take kindly to your moralising anyway, but only because what you were saying was true.'

'This is the sort of thing that happens, Jamie, when love goes wrong.' Charlie held his wrists up. 'This is the reality of affairs. The pain of broken promises. It's not all hearts and flowers and forgiveness and friendly little tête-à-têtes over the custody arrangements. Speaking of which – where is the lovely Pamela?'

'The lovely Pamela is sitting in the rather seedy-looking café just down the hall, nursing a coffee and probably contemplating which particular vice of mine to cite on her divorce papers. Do you want me to get her?'

Charlie shook his head. 'I'd rather she didn't see me like this.' He plucked disdainfully at his NHS nightie. 'Just give her my love.'

'I think I need to give her *my* love before anyone else's,' Jamie said wearily.

'Are things any better?'

'I don't think they've ever been worse,' he admitted. 'She knows about Teri.'

Charlie winced.

A look of concern crossed Jamie's face. 'Are you in pain?'

'No. I'm wincing for you, not me.' Charlie waved his bandaged wrist dismissively and winced again.

Jamie settled back in his chair and popped another grape in his mouth. 'Do you think things can ever get back to normal?'

'What's normal, dear boy?'

'Now there's a question.' Jamie rubbed his chin. It was heavy with stubble. 'You know, just Pamela, me, the kids, the mortgage.'

'I think that's really down to you, Jamie.'

Jamie stretched and yawned till the tears came to his eyes. 'You don't fancy getting out of that bed and going for a walk, so that I can have a nice lie down?'

'No, I don't.'

'I thought you'd say that.'

'It's time you were running along – you don't want to keep Pamela waiting. I'll be all right.' Charlie glanced at the slumbering occupant in the next bed. 'It would be nice if the fractured femur had some grapes left when he woke up, too.'

'Are you sure you'll be okay?'

Charlie nodded.

'Has anyone else been to see you?'

'No. I've told Richard to stay away.' He gestured at the nurses. 'These poor creatures have enough to deal with, without my histrionics.'

'What about your parents?'

'Mater and Pater? They don't know my circumstances. Old school, you know. Not sure that women should have the vote, men should still do National Service, bring back hanging. I don't think they'd understand. They think I'm a reprehensible rogue, nothing but a debauched dilettante. And I *do* have my reputation to keep up.'

'I'll come again tomorrow.'

'That would be nice.' He looked exhausted. 'Bring some grapes.'

Jamie put his hand on top of Charlie's. 'I love you, Charlie.' His voice was choked with emotion.

Charlie's eyes widened. 'That's a poofy sort of thing to say.'

'Naff off, Charles.' Jamie was embarrassed. He brushed his eyes with the back of his hand. 'You know what I mean.'

'I've never fancied you anyway. You're not my type.'

'I'm glad to hear it.'

'Go on, go and be nice to your wife.'

Jamie stood up. 'I'd shake your hand,' he nodded at the bandages, 'but I'm afraid it would come off.'

'Still firmly attached, old boy. I'm not much good at that either,' he said sadly.

'Stick to insurance then.'

'I'll take your advice, if you take mine.'

'No more amateur butchery?'

'Wouldn't dream of it, dear boy.'

'Good. I'll see you tomorrow.'

Charlie closed his eyes. 'Tomorrow.'

Jamie patted Charlie's hand and walked slowly down the ward. Charlie opened his eyes and watched him – his broad straight back and his mop of dark unruly hair even more unkempt than usual. He saw the nurse's eyes follow him, her attention distracted from the mundane task of tucking the man with the bandaged head and two black eyes back into his bed.

Charlie put his hand to his mouth. 'I love you too, James,' he said quietly.

Chapter Twenty-Four

Neither Jamie nor Pamela noticed the car parked just further down the road in Fraughton-next-the-Green. Teri had been sitting there for half an hour already. She had lured her mother from the house with the promise of an hour's shopping in Marks & Spencer's, but Mrs Carter was less than pleased when rather than the girlie expedition of retail therapy she expected, Teri had dumped her at the store's doors and promptly disappeared.

It had taken her ages to find Fraughton-next-the-Green. She knew her way to the shopping centre and back with her eyes closed, but once you strayed off the beaten track in Milton Keynes you were in uncharted territory. You could end up going round and round in circles for days and never find the place you wanted. All the houses looked the same, all the roads looked the same. And not knowing whether you wanted to be Vertical or Horizontal was a bit like not knowing your elbow from another part of your anatomy. She had even taken the precaution of studying her map book before leaving, but it was out of date and Fraughton-next-the-Green was marked as a pink blob with the words *Undeveloped Land* stamped unhelpfully on it.

Eventually, she had stumbled across it by accident and

at first she had thought it was a mirage brought on by severe disorientation. Fraughton was indeed next-the-Green. It was also next-the-olde-worlde-pub and next-the-village-pond, across which two swans swanned majestically. White-clad men played cricket on the Green, while people sat around in deck chairs and straw hats and clapped genteelly. Wild flowers grew in the neat grass verges and there was no litter or graffiti on the bus shelter. It was as if Milton Keynes had been involved in a head-on crash with *Trumpton*.

Jamie's house was set further down the road than the Green – away from the main 'action'. He was right when he said the house was a mix of architecture. It looked as if someone had cut several pictures out of *Homes and Gardens*, thrown them up in the air and then built what landed. There were pillars and porticoes, balconies and balustrades, all topped with a thatched roof – a peculiar blend of Regency, Georgian, Suffolk and Southfork.

The house had a circular gravel drive with a circular lawn in the middle of it, and in the middle of that Jamie pushed a Flymo about with purpose. Behind him Francesca followed with a child-sized rake. Jack sat in a plastic car with blue wheels and a yellow roof and Pamela helped him as he struggled to steer it through the gravel. She looked how she sounded. Cool, confident, controlled.

Collectively they looked like something out of Disney. All the scene needed was a few talking flowers and some cartoon rabbits hopping about, and they would have had their next blockbuster on their hands.

Pamela disappeared indoors and reappeared moments later with a tray of drinks. The family huddled together as she benevolently dished them out. Jamie took his drink and squeezed her affectionately round the shoulders. He squeezed Teri's heart painfully at the same time. Mr and Mrs Bun the Baker and their chubby-cheeked children Master Bun and Miss Bun had been less of a happy family than this lot.

How could she ever have thought that she was destined to share any part of his life? This was her dream – big house, two big cars, two angelic children, a look of quiet contentment and a hunk of a husband. This was what she thought about when she lay awake at night in her seventics box, imagining Jamie's humped shape slumbering beside her in the bed. It was her dream – but someone else was living it in her place.

So much for his wife not understanding him. It was the oldest line in the book and she had fallen for it. He was never going to leave all this for her. She must have been a fool to think that he ever would. Clare would put on her Sister Mary Bernadette voice and say, 'I told you so.'

As far as she could tell, Jamie had made only three lapses from utter perfection in his life. One was marrying another woman before he'd given himself the chance to meet her. The second was buying this house – which wasn't so much a statement of sartorial taste as a demonstration of cash over common sense. It was a house that screamed 'First Division footballer' – not 'insurance executive'. She could picture the architect now – the type of man who would park a Ferrari in the drive and would consider circular houses *de rigueur*. The type of man who would design the rooms with the lounge in between the kitchen and the dining room without a thought to the mess the transient food would make on the shag pile. It must be more his wife's style – although she'd had the good taste to marry Jamie.

The third slip was the flea-bitten hound that had just bounded into the Disney film set. It should have been white and fluffy and wagged its tail in time with the catchy signature tune written by Tim Rice that also should have been tinkling away in the background. This mutt was a cross between a doormat and the sort of Afghan coat that was briefly fashionable among the less discerning hippies during the late seventies. It clearly had more varieties than Heinz could ever hope to offer. Its fur stood on end, giving the impression its nose had recently been pressed into a live electric socket, and its tail wagged erratically in short staccato bursts that enhanced the effect.

This dog was the only thing that bound them all to earth. Its tatty presence reassured her that she hadn't slipped quietly into a virtual reality game of 'Mr and Mrs Perfect and their perfect lives'. This dog was the only anchor to sanity.

She looked away from the tableau in front of her. How was she going to face Jamie on the train tomorrow? It would be best to avoid him, but she needed to find out what had happened yesterday. She could consider commuting by coach. There was a coach that left from the end of her road at some ungodly hour in the morning. It took hours to get into London, but it was a fraction of the cost and they all drank whisky and played poker and had wild affairs with each other to pass the time. The locals called it 'The Love Coach'. She had tried it once. Whether it was the lure of cheap travel, whisky or the possibility of a wild affair, she was unsure now. On the first morning she had been violently sick just outside Hemel Hempstead and the driver had been forced to stop for her. Everyone had been very cross and unsympathetic and late for work, and she hadn't dared try it again. Not one of the men had looked like potential affair material anyway.

She drove away from Fraughton-next-the-Green unsure why she had come, and now that she *had* come, unsure exactly what she would do about it. Her biological clock was ticking away as loudly as the clock in the crocodile's mouth in *Peter Pan*. Except that unlike Peter Pan, this clock was reminding her that she was aging. She could feel her collagen fibres binding as she spoke. Her hormones were hurtling her headlong into hirsuteness – her oestrogen was on the way out and her progesterone on the verge of pulling the plug. That was why she was so desperate for a promotion: if she had fulfilment at work and a grotesque amount of money, perhaps there wouldn't be this empty yearning inside her, this desire to wear Laura Ashley smocks and float round the garden cutting roses, this ache to know that Braxton Hicks wasn't a character in *Dallas* but a kind of contraction, and talk about breaking waters and *not* mean the seaside . . .

Her mother, spent up at Marks & Spencer's, for once had the sensitivity not to break the solemn silence in the car. The deluge would probably come, but she seemed to realise that now wasn't the time, and Teri's heart went out to the chubby, elderly lady next to her who had the unfortunate affliction of sharing the Queen's hairdo.

The telephone was ringing as they pushed through the pile of free newspapers and leaflets advertising double-glazing bargains behind the front door. Teri was sure that every time she went out – even for five minutes – people leapt out of hiding in her bushes and pushed free newspapers and junk mail through her door. When she answered the phone, it was Clare.

Her friend sounded bright and bubbly, which made Teri feel even flatter. 'I'm sorry I haven't phoned, Teri. I've been terribly busy.'

'I thought you were sulking.'

'Me? No! I know that you can be thoughtless, heartless and totally selfish when you want to be, Therese, but I'm not one to bear grudges. Besides, I've been far too busy to sulk.'

'Go on then. What have you been doing?' Teri settled herself on the bottom stair. Her mother made a capital T with her fingers and Teri nodded.

'David came back to me!' she shrieked.

'Oh Clare, I'm so pleased for you,' Teri said gaily. Her heart sank deeper into the pit of her stomach. 'What happened?'

'Well, I decided to play it cool, after a month of sweating by the telephone, forcing myself not to ring. You know, Teri, I'm sure that giving up someone you love is worse than trying to give up chocolate – the withdrawal symptoms are terrible!'

This was just what Teri wanted to hear. Her mother opened the door and passed her a cup of tea. She mouthed, 'Thank you.'

'Anyway, after a month of no contact whatsoever – I didn't reply to his solicitor's letters, estate agents' calls, no midnight tearful phone calls, nothing – he simply abandoned the nubile bitch Anthea and begged me on bended knee to take him back. Can you believe it?'

'I'm really pleased for you,' she said numbly. 'What made him change his mind?'

'Sex,' Clare stated baldly. 'They were having it for breakfast, lunch and dinner with only a break for a Pot Noodle in between. And as you well know, Teri, Sister

258

Mary Bernadette always used to say "man cannot live by Pot Noodle alone".'

Teri twisted a tendril of hair round her finger. 'Actually, I think it was bread.'

Clare was affronted. 'I thought that was Marie Antoinette?'

'Er – that was cake.'

'Whatever,' Clare said dismissively.

Teri changed the subject. 'So how's it going now?'

'Heaven! I clasped him back to my bosom, Teri. I've ironed his shirts, I've performed sexual athletics in the bedroom, and in the back garden – but that's another story. I've fed him sumptuous specials from Delia Smith every night for dinner. Take it from me, Teri, even in the nineties the way to a man's heart is still first and foremost through his stomach rather than his genitalia.' Clare sighed. 'Generally, I've pandered to his every whim.'

'It sounds more like hell than heaven.'

'He has been languishing in my boundless stream of love and has thrown himself at my feet declaring himself a fool for ever leaving me.' Clare was jubilant.

'So everything in the garden of romance is rosy again?' Teri said with a twinge of jealousy.

'Absolutely marvellous,' she agreed triumphantly. 'I threw him out two weeks ago.'

'*What!*'

'Well, he was a bloody idiot! I knew that, you knew that, I just wanted him to realise it too.'

'So where is he?' Teri was stunned.

'I don't know. He's been phoning every night since declaring undying love to my answerphone.'

'I can't believe you,' Teri breathed. 'You're on a different planet from the rest of us.'

'You know he always had the hots for you, Teri. I'm surprised he never made a pass at you.'

'What's that got to do with anything?' she said warily.

'Mind you, I used to think you encouraged it sometimes.'

'That is grossly unfair – and untrue!'

Clare swept on, oblivious to her protest. 'Anyway, he's free now if you're interested.'

'Why should I want your cast-offs?'

'I seem to remember you rushing off with Stephen Whitely not five minutes after I'd broken his heart.'

'That was different! He had a Chopper bike and I was fickle then,' Teri seethed. 'Some of us have moved on since the playground.'

'Some of us have, Teri. Some of us,' Clare said benevolently. 'Still, that's another chapter of my life closed. Onwards and upwards. I'm dating a pilot called Dermot who, thankfully, is neither gay nor married. How are you and Thingy getting on, by the way?'

Teri checked that her mother was out of earshot. 'Jamie!' she snapped at Clare before relenting. 'I think it's grinding to a slow and painful halt. You can put on your Sister Mary Bernadette voice and say "I told you so".'

'Well, I hate to remind you, Teri, but I *did* tell you so.' She was right back at The Sacred Heart of Jesus primary school. 'If you would only listen to your Aunty Clare you'd save yourself a lot of pain. Remember when Michael Lacey wanted to meet you behind the bikesheds and I warned you that he was only after your body?'

'Clare, I was ten at the time.'

'And what did you get? Nothing but a quick snog and a—'

'Yes, thank you, Clare. I remember it very well.'

'You've suffered from cold sores there ever since.'

'Yes, you're right! I should have listened to you then.'

'And you should listen to me now. I'm so much wiser in the ways of the world than you are, Teri. You're an innocent abroad.'

'You were calling me a tart and a harlot and a ruthless adulteress last time we spoke.'

'I was cross because you were making me homeless. After begging me to come and stay with you –' Teri didn't actually remember any begging '– you then had the cheek to fling me out. Sometimes you can be so perverse.'

'You've spent months luring your husband back from the arms of another woman for the sole purpose of proving what a good thing he was missing – only to throw him out after two weeks – and you have the nerve to call *me* perverse!'

'I didn't phone to argue, Therese.'

Teri laughed. 'Why did you phone?'

'I want us to be friends again.'

'We never stopped being friends.' Teri sighed. 'I'm going to have to go, my mother's here and it sounds as if she's trying to demolish the kitchen.'

'Oh, give my love to her. I used to get on well with your mother.'

Teri nodded at the telephone. 'You have such a lot in common,' she said sweetly.

'Phone me,' Clare said.

'I will.'

'Teri,' Clare shouted, just as she was about to put the phone down.

'Yes?'

'Good luck with Jamie.'

'Thanks.' She was going to need it. Why did human

beings insist on making life unnecessarily complicated for themselves? It would be so much easier if we just simply fell in love with people who loved us back, who didn't have wives and children and life-threatening mortgages and emotional baggage and hang-ups and roving eyes and wandering hands and uncontrollable urges.

Teri padded back into the kitchen. Her heart still heavy from seeing Jamie in 'Toytown' with his wife and children. It put on a few more pounds when it saw what her mother was doing. Mrs Carter had removed the entire contents of the fridge, had spread them over every available work surface and was busy wiping down the inside with a J-cloth. 'How's Clare?' she asked, without looking up.

'Oh, she's . . . she's Clare,' Teri said philosophically.

'Good,' her mother replied. 'That's nice. I always liked Clare. She's got so much more *about* her than you have.' Teri stuck out her tongue at her mother's back.

Mrs Carter shook the J-cloth out. 'I'm going home tomorrow, Therese. You'll take me to the station, won't you, dear? You're looking much better now.'

She started to put the contents back into the fridge, examining them carefully – or as carefully as she could without her glasses – and wrinkling her nose at anything that looked remotely spicy.

'I think it was that nice young man who came to repair the television, myself.'

'Really?' Teri said sardonically.

Her mother ignored her. 'He seemed to buck you up no end. You know, you should ask him for a date. I watch *Top of the Pops*.' Mrs Carter wiggled her bottom. 'Take him to a rave or something – that's the sort of thing young people do these days.'

'That's the sort of thing sixteen-year-olds do these days, Mother. I'm over thirty years old.'

'Then you should have more confidence. You never used to be backwards at coming forwards. This is the nineties.' She wiped each egg with the J-cloth before putting them back. 'You've got equality. A boy only had to buy you two ounces of Uncle Joe's mint balls in my day and you were as good as engaged. One kiss outside the gate and the lights in our front room would be flashing on and off like the Blackpool illuminations. Things have changed. There's no need for you to sit on the shelf and wait for someone to take you down and give you a good dusting.'

'Thank you, Mother, I'll bear that in mind.'

'By the way, I bought some nice bits and pieces in Marks & Spencer's food hall. It's wonderful food, but I don't know how you can afford to shop in there all the time.'

'I can't.'

'I certainly can't on my pension. Anyway, you owe me thirty-two pounds and fifteen pence.'

'Thirty-two pounds and fifteen pence? What on earth did you buy – gold-plated chicken drumsticks?'

'I told you. Some nice bits and pieces.' Her mother lifted the Marks carrier bag on to the work surface and started to pull out the items one by one. 'I got some smoked salmon. Not my sort of thing really, but I'll force it down. I'd rather have a nice steak and kidney pudding, but I know you like it. Some rainbow-trout mousse. Some big prawns and some fancy-shaped little biscuit things.'

Teri had gone very pale. 'You haven't got any caviar in there, have you?'

'Don't be silly! Do you think I'm made of money? I did

get some sickly little meringues. Oh, and a bottle of their cheapest champagne. Still, it looks all right.' Her mother pulled the bottle out of the bag with a flourish. She frowned. 'What are you looking for, Teri? Is it your purse you're after?'

'No,' Teri said faintly. 'I suddenly don't feel very well at all, and this time I'm definitely going to need the plastic bucket.'

Chapter Twenty-Five

Pamela was going through his suit pockets. It was something that she had managed to avoid doing so far. She had also avoided pressing the last number redial facility on the phone every time he was out of the house, prising open his locked desk drawer and rifling through the contents of his briefcase – now that she had managed to work out his combination. He'd used their anniversary date – not very original, really.

However, this suit did need cleaning and Jamie had the habit of leaving a pile of business cards secreted in one of his pockets. There was something unavoidably grubby about commuting. She crammed his wardrobe with 'fragrance sachets' – nothing too flowery, woody scents of sandalwood, rosewood and patchouli – to dispel the lingering aura of city grime and diesel fumes. Despite using Sketchley's Gold Service, Jamie's suits could usually stand up by themselves within days. Collars and cuffs turned black at an alarming rate. Anti-perspirants might work well on television adverts showing people running around in the fresh air, but the manufacturers should do a bit of product-testing on commuter trains in the summer, when hot air belts out from the heating ducts unabated, and sweaty bodies are squashed together like

Swedes in a sauna. Just recently there had been an unseasonal hot spell, and the trains had been delayed all week.

There was a handkerchief in the top pocket of the suit – folded neatly, but decidedly dirty. Pamela pulled it out gingerly, holding it between her immaculate fingernails. It had been washed – but not by her. Whoever had done this didn't use Persil Automatic. There were faded red stains all over it that were probably lipstick, and when she shook it out to examine it further, a tidy little note fell out.

It was neat handwriting. Neat and girlish. She closed her eyes and tried not to look at it. This was a personal note between Jamie and his lover – she knew she shouldn't look, but it taunted her and teased her and tempted her to read it. She had found her mother's diary once – coincidentally, when she was looking for a handkerchief. It was hidden in the back of her underwear drawer, beneath the silky petticoats and sensible-sized knickers, and the lure of it had proved too great.

Pamela had read of things she shouldn't – her mother's irritation with her father, how they struggled to make ends meet despite the affluent lifestyle they'd adopted and how, although she tried to love her children equally, her mother couldn't help favouring Pamela's sister, who reminded her so much of herself. Pamela blew her nose hard on the handkerchief that she eventually found. Returning the diary to its secret place, she closed the drawer quietly, firmly and she never looked at it again.

It was with the same sense of foreboding that she viewed the note she held in her hands. She should tear it into shreds, she knew that. But now that she had seen the tiny, perfect script she wanted to know what it said. Jamie was downstairs. She listened for his footsteps, but none came. All she could hear was the faint murmur of the television drifting up from below. It was a comedy programme and someone was laughing too loud. She spread the square of paper on her lap and smoothed it out.

Her eyes filled with tears until the writing was blurred and she could read no more. Pamela sat on the bed, the grubby hanky looking up accusingly from the crisp cotton whiteness of the duvet cover. The note spoke of dreams. Shared dreams. Unfulfilled dreams. No protestations of love, no lustful lamentations, no sordid or smutty thoughts. Just sadness and regret – for opportunities missed, chances wasted and plans turned to dust.

Pamela held the note cupped in her hands. She could tear it up, destroy it, obliterate it – but what would that achieve? What was written would still be in her mind, waiting there for the darkest moments to regurgitate itself.

Was this what Jamie had really wanted from life? Had *she* crushed his ambitions, his goals, his spirit as easily as she could crumple this note between her fingers? Or had he simply abandoned them to devote himself to family, responsibility, commitments, duty? That didn't mean his dreams had gone away. Perhaps he felt them more keenly now that he knew they would never be achieved. She felt devastated. Why could he tell his lover about his innermost thoughts and dreams when he had shared nothing of this with her, his own wife?

She needed to see Teri. She needed to know what made her so special. She needed to know why Jamie could share with her things that he had never mentioned to another living soul. Now that she had spoken to her, it only made matters worse. Her voice was etched into Pamela's brain as if it had been scored deeply in cut-class. Was she dark? Was she blonde? Would Pamela be consumed with jealousy when she saw her, or simply wonder why Jamie had chosen her?

Pamela folded the note, following the previous creased lines carefully, like one does with a road map or a knitting pattern. She went to Jamie's wardrobe and put it back in the pocket of another suit that hung silently expectant in the wood-scented air.

Jamie was sprawled on the sofa, reading the remains of the Sunday papers and sipping a therapeutic whisky. He had been to see Charlie in the hospital again and had returned home pale and drawn. Pamela sat by his feet. 'I'm going to come into town with you tomorrow.'

Jamie lowered his paper. 'Why? You hate going into London.'

'I've got things to do.'

'What things?'

'Just stuff.' She picked up the glossy magazine which he had discarded on the floor. 'I wouldn't mind coming into your office,' she said over-casually. 'Perhaps we could meet for lunch.' Her face had coloured and she leaned earnestly over the magazine so that her hair would drape forward and hide it.

'You've never wanted to come to the office before.'

'Well, perhaps now is a good time to start.'

Jamie put his paper down. They had lit a fire to dispel the chilliness of the evening – a legacy of a clear, cloudless day. The embers cast a golden glow across the room which pooled where Pamela sat and picked out the unseasonal autumnness of her hair. Her face was pinched, her cheeks flushed, her pain transparent. 'I don't work with her,' he said.

Pamela started to protest and changed her mind.

Jamie massaged his hairline. 'I met her on the train.'

'I need to see her,' Pamela stated flatly.

'What good would it do?'

'None.'

'Then why?'

'It's a woman's thing.' She looked into the fire and her eyes flickered with the reflected dying flame. 'Like calories and hormones and stretch-marks.'

'Like masochism.'

She turned to Jamie. 'If it were me, you'd want to know, wouldn't you?'

'I *do* know!' Jamie tossed his paper to the floor. 'And believe me, it doesn't help one bit.'

Pamela sighed. She should explain about Tom, that it had all been a silly, stupid plot – a pretend revenge affair – and get this whole damned sordid business out into the open. Except that now she didn't want it all out in the open. She only wanted certain bits out in the open and, when pressed, would she feel the urge to confess?

However hard she tried, her Catholic upbringing would never really go away; there was always the underlying urge to purge the soul of stains of sin and guilt. Would it help or would it hinder? Could she really stand there and play the innocent party when she had courted the danger of temptation all along? And had finally not only succumbed but had actually instigated it? How could she explain to her husband that they both had more than a passing interest in room 405 of The Happy Lodge?

'Do you want to talk about it?' she asked.

'No.' Jamie sighed. 'My brain's about to explode as it is. I can't stop thinking about Charlie.' He had swung through the ward doors and had been at Charlie's bed before his friend had noticed him. The true pain had been

269

shining through there too, before he had put his carefree mask back on. He was bruised, bandaged and bereft.

At this moment, Charlie was a sadder character than Gordy. And that was so sad, it made you want to weep. Jamie had taken some grapes and a Get Well card, and they were the only things Charlie had received.

'So,' Pamela broke into his thoughts, 'do you mind if I come tomorrow?'

'Yes,' Jamie said. 'But you'll come anyway.'

Pamela hated railway stations – and airports. To her they were the epitome of purgatory. A place of disembodied coming and going – as many people happy and reunited with loved ones as there were devastated ones, cast out and abandoned, starting a life of enforced, eternal separation. These places were always so bleak. Bleak and windy, with the sort of wind that clings to your bones and chills you right down to the marrow. At least at airports there was the Duty Free to cheer you up.

Her thoughts turned miserably to Jack and Francesca, whom she had dragged screaming from their beds at an even earlier hour than normal to deposit – still protesting – with a bleary-eyed and infinitely obliging Kathy from next door. She and Jamie would be late home too and Pamela had asked Kathy to give the children whatever they wanted/demanded for their tea in the vain hope that copious amounts of junk food would buy their forgiveness for indulging in this selfish pilgrimage.

It was drizzling, and at her insistence they were waiting for the train – which was late – in the unpleasant waiting room, a cold glass box made up of windows two feet wide, banded by garish red aluminium. Three of the windows had no glass in them and the wind whistled peevishly through the gaps; the jagged edges of the broken glass looked like an evil smile. The floor was strewn with old newspapers and empty burger boxes, and it stank of urine. As soon as she had walked in, Pamela wished they had waited outside in the wind and the rain.

Jamie was subdued. No, morose. He hadn't tried to dissuade her from coming, but he hadn't spoken all the way to the station in the car, although he had held her hand as they queued to buy her a ticket. Now he stared out of the windows, peering past the numerous unmentionable substances that were smeared across them. When the commuters on the platform started to shuffle towards their favoured spot, Jamie and Pamela went out to greet the impending arrival of the train.

You could always get a seat this early. It was something Pamela had learned over countless dinners with friends who also commuted. They talked endlessly about the vagaries of British Rail and now Railtrack, the price of their season tickets and the comparative time they travelled. Their lives were measured by the length of their journeys. If yours was longer, more expensive and more hassled than your colleagues', you were lauded rather than ridiculed. It was worse than having dinner with a group of struggling golfers. (No. It was bad, but perhaps it wasn't *that* bad.)

The doors closed automatically, beeping like a demented microwave, and the train sped off towards London through the urban dereliction that was once Bletchley – a place not yet swallowed up by the greedy expansion of Milton Keynes, but no longer sufficiently attractive or economically viable to support its own town centre or to compete with the burgeoning megastores that crowded its limits.

It was at Leighton Buzzard that she got on. Leighton Buzzard – erstwhile scene of the Great Train Robbery and now the great husband robbery too. Teri – her husband's lover – swung on to the train jauntily, despite the fact that it was still only just after six-thirty in the morning. She looked as if she should be in a Tampax advert, with the strains of 'It's my life' following her and the confidence to wear white on days she really shouldn't. Her style was casual but expensive, and Pamela was surprised at the absence of the power suit she had imagined. She looked small and vulnerable and nice.

Her body was angled towards them as she moved between the seats and the train jerked out of the station. She shook the rain from her hair, flicking her eyes over the occupants of the carriage. When they rested on Jamie, who was looking suitably ashen-faced behind his paper, she smiled – but it froze on her face as she spotted Pamela.

Recognition was instant. Clever as well as beautiful. But it didn't give Pamela the pang of malice or jealousy she had expected. There was just a deep and abiding sadness to know that this woman, this girl, had been intimate with her husband. Intimate with his body and intimate with his thoughts. She would know the birthmark on his shoulder that looked like a map of Japan. Had Teri run her fingertips over its smooth, ragged outline and then lovingly nipped it as she once used to do?

Pamela tore her eyes away from the other woman and fixed them instead on the stylised mural at the end of the carriage, which seemed to depict the Swiss Alps and stippled clouds floating above what appeared to be two nuclear bunkers surrounded by navy-blue grass.

When she could bear it no longer, she glanced at Jamie and saw that he was mortified. It had been wrong of her to come. She shouldn't have done this to him. Throughout her childhood, Pamela's mother had insisted on accompanying her into the classroom and helping her to hang up her coat while all the other children had struggled valiantly with theirs alone. The final ignominy had been a warm, wet kiss on her cheek as her mother disappeared with a flourish of skirts. It had branded her a wimp in front of the class and she had longed for her maturity into junior school and out of such excruciating oppression. She could feel the same emotion emanating from Jamie and throbbing through her veins. It had been wrong.

At Euston the train stopped abruptly and the impatient commuters spilled out on to the platform. Teri left the train without looking at them. They followed at a polite distance, Jamie fussing with his newspaper to give her a head-start. Pamela watched Teri's hair bobbing in front of them, passing the hanging baskets over-flowing with garish red and yellow plastic geraniums, following the crowd of commuters through the ticket barriers like sheep being herded into a pen.

When she broke away from the mass of people and jogged up the slope into the main concourse, Pamela turned to Jamie, who was pretending not to watch her. 'You can go after her if you want to. I don't mind.'

'No,' Jamie said lifelessly. His face was a blank screen from which all trace of emotion had been erased. 'I'll stay with you.'

He tried phoning Teri all morning, but all he got was her jolly answerphone message, which said: 'Teri Carter isn't at her desk right now,' but infuriatingly offered no further enlightenment.

The office was very quiet without Charlie, and Jamie

listened to his secretary's dissection of *Animal Hospital* with even less fervour than usual. It was nearly midday when Joyless Lovejoy came out of his office and announced that he wanted to see Jamie in private straight away. He was staring out of his office window at the pigeons on the roof opposite when Jamie followed him in and closed the door.

'What do you know about Charlie?' he said, without turning round.

Jamie sat down. 'He's getting better. He should be out of hospital in a day or two. They've been keeping him in for observation.'

Joyless turned round and perched on the windowsill. He looked remarkably like one of the pigeons outside. Pointy-nosed, beady-eyed and grey – overwhelmingly grey. 'Is he mentally stable?'

'He's as stable as you or me,' Jamie answered laconically.

Joyless's head snapped up and he scrutinised Jamie's face for any sign of sarcasm. 'This is very inconvenient of him,' he said.

Jamie bristled. 'That's one way of looking at it.'

'Is he fit to do your job?'

'*My* job?'

'We need to be sure of a replacement before we can promote you.'

'*Promote* me?' He was aware that he was beginning to sound like Little Sir Echo.

Joyless glared at him. 'We're merging with another insurance group. All hush, hush. It'll mean reassessment, restructuring, reintegration, reorganisation and recentralisation. We want you to head up the IT Department.'

Jamie swivelled in his chair. 'I'm flattered.'

'We want you in Macclesfield next Monday.'

'Macclesfield!'

'Didn't I mention relocation?'

'No,' Jamie said. 'You mustn't have *re*-membered.'

'So you'll go?'

'Do I have a choice?'

'Yes.' Joyless nodded joylessly. 'Redundancy.'

'Chester?' Pamela's voice rose in disbelief. They were on the train on their way home. Jamie was feeling tired and emotional, and the last thing he wanted was a scene. His wife was nursing an ominously large Harrods carrier bag, which he was trying very hard to ignore.

'Well, near Chester,' he answered cagily.

'How near Chester?'

'Macclesfield.'

'Macclesfield!' Pamela's expression was pained. 'Chester sounds terribly salubrious. Macclesfield doesn't sound salubrious at all.'

'We live in Milton Keynes, for goodness sake. How much worse can Macclesfield be?' He was trying to keep his voice down. 'I think it would be a good move for us.'

'But the children will grow up speaking with Northern accents.' He wished Pamela would try to keep hers down too.

'*I* have a Northern accent.'

'Yes, but far enough north to have a certain rustic charm.'

'I'll take that as a compliment,' Jamie said tersely.

'It was intended to be.'

'Having a regional accent is hardly life's biggest handicap, Pamela. Even the BBC allow their presenters to veer from Queen's English these days.' Jamie gesticulated expansively. 'Take Michael Fish – there are days when I can barely understand the man. And these so-called "youff" programmes have presenters that are complete gibbering morons – they're totally unintelligible! If we keep letting the kids watch these they'll grow up being unable to string two sentences together – despite your best attempts with the Alphabites.'

'You've made your point,' Pamela said.

Jamie stared silently out of the window as they rushed through Watford Junction. It was a rare thing – rushing through Watford Junction. He normally liked to stop and read the platform sign which said PASSING TRAINS CAUSE AIR TURBULENCE. It made him smile and wonder how you could even swallow a train, let alone *pass* one. And heaven knows, he was in need of something to smile about today. 'I could stop commuting and live nearer to the office.'

'Is that some sort of veiled promise?'

'Yes, it is.' Jamie lowered his voice further. 'I would have thought with our current domestic predicament that you would relish the chance of moving away. Unless of course, there's something – or someone – that would keep you here.'

Pamela ignored the barbed reference to Tom. 'I didn't say I didn't want to move. I was just expressing distaste at Macclesfield.'

'What does it matter whether it's Mars or Macclesfield? This gives us a chance to make a fresh start.'

'Does that mean you're going to end it?'

Jamie looked around. The sea of raised newspapers and best-selling paperbacks jogged along with the steady motion. There was a pale-skinned Pre-Raphaelite redhead further down the carriage, with one button too many of her blouse undone. She had her face to the fluorescent

276

tubes, rosebud mouth parted expectantly, eyes dreamily closed, and picked her fingers constantly until they were red raw at the quick. Or what about the man diagonally across, who had chain-eaten painkillers since Carpenders Park washed down with Diet Coke. Were they struggling to hold their lives and their sanity together? He looked at the blank, expressionless faces and wondered how many of them were disguising difficult domestic situations that were straight out of *Brookside*. Probably all of them.

'We shouldn't be having this conversation on the train,' he said.

'Does it?'

'Yes.'

Pamela's eyes brimmed with tears and she started to cry. Slow, silent tears poured out of her eyes, rolling languorously down her cheeks and splashing on to her skirt.

'Oh, hell!' Jamie muttered. 'Don't cry.'

'You shouldn't tell someone not to cry,' Pamela sobbed. 'It negates their emotions.'

'You've been reading *Cosmo* again, haven't you?' He searched frantically in his suit for a handkerchief and finally pulled one out of his top pocket. The shock of recognition showed on his face. *It was the hanky panky*.

He hesitated in handing it over. What had once been white and pristine was a terrible mess now, anyway – stained and spoilt. Ruined. It was unlikely that Pamela would want to have it anywhere near her.

His wife had stopped in mid-sob and was staring at him. Reluctantly, he shook it out. A tiny, folded piece of paper dropped out of it and fluttered delicately to the grubby floor of the carriage. They both watched it, mesmerised by its meandering descent. He passed her the hanky, unable to take his eyes off the note on the floor. She took it but didn't use it, crushing it into a ball and twisting it between her fingers.

All the way to Milton Keynes the note lay on the floor between them, like a lone scrap of confetti, forgotten after the wedding had long since ended. Jamie listened to the wind-rush buffeting against the train, braced himself against the vicious jolt of a passing express and tried not to think of Teri.

The train slowed for Milton Keynes Central Station. Commuters gathered their belongings – newspapers, briefcases, coats from the overhead racks – and crushed towards the doors for their final burst to freedom. Jamie put his arm round Pamela to steady her as the train stopped. 'I need one last night,' he said. 'Just one night and then that's it. No more working late.'

Pamela chewed determinedly at her lip and nodded. A barely perceptible movement of the head, but a nod nevertheless. She was still wringing the hanky between her hands and there were dark smears of mascara under her lower lashes. The harsh fluorescent lights that flattered no one picked out the fine lines on Pamela's face. Jamie's heart twisted into a tight line like a wrung-out J-cloth. He swallowed the lump that threatened to fill his throat and helped her – and the still unmentioned Harrods bag – off the train.

The tiny note went unheeded, blackened and crushed beneath the weight of alighting feet. As the automatic doors closed, an eddy of wind caught it, whipping it and blowing it out of the train after Jamie and Pamela. It circled in the air, wheeling and soaring briefly before it plummeted to the platform. The train moved off and the wind blew along the dusty, grimy concrete, making the note skip animatedly. For a moment it teetered on the brink of the platform beyond the safety of the yellow line, before a final gentle gust tipped it over the edge.

The train was disappearing from view – whisking its passengers off towards the more exotic destinations of Crewe, Runcorn and ultimately Liverpool Lime Street. The scrap of paper lay on the track, forgotten, invisible, unnoticed by the people who pushed down the stairs on to the platform, cursed their bad timing and waited impatiently for the next train to come along.

Chapter Twenty-Six

'Jamie!' It was the tenth time he had called, but the first time he hadn't been answered by a recorded message. 'I didn't expect you to call.'

His heart still went into somersault mode at the sound of her voice, and it did a triple backflip now so that he wasn't disappointed. 'I need to see you.'

'I wasn't sure what to think after yesterday.'

He cut across her, impatient to get this over with. 'Can we meet tonight?'

'Of course we can.' She lowered her voice, so there must be people around her in the office. 'I'm sorry about what happened at the weekend.'

So much had happened he wasn't sure exactly what she was referring to, until he realised that Teri was still in the dark as far as most things were concerned. She still didn't know where he had gone when he left, or why Pamela had needed to contact him so urgently. He wasn't keen to shed any further light either.

'Is everything okay?' she asked, when he didn't answer straight away.

'Not really.' He sounded miserable.

'Do you want to tell me now?'

'Not really.'

'Shall I get some food for tonight?'

'No.' How was he ever going to break this to her gently? 'I thought we'd go to Steamers for a drink.'

'Neutral territory?' She wasn't just beautiful, she was razor-blade sharp.

'Something like that.' The silence hung heavy between them. 'I'll meet you outside the office.'

Teri's voice was quiet and he could tell it had nothing to do with the hindrance of eavesdroppers. 'I'll see you later then.'

He hung up and twirled round in his chair, propping his feet up on the desk. Why the hell wasn't Charlie here when he needed him? He would know what to do, what to say. He was aware that he was sounding like Joyless Lovejoy. Charlie was doing all right. The bandages had come off, revealing dark crusted slashes that would ultimately heal to nothing more than faint white reminders of a love gone tragically wrong.

One of the young nurses had been fussing around him, surreptitiously administering lavender oil to his wounds. They would heal quicker that way, she had told them earnestly. It was something she had learned on the part-time aromatherapy course she had done so that she could supplement her meagre National Health Service pay. Jamie wondered if lavender oil could help the mental scars too.

He sat alone in the corner of the Clog and Calculator at lunchtime, not noticing the tasteless pint of bitter that sat in front of him and avoiding Gordy and three more of his cronies from the office. They were talking loudly and laddishly about the barmaid's breasts, while she leaned lazily on the pumps, absently picking peanuts from the dish on the bar and popping them into the red gash of her mouth. He had taken a detour on his way back to the office and had stopped at the flower shop – Blooming Marvellous – which announced: *Say IT with Flowers!* in the window. Which flowers were suitable for saying his particular IT, was anybody's guess.

He chose roses, the blooms of lovers. How romantic. They were deep dark red, the colour of let blood. The colour of hearts torn and mangled. The colour of the congealing wounds on Charlie's wrists. The soft, velvet plush petals deceived the unwary and made them prey to the spiking thorns on the stems.

The florist offered to trim the thorns, but Jamie refused. They summed up perfectly the way he was feeling, particularly when she cheerfully pointed out that there were always more thorns on roses than there were petals. It was a thought that sent him further into his depression.

The florist wrapped the roses in copious layers of paper tissue and bound them tightly with a scarlet bow. He paid and clutched the bouquet to his chest. As he stepped on to the street, a thorn pushed through the protective layers and drew blood from the finger on which he used to wear his wedding ring. Blooming marvellous.

The roses spent the afternoon unfurling on the office floor, while Jamie went over in his head the best way to tell Teri that it had to end. By the time he left, they had gone from tight curled buds to full-blown but tired-looking blooms. He knew how they felt. The heating in the office was rather like that on the trains. It made sure they froze to death all winter, and with the onset of the balmy days of spring it miraculously burst into life and fried them all through the summer. Armpits sweated, shirt collars chafed and shoes squelched. It was a blessed relief to be standing in the fume-choked, car-filled excesses of Euston Road waiting for Teri.

She burst out of the revolving doors chatting animatedly to a colleague and, despite the fact that he had made up his mind to do it, he wondered how he was going to manage without her. He kissed her cheek and gave her what was left of the dying roses. They walked up Euston Road arm in arm, making no attempt at conversation. At the station the concourse was, as usual, thronged with people. They made their way across towards Steamers. Jamie opened the door and a wall of sound met them – the high-pitched hubbub and hearty laughter of aimless conversation.

'Not in here.' Teri pulled his arm. 'If you're going to end it, the least you can do is afford me some dignity.'

Jamie's face crumpled. 'How did you know I was going to end it?'

'I may be green, Jamie, but I'm not entirely cabbage-coloured.' She smiled at him wryly. 'Come on, I've a bottle of fizz in the fridge at home and I have got something to celebrate too.'

Jamie hesitated. 'I promised Pamela.'

She looked straight at him. 'It's far too late to start worrying about telling porky pies now, Jamie. One more isn't going to make the slightest bit of difference. We'll both be prodding the coals in hell as it is, and you'll be lined up by that tiny little guillotine. Come on, or we'll miss the train.'

Chapter Twenty-Seven

There was a policeman on the screen wearing a fluorescent yellow vest which said POLICE INCIDENT OFFICER in bold capital letters.

Pamela looked up from her sewing. It was nine o'clock and the first time she had sat down that night. Jack and Francesca had squabbled incessantly since teatime and had forced her brow to crease into a permanent furrow and subsequent headache. Now she was stitching name tags into Francesca's school sweatshirts in the vain hope that she might at the end of term have the same ones she started with.

It was the tangled mass of trains and the mention of Euston Station that made her prick up her ears and prick her thumb. In the background, ambulance sirens wailed, the surging discordant noise still sounding strangely American rather than British. There were shots of bloodied, bandaged people being stretchered away from the trains by men in tight-fitting orange jumpsuits who whisked them into waiting helicopters. In the background, firemen held clear plastic drip bags attached to patients lying bleeding on the ground – they looked like something they had won at the fairground and should have had the orange flash of a goldfish swimming round in them.

Horrified, Pamela learned that this was the 18.07 out of Euston – a packed commuter train that had crashed into an empty goods train heading south from the depot of Bletchley. The collision was just south of Watford Junction. The train had been carrying over four hundred people. There was one fatality and over one hundred other injuries. The POLICE INCIDENT OFFICER said that it was a miracle more passengers weren't killed. Pamela's throat went dry.

The news cameras switched to a harassed BBC reporter, standing outside Watford General Hospital. Every ambulance that arrived at the ugly grey concrete building was greeted by a swarm of nurses in pale blue uniforms and matching plastic aprons who fussed around the casualties and hurried them inside. A large red sign bearing a large red arrow said: WALKING WOUNDED THIS WAY, PLEASE.

Pamela couldn't hear what the reporter was saying. There was blood rushing in her ears and she scoured the faces of the injured, imagining them without their bandages. One fatality. *Oh God, please let it not be my Jamie.*

The news flash continued interminably – eyewitness reports of crashing sounds and flying glass and flowing blood. The trains hung precariously from an embankment, looking like toys sadistically smashed by a child who hadn't yet learned how to play nicely. In the houses below the carnage, people had been evacuated while they were having their tea. One man complained to the reporter about his chips going cold.

A haggard-looking spokesman from the Railways Inspectorate made a vacuous statement to the camera, citing unblemished safety records and assuring the general public that an internal enquiry was being launched. He, too, echoed the sentiments of the Incident Officer that it was a miracle there weren't more dead, then delivered his well-rehearsed uncomfortable condolences to the families of the dead and injured. Already the press were looking for someone to blame. All Pamela was looking for was Jamie.

Chapter Twenty-Eight

Teri found the only vase she owned, which was lurking at the back of her under-sink cupboard gathering dust. She unwrapped the fading blooms, which were now shedding their petals due to the warmth of the train and the battering they had taken because they had both been forced to stand until Watford Junction. It was a shame that the only flowers she'd had in years seemed destined to be a farewell present.

She clinked two lone ice-cubes from the tray into the vase and tossed the tray into the sink. Somewhere she had read that ice could revive wilting flowers. This lot would need a small iceberg to do the trick by the look of them. Either that or a small miracle.

What would revive a wilting love affair, she wondered. Certainly not an iceberg: this relationship was beginning to feel as though it had been struck a cruel and fatal blow by one. It seemed unlikely to survive. Look at the *Titanic* – how indestructible that had seemed at the time. Had she and Jamie ever seemed indestructible? No, she had to admit, they hadn't. They had always been a leaky tub – the water of commitment and loyalty seeping in too steadily for them ever to venture too far from the shore.

She had seen this coming. After the debacle of the

weekend and then Pamela on the train yesterday, what else could she expect? They were up to their ears in water – the moment of sink or swim. There was no question about what Jamie would do – there never really had been. It was why she loved him – the kindness, the loyalty, the inherent goodness. She had vowed that she would be brave and smiling as their ship slowly sank. Jamie would strike back for the safety of the shore and she would silently and with dignity let the water engulf her.

Teri tucked the champagne under her arm and carried the vase into the lounge, where Jamie was perched uncomfortably on the edge of the sofa, scattering petals across the carpet as she went.

'Here, you can open this.' She passed him the bottle and slid two slender glasses across the coffee table at him. 'Open it carefully. I don't want another dent in my ceiling.'

He squeezed the cork expertly out of the bottle and poured the champagne into the glasses. 'What are we celebrating?'

Teri took a glass and knelt on the floor in front of him. '*We're* not celebrating. *We're* in mourning. *I'm* celebrating.' She lifted her glass. 'May I propose a toast to the new presenter of City Television's most popular youth culture show – *Out and About!*'

A smile creased Jamie's face and his eyes sparkled with the reflected bubbles from the champagne. 'You got your promotion!'

Teri sipped the champagne and put it to one side. 'And about time too!'

'That's incredible.'

'I know. It was such a fluke too. My producer – I told you about him – Richard Wellbeloved . . .'

Jamie's blood ran cold. 'I don't believe it,' he said.

'Thanks!' Teri pouted. 'You need an ego the size of a very large house to be on television, and at the moment mine's already smaller than my downstairs loo!'

'That wasn't what I meant.' He waved his hand dismissively. 'Carry on!'

'Well, he's gone! Under a cloud, by all accounts. The rumour is, he's been given the big heave-ho from on high. Gross misconduct. And that irritating little twerp Jez – I told you about him too. Gone! Apparently, they've run off together . . .' Teri prattled on, but Jamie was only half listening.

How could he tell her about Charlie now? Why did it always work out that one person's pain was another person's pleasure? Why was one man's grief invariably another man's glory? One's loss another's gain. Was that why funerals were so much like weddings? Flowers, cars, hymns, crying and slap-up food afterwards. No one wore black at funerals any more and everyone seemed to wear black at weddings – with the possible exception of the bride. And even that wasn't a certainty. As far as he was concerned, there was only one obvious difference – one was most definitely an end and the other was a beginning. And, of course, no one tended to video funerals.

'. . . There was some scandal involving the programme controller's desk, some cocaine and a banana. But you know what office gossip is like. You can't believe everything you hear.'

'It's true,' Jamie said.

Teri's eyes widened. 'What – even about the banana?'

Jamie shook his head. 'I don't know about the banana – or the rest of it – but Richard Wellbeloved has definitely run off with Jez.'

'Well,' Teri said, 'who would believe it?' She shot bolt upright. 'How do you know?'

'That's why Pamela was looking for me on Saturday. Charlie's in hospital. Richard was his lover, partner – I don't know – whatever you call it these days. Charlie's taken it very badly. He tried to top himself.'

'We *are* talking about Charlie "I'm one of the boys, tits and bums, ten pints of bitter and big-breasted ladies" here?'

'The very same one.'

'And he's gay?'

'As Elton John. He just doesn't play the piano as well.'

'I'm stunned.' Teri looked it. 'I was going to try and fix him up with Clare.'

'It's just as well you didn't.'

'I can't see why Richard Wellbeloved is attracted to Jez. Charlie is a much better catch,' Teri said philosophically.

'Apparently, he's got a sperm whale tattooed on his penis.' Jamie filled his glass again.

'Richard Wellbeloved?' Teri's voice was a squeak.

'No, Jez. And pierced nipples.'

'That figures.' Teri pulled her fringe away from her face. 'But I still can't see the attraction.'

Jamie shrugged and smiled. 'Perhaps it's a life-sized sperm whale.'

Teri stopped to think about it, then: 'Look, I'm not going to sit here all night discussing other people's love lives when our own is on the brink of catastrophe.' She took his glass from him. 'Come upstairs and make love to me.'

'I can't.' He put his face in his hands. 'It would only make things worse. I think it would be best to end it quickly.'

'No, it wouldn't.' She pulled him towards her by his tie. 'It's best to end it slowly and seductively. Then at least we can look back when we're sitting in our rocking chairs reminiscing in our Alzheimer-riddled heads and remember what irrational and irresponsible ravers we once were.'

There seemed no appropriate moment to tell her, so Jamie blurted it out. 'I'm moving to Macclesfield.'

'Macclesfield!' She let go of his tie and he recoiled on to the sofa.

'It isn't the end of the world. Or even the end of civilisation as we know it.' He adjusted his tie, tidying it back into the right place. 'Though Pamela thinks it is.'

'Why Macclesfield?' Teri shook her head in disbelief.

'My company's relocating.'

'That still doesn't answer the question.'

'I don't think there is an answer – other than why not?'

Teri's face had fallen and she looked as if she was about to cry. 'We'll never see each other again.'

He could tell he wasn't making a very good job of breaking this gently. He suspected bulls in china shops broke things more gently than he did. 'That was the general idea.'

'I didn't think it would be so final.'

He pulled a petal off one of the roses and rolled it absently between his fingers. 'You can't end an affair and then still go on seeing each other – it doesn't work like that.'

'I thought we might at least accidentally bump into each other sometimes on good old Platform Eight. You know, you could ladder my tights and sprain my ankle again. And I could ruin another one of your hankies. It would be just like old times. And we could shoot the breeze over a coffee at the End of the Line like good buddies do.'

Jamie shook his head. 'You know it wouldn't work.'

'I must say you're taking this very calmly.'

'I'm not calm – my insides are churning more than they do when I've had a chicken vindaloo.' He discarded the petal which was bruised and broken. 'I'm just resigned. There's a difference.'

Teri twisted and leaned against his legs. 'Did you ever love me?'

It was a stupid thing to ask. She should know he did. He had risked everything for her. But he could feel the uncertainty prickling from her like the edgy palpable static electricity that comes from VDU screens. He smoothed her hair with his hand, expecting it to crackle under his fingers. It didn't.

'You know I did. I still do,' he whispered.

'More than Pamela?'

How did he ever think this was going to be easy? He didn't answer and when she looked up at him, his eyes were closed and he was resting his head back against the sofa.

'More than Pamela?' she repeated.

'I love my wife,' he said, without opening his eyes.

'Look at me and say that.'

Jamie turned his head and his eyes met hers and he said levelly, 'I love my wife. I always have.'

'You bastard.' Teri sounded sulky. 'You do, don't you?'

Jamie nodded wordlessly. 'It's a different love. There's not the need – the greed. It's steadfast and stoic. It's corny and dated – and it's, well, it's *there*.'

'So a bit like Rolf Harris, really.'

Jamie sighed. 'A lot like Rolf Harris – but without the

didgeridoo.' He bent down and kissed the top of her head. 'I wish I could turn back the clock. I wish that we'd never met and then I wouldn't have to hurt you now.'

'I wish you wouldn't keep making wishes. I've already told you once that you're too old. The last ones you made didn't come true or we wouldn't be in this situation now.'

He wrapped his arms around Teri and pressed her to his chest. Her body was tight and angled, every muscle taut with tension under his hands. She felt considerably less in control than she sounded. 'How am I going to live without you?'

She looked up at him. 'I used to think that about Häagen Dazs ice cream, but somehow I managed.'

'You just eat Ben and Jerry's instead now, don't you?'

Teri looked puzzled. 'So I do.' It was an analogy that Jamie didn't care to dwell on.

She lay watching his sprawled dozing body on her bed, remembering every line of his face, the way his hair curled, the birthmark that looked like a map of Japan on his shoulder. This would form the Polaroid photograph that she would store in her memory. She had taken no proper photographs of him and it seemed too late and too sad to start now. How could she ask him to smile and say cheese when that same mouth would say goodbye to her in just a few short hours?

His heart was beating loudly and solidly in the silence and she strained her ears to listen in case it was one of her neighbours with their bass boost turned up too loudly. Teri kissed his ear lobe and he swished his hand as if to swat an irritating fly before he opened his eyes and realised it was her.

He smiled, a lazy, lopsided smile – *store in the memory* –

and his eyes crinkled. Three more lines to memorise. She kissed him full on the mouth. There was a need inside her that was more raw than a plateful of sushi. 'Make love to me again.'

'I don't know if I can.'

She trailed her hand over the flat of his stomach. 'Just one last time.'

He held her away from him. 'This is the third time you've said that.'

'We all have to find previously untapped reserves of strength during times of adversity.' She padded to the stereo, seemingly unaware of her nakedness, and put on a CD – *Touch Me in the Morning*. 'Indulge me before you break my heart.'

'Teri!' He looked at her accusingly. 'This is a real tear-jerker!' She came back to the bed and Jamie took her hand. 'Don't torture yourself like this.'

'I'm not torturing myself. It's you that's torturing me. Besides, if it was good enough for Diana Ross it's good enough for me.' She lay beside him on the bed, head nestling on his chest. 'Anyway, I'm a big girl now. I'm not going to cry.'

'Come here,' he said gruffly.

This time they made love silently and seriously – afraid to touch each other unless one of them should shatter into a thousand brittle fragments. The tears slid silently down her face and Jamie's face was wet, too – although she couldn't tell if it was from her tears or his own.

He traced the line of her tears over her cheeks. 'I thought you said you weren't going to cry.'

'I lied,' she said.

When she had laid curled in his arms for some time he said gently, 'I have to go.'

He prised her away from him and twisted out of bed and sat with his back towards her. She pulled the sheet over her head and stayed there. Jamie went into the bathroom. She could hear the tap running into the sink and solitary splashes of water, but there was no singing like there usually was. Eventually, he returned.

'I'm ready to go.' His voice was tight with emotion. There seemed a necessity for this sharp cruelty, this detachment from the pain, if he was ever going to be able to go at all.

'Goodbye,' Teri said from beneath the covers.

'Don't let me go like this.' Jamie pulled at the sheet tucked tightly over her head. 'Come out and say goodbye like an adult.'

'I don't feel like an adult. I was going to be brave and sophisticated and light-hearted but I can't.' Diana still crooned on the CD player.

He pulled the sheet down. Her eyes were red-rimmed, her face tearstained. He brushed her hair from her face and kissed her forehead. 'I love you,' he said and walked out of the door.

Teri closed her eyes and hot tears squeezed through her lashes again, burning a track across her already feverish cheeks. 'I wish you weren't married, that we weren't hurting anyone by loving each other, and I wish more than anything that when I opened my eyes you'd still be here.'

She opened her eyes at the same time as the front door slammed brutally and irrevocably shut behind him.

So that was it. Their brief encounter was over. Trevor presumably chuffed unhappily away alone on his train, while whatsername stood pathetically waving a damp hanky. It was bound to be something like that. It always was.

Life was nothing but a bitter journey on the rails to nowhere. A series of horrible tacky stations, unexpected delays and, sometimes along the way, the odd devastation of a major derailment. That's what Jamie had been – a major derailment on life's tortured track.

Anyway, she'd never know how the stupid film ended – and what's more, she no longer cared. How could she ever bear to watch it now? Whatever happened THE END would come up in big white capital letters. And she'd reach for the man-sized Kleenex once again.

Chapter Twenty-Nine

The emergency number that they gave out for friends and relatives was constantly engaged. She sat with the phone in her hand, pressing and re-pressing the redial button and imagining that by sheer will she could force the incessant, negative bleeping to change to a comforting, informative ring.

There was a news update every half-hour, and still she hadn't recognised Jamie among the battered and tattered travellers. Surely, he wouldn't be on that train. This was to be his last night with *her* – with Teri.

What were the chances of them being trapped and tangled together on the train? A million to one? There was more chance of them winning the National Lottery.

Somewhere, she had read that it was more likely for a thirty-seven-year-old man to die of a heart attack immediately after buying his lottery ticket than it was for him to win 'The Big One'. For one mad moment, Pamela clung to the safety of that thought.

Jamie must surely have been well on his way to Teri's place by the time the train crashed. You're hardly likely to hang around at the office if there's a passionate night of sex on the cards, are you? To Pamela it seemed a cruel and ironic twist to be praying fervently that her husband was safely tucked up in bed with his lover. Somehow, she thought hysterically, it wouldn't be what Relate advised.

For the last time she tried to get through to the emergency number, but it was still frustratingly unavailable. There was only one other option. She stared at the phone, wrestling with her indecision. Perhaps he would come home soon? Safe and well and hopefully sexually unencumbered, too.

The minutes squeezed by on the hall clock in exquisite slowness until another twenty had passed into the vacuum of oblivion and there was still no sign of Jamie. She had lasted out this long, sweating and trembling beside the phone like a heroin addict who tries to prolong her fix as much as possible – but knowing full well that she will eventually succumb. Her hands trembled as she dialled Teri's number for the second time that week.

'Hi.' A quiet, subdued voice answered the phone.

Pamela swallowed. 'Is that Teri?'

'Yes.' Her voice was instantly cautious.

It was horrifying how nice she sounded. Pamela wanted to hate her and be set against her but she couldn't find it in her heart. 'I promise I won't make a habit of this,' she said politely. 'Is Jamie there?'

'No.'

Oh my God. Pamela tried to breathe deeply. She closed her eyes to keep the blackness at bay. 'There's been a train crash, at Watford Junction. I just need to know that he's safe.' She steadied her voice again. 'Has he been with you?'

There was a moment's hesitation before Teri answered. 'Yes,' she said. 'He's safe. He's already left.' She paused and Pamela heard her clear her throat. 'He's on his way home to you.'

Pamela stood against the wall, her emotions scattered like a tub of hundreds and thousands dropped on a kitchen floor. Relief flooded through her, making her giddy with happiness. 'Thank you,' was all she managed to say. 'Thank you.'

'You love him very much, don't you?'

'Yes,' Pamela said. She was crying and smiling at the same time. Tears of joy, of relief, of sadness and regret.

'I do too,' Teri said sadly. 'I'm sorry about all this. We never meant it to happen.'

'These things can take us all by surprise sometimes,' Pamela said. She thought of Tom and Shirley, of Jamie and herself, and her heart went out to the sad and lonely young woman at the other end of the phone.

'You're a very lucky woman, Mrs Duncan.' It sounded as though she was crying.

'I know,' Pamela said softly, and put down the phone.

Chapter Thirty

Jamie drove home along the main roads. His mind was too full of images of Teri to risk the twists and turns of the village roads in the darkness. The yellow-orange glow of the street-lamps soothed him, and the concentration of his driving helped to stop him thinking too much.

He wondered how they would settle down in Macclesfield. It would be good for them to make a fresh start. He would make it up to Pamela – and the children. The thought of how close he had come to blighting their lives made him shudder. He had never wanted them to become just another blip on the broken-home statistics.

How could he have coped with seeing Teri on the train and not holding her and smelling the fresh, clean scent of her hair – pretending that they were just friends and that they had never really been lovers? Would there come a time when he would be able to remember something she had said, but not be able to hear her voice, its tinkling intonation and the effervescence of her laugh? Would he remember the colour of her eyes, but not be able to picture her as sharply as he could now? Would he ever feel the softness of silk against his skin and not think of her? Would there be a time when he would look back and know that what he had just done was the right thing? Or would she remain gouged in his heart for ever like the initials carved on a tree by a young and hopeful courting couple? Although he was married to someone else, the scar would remain with him always – lessening, fading with age but never entirely disappearing.

As he turned into the drive and pulled up at the garage doors, the security light flashed on, flooding the sweep of gravel with a harsh glare, picking out the colours of individual pebbles. It had been fitted for them by Secure Home Limited. There had been precious few perks in Pamela's job, except for this state-of-the-art burglar alarm and a house that had more security lights than a NATO base. It was funny how they had taken so much trouble to defend their house, yet had left themselves so open and vulnerable to attack. He hoped Pamela would be able to forget Tom. She hadn't been into work since the curry-flinging episode, and there hadn't been any 'hang-up' phone calls, so he was quietly optimistic.

He parked the car and set the alarm, closing the garage door behind him. This was one thing he wouldn't miss about Milton Keynes – the car crime was rife here. Although he doubted that Macclesfield was very much better. You probably would have to move to Mars these days if you didn't want your car to be nicked. If the truth was known, they probably already had little green joyriders there.

Jamie pondered briefly how many vehicularly challenged juvenile delinquents would want to half-inch a Volvo with infantile vomit all over the upholstery and a baby seat in the back. No street cred or what. Still, there was something intrinsically embarrassing about having to make a claim of your own when you worked in insurance. It was better to be safe than sorry. And he had always been a cautious man.

* * *

Pamela was waiting in the kitchen. She heard the car and the crunch of his feet walking heavily across the gravel. Her face was freshly washed and her make-up re-applied. There was an envelope in front of her and she fingered it tentatively, brushing unseen specks of dust from its surface with shaking hands.

The envelope contained tickets for the Monaco Grand Prix. In Monte Carlo. A million miles from Milton Keynes or Macclesfield. She had stretched her flexible friend to the limits of its pliability and had booked a five-star hotel too. It would be her last wanton extravagance, and it would be worth it. The room had a jacuzzi – perhaps they would make love in it.

There were only two tickets and they would abandon the children to the tender mercies of her mother and go alone. Husband and wife. Man and woman. The tickets had been difficult to get hold of and extortionately priced, and she would probably hate it – the noise, the crowds, the cloying smell of oil, the environmental pollution, the French. But she would go for Jamie's sake and she would make sure that she enjoyed it and that he enjoyed it too.

Pamela realised it was a small and hideously inadequate gesture, but it was an attempt to compensate for the things Jamie had sacrificed for them. The things that his heart most desired. The things that he had confided to Teri and hadn't been able to tell her. It was an attempt to say that she would try to make more time for him, to understand him and to show that she really did love him.

They would have a smaller house in Macclesfield, she decided – one without an *Alien* mortgage. One that didn't strangle the life out of their relationship and make a prisoner of their dreams.

She heard his key in the lock and as she turned to greet him, her eyes glanced along the work surface. The stained and ruined handkerchief was lying on top of the pile of bills that waited patiently for someone to pay them.

'Hi, I'm home,' he shouted breezily. She heard the catch in his voice and the way it didn't quite match the heartiness of his words.

She picked up the hanky and clutching it tightly in her hand, she walked to the swing bin. Pushing the lid deftly to one side, she dropped the hanky inside.

Chapter Thirty-One

Teri went back upstairs to the bathroom. There was a wet towel on the floor – it was clear no man was perfect – and a sprinkling of Johnson's Baby Powder on the carpet that looked like a case of seriously bad dandruff. How could he think of using baby powder at the moment their relationship was turning to dust? There was a damp footprint in it – a Jamie-sized one – and she put her own foot down inside it and a flurry of soft white talc clung desperately to it.

She had bought them both new toothbrushes. A pink toothbrush and a blue toothbrush – a jokey reference to the old Max Bygraves song. She picked Jamie's blue toothbrush up and threw it in the bin. Her own looked so forlorn now. There was nothing in this world sadder than a toothbrush-holder with only one toothbrush in it. It summed up the essence of loneliness. If only life was as easy as Max Bygraves had made it sound . . .

Teri ran her hands over the flatness of her stomach. Was she the only person in the world who was becoming fraught about a continued lack of cellulite and stretch-marks? She sighed and opened the bathroom cabinet. The box she had bought a few days ago sat staring at her insolently from the shelf. There were only so many earlyorning vomiting sessions that could be blamed on an xcess of champagne and smoked salmon and tiger prawns and cream-filled meringues.

Teri lifted the pregnancy test out of the cupboard. It was quite predictably called THE PREDICTOR and she thought it sounded like the latest Arnold Schwarzenegger film. Perhaps the baby would burst forth from the birth canal brandishing an Uzi eight millimetre and blast the obstetrician into oblivion. Perhaps not. She placed it on top of the toilet. Perhaps she would use it tomorrow. Then again, perhaps not.

She felt no guilt or shame or regret. Which for a Catholic, convent-educated girl was quite a departure from how she had conducted most of her life. The Catholic ethos seemed to her to be one wrought in guilt and shame. It had been enforced wholeheartedly by a mother who had in a former life been a Spanish Inquisitor, and a best friend who prided herself on being an incarnation of Sister Mary Bernadette – commandant of The Sacred Heart of Jesus primary school. If there was a child, it would be born with pride and joy.

She would call Clare and grovel and ask her to come back. Stoically, she would listen to all that crap about bindweed in the garden of romance again and she would agree that Clare had been right all along, and that she could have avoided all this pain and suffering if she had only listened to her in the first place. And, for once, she would probably be right.

If the test was positive she would tell Clare first, knowing that her friend would scold her and bully her and support her. And she would be there for her as she always was. Clare would get drunk and Teri would sip a glass of orange juice so as not to inflict any damage on the brain cells of the tiny tadpole inside her that would miraculously turn itself into a child.

They would work their way steadily through a box of man-sized Kleenex and pontificate about what heartless bastards men really were. But she would say quietly to herself so that Clare couldn't hear – *not Jamie*. If Jamie had been heartless, he would be here right now and not with his wife and children where he belonged.

With unfaltering fingers she unwrapped the cellophane on THE PREDICTOR. She would definitely do it tomorrow. The sooner she knew the better.

It was a good job that she had signed her contract for *Out and About* as soon as she had received it. She wondered what her new producer would think of a children's television presenter who was not only unmarried but pregnant, too.

It would certainly be more trendy than John Craven had ever been.

Best of Enemies

Val Corbett, Joyce Hopkirk and Eve Pollard

Charlotte – 'Charlie' – Lockhart has it all: a devoted MP husband, Philip; an adorable toddler, Miranda; and an absorbing television career. But things aren't quite perfect. There's another woman in Philip's life: his ex-wife.

Five years after her divorce, Vanessa Lockhart would love to remarry. But dates are rare for fortysomething divorcées. At least she's close to her two girls, and she's made sure they know *exactly* how she feels about Charlie.

A rare face-to-face meeting between Charlie and Vanessa brings hostilities into the open. And there's worse to come. Someone is on the trail of a long-buried secret – a secret that could create scandalous headlines and destroy Philip's career. The slow torture of two families is about to begin . . .

'Kept me reading far too late into the night' Maureen Lipman

'A page-turner . . . great fun' *The Times*

'Enjoyable blockbuster' *Sunday Times*

0 7472 4968 7

HEADLINE

The Real Thing

Catherine Alliott

Everyone's got one – an old boyfriend they never fell out of love with, they simply parted because the time wasn't right. And for thirty-year-old Tessa, it's Patrick Cameron, the gorgeous, moody, rebellious boy she met at seventeen; the boy her vicar father thoroughly disapproved of; the boy who left her to go to Italy to paint.

And now he's back.

'You're in for a treat' *Express*

'Alliot's joie de vivre is irresistible' *Daily Mail*

'Compulsive and wildly romantic' *Bookseller*

'An addictive cocktail of wit, frivolity and madcap romance . . . move over Jilly, your heir is apparent' *Time Out*

0 7472 5235 1

HEADLINE

Now you can buy any of these other bestselling Headline books from your bookshop or *direct from the publisher*.

FREE P&P AND UK DELIVERY
(Overseas and Ireland £3.50 per book)

Olivia's Luck	Catherine Alliott	£5.99
Backpack	Emily Barr	£5.99
Girlfriend 44	Mark Barrowcliffe	£5.99
Seven-Week Itch	Victoria Corby	£5.99
Two Kinds of Wonderful	Isla Dewar	£6.99
Fly-Fishing	Sarah Harvey	£5.99
Bad Heir Day	Wendy Holden	£5.99
Good at Games	Jill Mansell	£5.99
Sisteria	Sue Margolis	£5.99
For Better, For Worse	Carole Matthews	£5.99
Something For the Weekend		
	Pauline McLynn	£5.99
Far From Over	Sheila O'Flanagan	£5.99

TO ORDER SIMPLY CALL THIS NUMBER

01235 400 414

or e-mail <u>orders@bookpoint.co.uk</u>

Prices and availability subject to change without notice.